	DATE DUE		

MAR - - 2002

COLOR
OF
JUSTICE

ALSO BY GARY HARDWICK

Supreme Justice

Double Dead

Cold Medina

COLOR
OF
JUSTICE

A NOVEL OF SUSPENSE

GARY HARDWICK

WM

WILLIAM MORROW

An Imprint of HarperCollins*Publishers*

COLOR OF JUSTICE. Copyright © 2002 by Gary Hardwick. All rights reserved. Printed in the United States of America. No part of this book may be used or reproduced in any manner whatsoever without written permission except in the case of brief quotations embodied in critical articles and reviews. For information address HarperCollins Publishers Inc., 10 East 53rd Street, New York, NY 10022.

HarperCollins books may be purchased for educational, business, or sales promotional use. For information please write: Special Markets Department, HarperCollins Publishers Inc., 10 East 53rd Street, New York, NY 10022.

FIRST EDITION

Designed by Paula Russell Szafranski

Printed on acid-free paper

Library of Congress Cataloging-in-Publication Data has been applied for.

ISBN 0-688-16514-1

02 03 04 05 06 QW 10 9 8 7 6 5 4 3 2 1

For my father, Willie Steve Hardwick,
who cheated death, but could not cheat life

white (wīt) n. 1. An achromatic color of maximum lightness, the complement or antagonist of black, the other extreme of the neutral gray series. Although typically a response to maximum stimulation, white appears always to depend upon contrast. 2. The white or nearly white part of something. 3. One that is white or nearly white. Caucasian. 4. Pale, colorless. 5. Incandescent. 6. Fair or fair minded, honest. 7. Silvery and lustrous. 8. Clean, unsoiled, unmarked, unblemished. 9. Unsullied, pure. 10. Good, angelic, devoid of sin.

—Various American dictionaries

black (blâk) adj. 1. Being of the darkest achromatic visual value; producing or reflecting comparatively little light and having no predominant hue. 2. Having little or no light. 3. Belonging to an ethnic group having dark skin, esp. Negroid. 4. Dark in color. 5. Soiled, as from soot; dirty. 6. Evil; wicked. 7. Cheerless and depressing; gloomy. 8. Marked by anger or sullenness. 9. Attendant with disaster; calamitous. 10. Deserving of, indicating, or incurring censure or dishonor.

—Various American dictionaries

Every man carries a secret knowledge of himself, what he truly is, like a burden.

—Joe Black (2000)

COLOR

OF

JUSTICE

Prologue

NEW KID

The playground of Davison Elementary School was full of life. The kids ran, slid, yelled, and jumped under the morning sun, releasing the unexpendable energy of youth. Dust rose from the hard gravel and dirt that composed the yard, wafting in thin clouds blown away by the fall wind.

The school had long ago abandoned the notion that it could have grass in the yard. If it wasn't killed by the hundreds of stomping feet, or the lack of funds to maintain it, the hardness of city life itself seemed to do it in eventually.

The kids played within a high steel fence. DO NOT CLIMB signs hung about ten feet below the top, and there were still remnants of the razor wire that had been atop the enclosure. It was an experiment that was desperate and had failed when everyone involved realized it made the school looked like a miniature prison.

Cars and trucks roared by on the freeway just in front of the school, the muted engine noise a hard background to the day. Slow-moving vehicles drifted down Jos Campau Avenue to the east, their occupants eyeing the playground then moving on.

The school security officer who watched the kids glanced at the cars as they slowed, then sped up, moving on. These cars and their occupants had been the catalysts for the razor-wire experiment. The men inside them always looking for opportunities to sell corruption and poison to the innocent. The school was in a once proud, blue-collar land, which was crumbling each day as the exodus of families, the influence of drugs and criminality, encroached from all sides.

The morning bell rang loudly as the day began. As it cut through the joy of playtime, a collective sound of disappointment rose from the kids. The doors to the school swung open. Teachers and guards beckoned the kids inside.

The students filed in as a police cruiser pulled up to the front of the school. Immediately, everyone stopped to look, to see where it was going. Neither the siren nor the cherry lights were on, so there was no great urgency. Still, a cop car in this area usually meant trouble.

All eyes watched as the car slowed, stopping in front of the building. This was an elementary school, but trouble had come before. Any minute, the doors would fly open, and the officers would get out, guns at the ready.

But no one got out of the cruiser. The blue-and-white patrol car just sat there, DETROIT POLICE emblazoned on the door.

The cop in the front seat talked to someone who could not be seen. Then he opened the door and got out.

The cop was a big man. To the kids, he seemed to be a giant. His dark blue uniform sparkled with silver buttons and a badge that caught the sunlight. Under his policeman's cap they could see the edges of his hair.

The cop moved to the passenger side of the cruiser and opened the door. Out stepped a little boy. The man walked the kid to the front of the school. The kid tried to keep up with his father's big strides, but he had to hurry to do it.

The eyes of everyone were on the cop and the kid as they made their way to the front office. The cop was indeed huge among the little kids who strained to look up at him. The pair cut a path through the student body and teachers as they went inside the main office. Another bell rang, and the classrooms filled up.

The cop and the boy came out a few minutes later, now accompanied by an assistant principal. She escorted them to a classroom on the corner of the first floor. They went inside and talked to the teacher, who was just about to start class.

The teacher looked alarmed as they spoke in whispers and the cop handed her a paper. The teacher examined it, then smiled at the little boy.

"Well, first day?" she asked.

The little boy nodded. The teacher pointed him to a seat, and he took it, settling into the hard, wooden desk.

The cop clapped his son on the shoulders. A gesture that seemed to be meant for a boy much older. The little boy smiled as his father left the room.

The teacher's face took on a concerned look after the cop was gone. She welcomed her new student and asked the class to do the same. They did, with cautious and tentative voices.

The teacher started the day's lesson, writing something on the board. She glanced at her pupils and focused on the cop's son sitting in the middle of the class, the only white face in a sea of black students.

PART ONE

Shadow of
Justice

Everybody dies for a reason.

—DANNY CAVANAUGH

1

HALF-MOON

The half-moon's bright side flashed as it came out from behind a thick cloud. Its dark half was a pitch hole, blocking out the stars. The sky stretched behind the lunar vision, big and dark like a child's blanket pulled over frightened eyes.

A man crouched behind a bush on Seminole Street in Detroit's Indian Village, looking up at the half-moon with intensity. The stars beyond the moon's dark side seemed stuck in the murkiness of the night sky, held prisoner by its density. A chill was in the air. It was spring, but the long arm of Michigan's winter still held the city in its embrace.

The man behind the bush rose, pushing up like a weed from the cold earth. He stood still a moment, looking at the area from a new vantage, then quickly walked across the street to the large white house. He counted his steps, a curious habit he could not break.

". . . nine, ten." He counted in his head as he moved into the street. ". . . sixteen, seventeen . . ." He crossed it and stepped on the soft grass of the home he watched. ". . . twenty-three, twenty—"

Suddenly, he saw something from the corner of his vision. He turned quickly, a movement so fluid and fast that it seemed like a practiced motion. He stood motionless on the sidewalk, his back leg pointed out and his weight shifted onto the forward one, like a dancer.

A stray dog walked toward him, each skinny limb rising and falling with a deliberateness the man didn't think a dog possessed. The man faced the animal. The dog stopped in its tracks, too, assessing. The animal's eyes gleamed evilly in the dark. The man met the gaze with one of his own. He grew worried. He was not afraid of the mutt, but thought he'd have to kill it and the noise would ruin his plan. He saw himself stepping on the dog's neck, crushing it, and hearing its plaintive cry echoing in the cool night air. He wanted to do it, wanted to end its worthless life.

Shifting out of his dancer's pose, he took on a defensive stance, then glared at the animal, trying to put his desire to kill the animal into his eyes. The dog seemed to sense this and backed off slowly, then it turned and ran, conceding the staring contest.

A little disappointed, the man turned his back on the mutt and moved on. Soon he was in the back of the house. He crept to a window and glanced inside. The interior was dark, but he could make out the alarm system's control box. A row of lights glowed on it.

Without hesitation, the intruder moved to a thick bush at the base of the home. He pushed the bush aside, revealing a power box with a padlock on it. The bush was strong and he had to lean on it to keep it down as he worked. He jimmied the lock and opened the power box. Then he unscrewed the master fuse, cutting the power in the house.

Quickly, he ran to the back door and forced it open. The intruder stopped in the pantry just inside the entrance. It was filled with plants, soil, foodstuffs, exotic spices, and imported canned goods. The smell of garlic and onions was thick in the atmosphere.

He entered the kitchen, moved to the right wall, and quickly dismantled the alarm system. If someone turned the power back on, it might send off a distress signal, and then he'd have to abandon his plan. He broke the box's housing and ripped out the wires, uttering a grunt as he did. Satisfied, the intruder stepped away from the wall and went through the kitchen.

Suddenly, a small sense of panic filled him. It was too easy. Now he was worried because nothing in life came this easy. He took a second to compose himself and when he was sure that destiny was with him again, he moved on.

He walked through the big kitchen into the den. A wide-screen TV and overstuffed leather sofa dominated the area. He glanced to his right and saw the dining hall, an expansive room with a crystal chandelier and a great oak table.

The intruder walked into the living room. The blinds on the windows were only half shut and the moonlight crept in, cutting the room into light and shadow. He moved across the expanse, taking cautious, measured steps on the hardwood floor, careful not to make noise. The streaked light rolled across his body like waves of intermittent energy. It obscured his visage like a strange, floating caul. Moving faster now, he appeared to be a man caught in limbo, drifting on a sea of light and shadow.

He stopped. On the walls above him were pictures. The faces stared down with cold malevolence and he felt himself step backward involuntarily, afraid the apparitions would tear themselves from the frames and attack. He stood in fear for a long moment, not knowing what was real and what his mind had created. His heart beat loudly and he could feel it in his eardrums, pulsing, like a warning. Finally, he pushed himself forward and began to walk again, heading for the stairs.

Climbing the staircase slowly, the intruder stepped lightly. Like the floor, the stairs were hardwood and heavy feet would make too much sound. With each step, he forgot about the frightening people in the pictures and felt a new intensity for his undertaking. He was ascending toward the future.

On the first-floor landing, he looked down a long hallway. A long ornate rug ran down the middle of the floor and five doors were on the hallway. He headed straight for the first one to his left, turning the doorknob, again careful to keep quiet. The door opened with a soft click and he moved inside.

The intruder stopped again as he entered. More of the cruel pictures hung on the walls of the bedroom, guarding the sleeping couple. He fought his fear, knowing he had the power this night, and not even the monstrous countenances could change that.

He moved to the brass bed in the center of the room. A man and woman slept with their backs to each other. The woman looked blissful and content. The man's face held concern in his slumber. Suddenly angered by the man's face, the intruder felt his fist clench tightly.

He could do it now, he thought. Dispatch them to the other side, never letting them awake. But that would do him no good. He needed to find out what they knew first, and for that he had to wake them.

Quietly, he removed a brown bottle from his pocket, poured a substance on a rag, and placed it over the sleeping man's face. The man struggled a bit, then stopped moving. The intruder approached the woman next. Her struggle was not nearly as great. He gagged them, then removed some rope and tied them to the bedposts.

He sat and waited, checking his watch from time to time. After about ten minutes the man came to. He tried to yell, but the gag was firmly in place. The intruder brought the woman out of it, gently slapping her face like a concerned caretaker. She, too, struggled, but the binds held fast.

The man looked into the couple's terror-stricken faces. He wore no mask, and they understood what that meant. The woman was crying now, tears streaming down her plump cheeks. The man slumped into himself, giving in to the fatality of the situation.

The intruder stood and checked the bonds on the couple. They had not given, but he was taking no chances. He mechanically pulled at the hand and foot restraints and checked the gags. They were secure.

He smiled at them. He was smart, much too smart for the couple, and they were surely at his mercy. He pulled out a small weapon. He placed it on the chest of the fear-stricken man and looked directly into his strained eyes.

"Listen carefully to me," he said.

Then he fired into his body.

The man jerked and shook from the impact but did not lose consciousness. The intruder repeated his statement to the woman then quickly fired into her side, sending her into spasm of shaking.

Watching as the helpless couple convulsed before him, he was neither elated nor repulsed. He was calm in his mission, his pulse was steady, his mind focused.

He waited until they stopped shaking, then he checked to make sure they were still breathing. They were.

He pulled out another instrument and covered the wounds he'd just inflicted. Then he removed their gags and asked his question. The victims answered, pleading with him. Unsatisfied, he replaced the gags and fired again.

2

RESTRAINT

The old woman moved slowly toward the end of the hallway. The place was quiet and she heard the soles of her sensible shoes on the just-cleaned hardwood floor. Her footfalls were lazy, sliding things, the sad, step-drag of a weary woman.

She was barely aware of her surroundings, of the house in which she had spent more than thirty years. Familiar faces, family, friends, and memories passed by her like ripples of time, hung from the white walls of her life.

Suddenly, she wasn't aware of walking. She no longer heard her feet hitting the floor. She was floating, drifting toward the staircase at the end of her path. For a moment, she thought it was over. Then just as quickly, she was back on earth, feeling gravity pull her down to the shiny floor.

She took in a sharp breath as her left foot sensed the top of the long staircase. She hesitated only a moment then continued on her way. Her next step was airy, like floating again, but it didn't last. She felt her balance fail. The world tilted, then rushed up to her as she fell into a void.

Her body twisted and she reached for the wooden banister, feeling it for a second in her grasp. As she let go of the railing, she spun *completely around and caught a glimpse of the pictures on the wall just before the first impact jolted her head. It was followed by another, then another, until they sounded like dull thunder from some far-off storm.*

Her body weight fell on her fragile neck and it snapped, turning her head to its limit, then beyond. Her vision clouded and her mind filled with dark stars. Her torso landed at the base of the stairs in a heap, extremities still twitching from reflex and trauma.

She was dead.

The house was quiet again. Somewhere a clock clicked dully. The phone rang, splitting the silence, filling the place with sound. . . .

Detective Danny Cavanaugh pushed himself out of bed as his phone rang loudly. Normally he'd be pissed about being awakened before his shift, but the phone had pulled him from the terrible dream about his mother. He'd imagined her death many times, but never had he'd seen it so vividly. He was faintly aware that he was breathing heavily and that his hand was shaking. He felt his heart pounding, pulsing blood. He steadied his hand, moved it to the phone, and picked up the receiver.

"Yeah," he said calmly.

"Ass in gear, Cavanaugh," said the familiar voice on the other end. "We got a tip on your boulevard shooters. Team's assembling in an hour."

"Yes, sir," said Danny, and hung up. He got out of bed, looking at the still neat side where his girlfriend usually slept. He pushed the last images of his mother from his head and scrambled to get his clothes.

Forty-five minutes later, Danny approached the small house just off Tireman in Detroit. The residential street was unusually narrow, making it seem almost like a path. There were five streetlamps on the way, and they had all been shot out. He knew right then they were on to the right place. Dealers did shit like that to darken their hangout. It made it easier for them to see you coming, and harder for you to see them watching you.

Danny and his partner, Erik Brown, moved carefully down the

street. Two junked cars on blocks, probably stolen, sat halfway up the block. Debris lined the street and gutter, and a dead cat, frozen in death, lay on the hard ground in front of one house.

The houses that looked inhabited had a sad, desperate loneliness about them that seemed to push you away from their darkened windows and bare lawns. This is the city, Danny thought. Somewhere in this place of quiet doom were the men he was looking for.

Danny and his partner saw one of the detectives from the command post coming their way. He was out of place, and so Danny knew something was up. He went to the man quickly.

"Wha'sup?" asked Danny. "We got a problem?" Danny was white, but the voice that came out of him sounded black, a resonant baritone with hints of Southern accents and the rhythmic timing of languages long forgotten. Danny had acquired this pattern of speech from spending his entire life in the neighborhoods of Detroit.

Those who met Danny were initially surprised to hear that sound coming from the face of the big Irishman with the reddish hair and green eyes. This detective was not shocked, he was a friend.

"I changed my position up the street," said the detective. "Felt more comfortable. I didn't tell the boss. I didn't want it to go out over the radio."

"Cool," said Danny. "Just be careful. They already put one man in a box."

The detective nodded and moved back. Danny and Erik settled their gaze back on the target house and walked on.

Danny struck an imposing figure. He was six four and about two-twenty. A former marine, he kept himself in good shape. He had a disarming, friendly demeanor that belied the street swagger he'd attained over the years. He was the kind of guy who seemed like an old friend right after you met him. Danny's disarming manner masked an astute, deductive mind that never missed anything.

Danny was in his early thirties and a newly minted detective. He'd gotten the promotion after he'd helped the feds catch the man who'd assassinated Supreme Court Justice Farrel Douglas. It was a national story, and it got him out of a nasty bind involving a police brutality charge involving a robber who'd shot Danny's girlfriend and former police partner.

Before he became a detective, Danny had carried two guns, a Glock and a Smith & Wesson .45 ACP revolver. He was ambidextrous, and so was good with either weapon, and deadly when he used both. Danny's father, a retired cop, was a big fan of old westerns, and had taught his son how to shoot using two guns when Danny was a teenager.

When Danny got his gold shield, he was forced to carry the standard-issue 9 mm. He hated this, but complied because he desperately wanted to make good on his new job.

Danny and his team's targets this night were a trio of gunmen who had shot and killed a rival dealer who worked the neighborhood on the south side of Grand Boulevard, not prime real estate but, in the drug trade, worth something. The dead dealer was shot by a Uzi sub-pistol, illegal and very lethal. Two days later, while the mayor was inspecting the new MGM Grand Casino, a police cruiser was fired on after signaling a vehicle to stop in Cass Corridor only a few miles away, same MO, same shell casings—same suspects.

That's when Detroit's Special Crimes Unit was called in. They were given a simple job: find these guys before they turned that area of the city into a graveyard, embarrassed city hall, and put a damper on all of the big-ass, big-money development in downtown Detroit.

Earlier in the day they'd gotten a tip from a man who had to be a rival dealer, and who apparently didn't want to be the next one killed. That led the SCU to the place where they were now.

Danny stopped as he saw the vehicle that had been involved in the shootings.

"Got a triple black GMC in front of the house," said Danny.

"Copy," said a man's voice on Danny's radio.

Danny had been through anger management as a way of cleaning up his record as a uniformed cop. He also had to go to a shrink. The department psychologist told him that each gun was the embodiment of his divided soul, the black Glock, and the steel (white) .45. Danny thought it was bullshit, but he needed to get through the sessions to help his career, and what man really knew what he thought subconsciously.

Since he'd become a detective, Danny had adopted a new outlook on police work. Gone was the bull who'd plow through any situation, shooting first, then maybe asking questions later. Now, he was a homicide detective, a thinking man's cop. It was his job to avoid death, prevent death, not cause it. So *restraint* was the word foremost in Danny's mind as he approached the suspect house with the deadly men inside.

"I hope these muthafuckas are tired," said Danny to Erik.

"Don't count on that shit," said Erik. "Anybody who'd smoke people as casually as these guys don't take downtime."

Erik was a funny, good-natured brother who prided himself on what he called his TWA, Teeny Weenie Afro. Erik was just under six feet tall, in great shape, and considered himself to be a fairly good-looking man. He was unassuming in his manner, but you could see in his large brown eyes a mind that never stopped working.

Erik had two years more on the job than Danny. Their boss thought they were a good match, and he was right. Erik and Danny had fit together nicely right from the beginning, Danny's brooding, analytical cop to Erik's outgoing veteran.

"Second team in place," Danny heard on his radio.

"First closing," Danny said.

Danny had assumed a leadership position in the partnership. Erik preferred persuasion to ass-kicking. Danny, on the other hand, was always willing to put himself in harm's way. He didn't know if this really made him the leader, or a fool, but it worked, and the two men got along just fine because of it.

The cops were closing in on the suspect house. The first and second teams were detectives, and there were two teams of uniforms as backup. They were all wearing protective vests. Erik carried a riot gun. Danny carried the 9 mm, trying to rid himself of the feeling that his other hand was empty.

There were fifteen residences on the street, and of these, only about ten were occupied. The rest were abandoned or burned-out shells. Danny always wondered what killed peaceful homes, turning them into ghost houses, and what became of the lives that had inhabited them. He'd seen families destroyed by drugs, alcoholism, and hopelessness. Who knew which of these demons had robbed these houses of their joy.

Danny and Erik moved past an abandoned house with what was once a blue door. It was now peeled and dirty, its knocker hanging on by one screw, mocking itself. The stairs leading to the place were stone, but the middle steps were broken, caved in on themselves, a gaping maw in the ascension. For some reason, that sent a chill up Danny's back.

Next to the house with the blue door was another house, better-looking and definitely inhabited.

"First team at point," said Danny. He exchanged a look with Erik, and they moved closer to the occupied house. Danny was going in first, and his heart was already racing. But he wasn't nervous. He was excited. This was why he'd bought the ticket to be a cop.

Danny and Erik edged up to the suspect house. The door glinted in the dim glow of the streetlight. It was matte gray and had two lines of large rivets in it. There was no guard on the front of the house, but from the looks of that door, it was reinforced steel.

"Got a big-ass steel door in front," Danny said into his radio.

"Same back here," came the reply.

"The windows are all boarded up," said Danny to Erik. "Locked in tight."

"You know what?" said Erik. "I bet them brothers ain't really up to no good. I bet they're in there just playing a nice game of bid whist or something."

Danny smiled a little. Erik was always good for breaking tension. Danny waited for the team leader to respond. They were safely tucked away a street over. If the team couldn't get in, they'd have a standoff, and for sure, the killers inside would resist and that could get ugly.

"Stand by," said the team leader.

"Standing by," said Danny.

"I'm hungry," said Erik. "We should get some of that plastic explosive the tactics guys have, blow this damned house off the face of the earth, and all go get some White Castle burgers."

"I heard that," said Danny. "Wish we could. Lord knows I need a rest from this shit."

"The only good thing is, they can't see us out here through these boarded-up windows."

This gave Danny a thought. He looked at the base of the house. Sure enough, the killers had neglected to board up the basement windows. Most of the homes in Detroit had basements, and this house was no exception. These guys were typical dealers, he thought. They spent a grand on a steel door, but left the basement vulnerable. But if they were smart, Danny thought, they wouldn't be drug dealers.

"We can get in through the basement," said Danny. "They didn't close it off."

"Like hell," said Erik. "These drug boys all have attack dogs to guard the basement. That's why the basement's unprotected. You wanna get your nuts chewed off by some pit bull?"

"We don't know that," said Danny. "Besides, I can take care of a mutt-ass dog."

Danny called the team leader and requested permission to try it. He waited for what seemed an eternity. He knew what they were thinking. All they had to do was wait until morning, and when the men came out, the cops'd have them. The only problem with that was it would be light, and the suspects would check the area. If they saw anything that looked like a cop, all hell would break loose.

"Team one, go in," said the team leader. "Be careful. Radio if you get in a jam. We'll come full force."

"You crazy muthafucka," said Erik.

"And you my partner," said Danny. "What does that say?"

Danny and Erik moved over to the side of the house next to the abandoned one. Danny crawled to the basement window closest to the back. He figured the suspects were all in the front, so he'd have a better chance of not being heard if he stayed in the back.

Danny checked the window. It was old and filthy. He couldn't see much inside. The window was locked. It had a latch on the inside. Danny pulled out a knife and jammed it in the opening in the base of the window. He felt the blade hit the latch. He applied more pressure, and there was a soft creaking noise as the latch gave way.

Danny pushed the window in slowly and stuck his head inside. It was dark, but he didn't see anything. He pulled out his gun and pushed himself in headfirst. Going in feetfirst would have been smarter, but he wanted to see whatever there was waiting for him inside.

Hanging inside the basement, he found it empty. Nothing but old furniture and rotting cardboard boxes.

Danny put his gun away, then asked Erik to hold his legs. Erik grabbed them and Danny slid down the wall onto the floor. He got up and helped Erik inside.

"First team in," said Danny.

"Standing by," came the reply. "We'll let you know when we breach the door."

Danny took out his weapon and made his way to the stairs. Erik raised the riot gun and followed.

"Now what, Danny boy?" said Erik.

"We go up, call in the team, and hope nobody makes us kill them."

"Not the best plan I ever heard, but let's do it."

Suddenly, they heard voices from above them. Erik and Danny froze where they were and listened. They heard a muted cheer.

"Somebody playing tonight?" Danny whispered.

"Pistons-Cavaliers," said Erik.

"Let's move, they might all be into the game and we can catch them off-guard."

Danny and Erik slowly crept up the old wooden stairs, careful not to make too much noise. He got to the door at the top of the stairs and found it open. He peeked inside. The basement door led to a kitchen. It was messy, and Danny smelled the odor of spoiled food. Danny heard the game being broadcast from a room on his right and assumed their targets were in there watching the game.

Danny was about to go through the door, when he heard a woman's muffled cry.

"Shut da fuck up, bitch!" said a man's voice.

Danny heard the sound of someone being struck, then laughter.

"Ow!" yelled the same man. "Yo, dis bitch kicked me! I got somethin' fo' yo' ass . . ."

This was followed by a muffled scream from the unseen woman.

"Shit," Danny whispered.

"Fuck," said Erik. "Call the shit in."

"They'll kill her. They ain't got nothing to lose at this point."

"Danny, don't be fool—"

"Back up, then hit the door in five," said Danny, adding "Get my back." And Danny had no doubt that Erik would. Danny rushed into the kitchen, his gun out in front.

Danny saw the flash of the kitchen with its dirty walls and sink filled with broken dishes and pots. It was about ten strides to the room where the killers were watching TV.

Danny entered, yelling that he was a cop, and demanding that they all hit the floor. He heard Erik behind him and the first explosion of the battering ram hitting the reinforced front door.

Two of the three killers were only about twenty or so, and one of them held a kitchen knife in his hand, bloody from having cut someone. The third was older, maybe thirty and hard-looking. He was obviously the leader. In the far right corner was the girl. Danny could see just a hint of her, but he couldn't look because he would have had to take his eyes off the men.

The young man with the knife dropped his weapon immediately. The other man was unarmed. He raised his hands into the air.

The leader sat by a chair with a Uzi in his hand. He had it pointed at the bleeding girl. He saw Danny and both men froze. Slowly, the leader stood up. He looked at Danny quickly then his eyes darted back to the girl.

"Hold up!" yelled the leader. "Or that's it for her ass."

Danny kept his gun trained on the leader as the battering ram hit the door again, like thunder. The leader was startled for a second, but he never took the weapon off the girl.

"Go ahead and cap her," said Danny.

Erik kept his riot gun on the other two men, but he wanted to jerk his head around at Danny's statement.

"Put y'all's guns down and I won't shoot her," said the leader.

"You trippin'," said Danny. "This ain't about her. Are *you* ready to die?"

Slowly, Danny started to move toward the man, never taking his eyes off his face. Danny could see in the man's eyes that he was the real deal, a killer. But Danny couldn't put his weapon down, even if it meant the girl caught one.

"You got five seconds to drop that gun," said Danny. "Your choice, walk out or get carried out."

Danny waited as the leader thought. He wasn't too bright and Danny knew the simple alternative in his hand was one the leader understood. These drug boys were all about bullshit macho. This fool was going down for murder with little hope of ever getting out of prison. So Danny knew he was thinking that if he fired on a cop maybe he could go out like a man and that might be worth something to the sorry-ass story that was his life.

The leader looked down the barrel of Danny's gun, then into his eyes. He took in a sharp breath, then lowered the gun and dropped it. Danny walked over and forced him to the floor where he quickly cuffed him.

The cops hit the steel door again, and it popped its hinges and fell inward. Two more detectives poured into the room.

Erik yelled that he had the two unarmed men covered. Danny read the leader his rights, then let two uniformed officers take him away. The other two members of the crew were carted off as well.

The cops searched the place and found drugs and about five grand in small bills. Dealers always had small bills. The girl they'd kidnapped turned out to be the leader's cousin, a girl who'd stupidly threatened to go to the police about what he was doing. Everyone there was sure they had saved her life.

Danny and Erik were congratulated by the team leader, a cop named McDonald, whom everyone called Big Mac. Danny and Erik mumbled responses, each of them not wanting to discuss their feelings in public about what had just happened. Soon, Big Mac moved on, and almost immediately, Erik turned to Danny.

"Do I even have to say it?" asked Erik.

"No," said Danny. "I know I was wrong, but we only had the one chance. That girl was—"

"One of the things I hate about this job is the random chance that I might get my balls blown off," Erik said, ignoring Danny. "I don't need your ass increasing that shit on me!"

He was mad and Danny knew that he was in an indefensible position. Even though it had all turned out okay, they had to go out again tomorrow, and the next day, and Erik was not pleased about that.

"I'm new at this," Danny said. "You know that." It was a lame-ass excuse and he regretted it as soon as he'd said it. He'd been a cop too long to have that be a legitimate excuse.

"Look, I'm just upset now, man. So, don't talk to me for a while."

"How long?" asked Danny.

"You still talkin', dammit," said Erik.

Erik walked away and Danny didn't try to stop him. His partner was totally right. Danny had had no right to force him to follow into that situation. Even though they might have saved a life, Danny had put others in peril. What Danny did was heroic, but to your partner, it was screwed up. Danny was much more reckless than Erik, and they were still getting used to one another.

Danny went out the front door into the night. He breathed in the cool air, and tried to clear his head. Erik was on a cell phone, probably talking to his wife and kids. Now Danny really felt like shit.

Danny watched as they loaded two of the killers into a squad car. The leader was put into a different car so they could get conflicting stories if anyone talked. Danny sighed as he realized that he'd have to spend all the next morning filing reports on the incident.

Erik finished his call and gave Danmny a look that was not nearly as angry as he had expected. They didn't speak, but Danny could tell his partner had already started to forgive him.

Glancing up into the dark sky at the hanging half-moon, Danny imagined the other part of it from its visible half. The stark white divided against the blackness of the eclipsed part seemed to fill the night sky. He broke away from the vision and the obvious thoughts in his head. Then he went back to his job, happy that no one had been killed this night.

3

WHEN LUCY FELL

There's an old joke that God invented liquor so the Irish couldn't take over the world. This would have been true in Danny's family many years ago. His father, Robert Thomas Cavanaugh, was a hard-drinking cop with a fiery temper and little concern for his family. Danny had inherited his father's strength, but his temper had come along with it, a familial mixed blessing.

These were the things Danny thought of as he raised his hand to knock on the door of his parents' house on the east side of Detroit. The neighborhood was nice, having fought off encroaching criminality over the last ten years. Being home brought back memories, some great, others awful. Danny felt his gut tighten as he heard someone walking toward the door.

Robert Cavanaugh opened the door and glanced up at his son. Robert was going on sixty-five and was slowing down. He'd developed a bad habit of crouching when he stood, and the last few times Danny had been by, he was always in his pajamas, as was the case today. Still, Danny saw the handsome, straight-arrow cop with the square jaw and reddish hair who used to strut around as if nothing could touch him.

Danny remembered when his father had taken him to his new

school that first day so long ago. He'd glanced up at him and his father's head had been framed by the morning light of the sun, creeping around the edges of his policeman's cap, almost godlike. That was always Danny's picture of what it meant to be a cop, something powerful, beautiful, and mysterious.

Robert pulled his plaid green robe around him, mumbled something like a hello, then walked off. Danny followed him inside.

"Wha'sup?" Danny asked.

"You don't have to come over every day," said Robert. His Irish accent was just barely detectable. It was a sign that he was upset when you could discern it in his voice.

"I worry," said Danny. "You live alone now."

"I can take care of myself," said Robert. He produced a .38 special from under his robe, then just as quickly, it was gone.

Robert moved into the kitchen. Danny went after him for a few steps, then stopped and looked at the pictures in the room. His mother's face stared at him from all directions.

Lucy Cavanaugh had died about a half year ago. She'd taken a bad fall down the stairs, struck her head, and never woke up. It had hit his father hard. Robert seemed to age twenty years inside of a month. He'd dropped twenty pounds and his disposition was as bad as it could be, not that it had ever been all that good to begin with.

Danny had been devastated, too. He and his mother had not gotten along very well and she'd passed before he could make it better. Since her death, he'd been haunted by her demise, dreaming of her falling to her end with him powerless to do anything.

Danny's parents had been having a rough go of it before the accident. They argued about everything and didn't speak for days at a time. He could never figure out how they could be married for four decades and still have problems. His parents had just had a fight when Lucy fell down the staircase. Now she was gone, and neither Danny nor his father could ever set things right with her.

Danny's mother had never approved of his life. He was unmarried and living in sin with a woman, a black one at that. Lucy didn't say much about Vinny's color, but Danny knew it bothered her as it did most people. On the other hand, Robert, for all of his flaws, didn't have a prejudiced bone in his body, a rare thing for cop.

Danny walked past the long staircase and tried not to think of his mother tumbling down them. He went into the kitchen and found Robert Cavanaugh sitting at the table eating a breakfast of leftover pasta and orange juice.

He wanted to say so much to his father, but every time he tried to talk about Lucy dying, Robert clammed up, becoming sad and angry. Maybe it was better not to talk about, he thought. The two men had only each other. There was Danny's brother, but the family had dropped contact with him years ago. No one tried to find him for the funeral. Hell, no one even knew if he was still alive.

Danny wanted to discuss it. His mother's death bothered him greatly, and it was more than the normal reason. There was something not right about it, something that tingled the police instincts he'd inherited from his father.

"I've been thinking about Ma lately," said Danny.

Robert didn't respond. He looked over his plate at Danny with an annoyed expression.

"I've been having this dream about how she died." Danny knew he was treading on dangerous ground, but he'd never gotten anywhere with Robert by pussyfooting around.

"You know how she died. We all know, Danny," said Robert pointedly. "So what's your problem?"

"I don't know if what the medical examiner said was right, you know—"

Robert's face contorted into mild anger. "It's too early for that shit," snapped Robert. "For God's, sake can't you ever leave it alone! Fuck, just fuck it!" Robert grabbed his juice and stomped off, mumbling.

Danny listened as his father stomped-cursed his way into the other room. He poured himself a glass of orange juice and said nothing more. He just sat for a while, waiting. Then when he felt Robert had calmed down enough, he went into the living room. He took a moment, watching his father, his mind flooding with memory. Danny kissed his father on the top of the head and headed out, leaving the pain and memory of his mother behind.

"How are you feeling today, Danny?" asked the therapist.

"I'm cool," said Danny. He settled into the big leather chair and let it envelop him.

The therapist was Dr. Donald Gordon. He was the department psychologist and a former detective. A white man of about forty or so, he had a medium build and was beginning to lose his salt-and-pepper hair.

On Gordon's desk was a picture of him and his wife of fifteen years, Patty, and their daughters. When he got his degree, he'd left the department after ten years to be a shrink, but he'd been drawn right back into the game a few years later.

"So what's on your mind?" asked Gordon.

"I visited my father again today," said Danny. "He still won't talk about it."

"How does that make you feel?" asked Gordon.

"It's fucked up."

"You said that you had questions about your mother's death, that everything didn't fit. You still feel that way?"

"I'm a cop. Nothing ever fits for us." Danny was trying to get away from the discussion, but Gordon was right. The death of his mother was something he thought about each day. Lucy had descended those stairs thousands of times and never had she slipped. Sure she was old, but she was in good shape. He didn't like to think about it because if she didn't slip and fall, then the alternative was too terrible to imagine.

"I only bring it up," said Gordon, "because you always do at some point. Let's see if we can get to the bottom of it this time."

Danny had successfully completed an anger management course, but it was strongly suggested that he see the department shrink in order to solidify his hold on a gold shield. Danny's history of overzealous law enforcement was not a help to his career. These days, a violent white cop in a black city like Detroit was a lightning rod for trouble of all kinds.

Danny didn't like the idea of seeing a shrink. Crazy. It was an old notion, but one that hung on in the blue-collar world he lived in. A man took care of his own problems, and he certainly didn't go to a doctor and whine about them. And yet Danny was finding comfort in his weekly visits. Gordon was laid-back and knew the police game well enough never to need explanation. It was like having another partner, or at least that's what he kept telling himself.

"Okay, Doc," said Danny. "If my mother didn't fall down those stairs then my father . . . he was the only other person there. They had been having trouble, fighting a lot."

"Your father, Robert, the *cop*?" Gordon said with emphasis.

"Yeah, he'd know how to do something like that."

"Like what?" asked Gordon. "Say the words, Danny. It's the first step to dealing with this."

"He'd know how to kill someone and make it look like an accident," said Danny with a hint of sadness in his voice.

"Do you think he did it?"

Danny thought long about his father. Robert Cavanaugh was a hard man, tough and uncompromising. He'd shot two men during his tenure as a cop—one of them died. Yes, he could do it, but *why* was the question.

"I don't know," said Danny. "I'm just a little fucked up about it, you know. My mother and me wasn't all that close."

"And you never got closure?

"No," said Danny, laughing a little. "We never seem to get that closure shit down in my family."

"Maybe thinking your father did something bad is just your own guilt about the accident, trying to blame someone else."

"I wouldn't do that to my father. It's just that . . . he was supposed to take care of her. He didn't. That's all."

"Then you have to talk with your father about it at some point," said Gordon.

"I try," said Danny. "My old man just won't let me go there. If I push, he'll probably try to kick my ass." Danny laughed a little.

"I try to get people to take action to solve their problems," said Gordon. "If you won't do anything about this then you have to stop punishing yourself with all these unanswered questions."

"Shit or get my ass off the pot, huh?"

"That would be another way of saying it, yes."

"Then let's forget about it," said Danny. "I'll just let it all go."

Gordon made a few notes in a book he always kept nearby. Danny watched him and knew that he'd lied about letting it go. He was playing out the scene in his head again. He saw his mother come out of the bathroom and walk to the stairs. He saw her lose her footing and tumble. He watched as she hit the bottom of the landing, twisting her neck, her head slamming into the floor. He saw his father running feebly after he tried to stop her fall, almost falling himself.

"I want to get back to why you came here," said Gordon. His voice jolted Danny back into reality.

"Why I came?" asked Danny.

"Well, we've been here for a long time trying to get to the root of your problems with aggression. We got to a point where we decided that it had something to do with growing up in an all-black neighborhood. Then your mother passed and we got sidetracked."

"I guess we did. What do you want to talk about?"

"Black people," said Gordon.

"What about them?" asked Danny.

"You think being an outcast made you overly aggressive?"

"No," said Danny. "It's not like that. I was accepted eventually, it's more like . . ." He stopped a moment to collect his thoughts on this. These sessions were helping, but they challenged him mentally. He was good at being a cop, but talking about his feelings was crippling. "Black people are sick."

Gordon's eyebrows raised. "How so?"

"Not sick like physically," said Danny. "They're sick in the heart, down where we can't see it, can't touch it, down where if you want to help, you'd better have a damned good reason for asking, or it might be your ass."

"Personal things?"

"Yeah, that's it, personal."

"Why are you so comfortable talking about this?" asked Gordon. "I mean, I'm a white guy and it makes me nervous to analyze black people in such a generalizing way."

"But I'm not a white guy," said Danny casually. "That's what I'm saying. I mean, not really. I have that sickness in my heart, too. So, I'm really talking about myself."

Danny had lived around black people since he was a kid. His father, Robert Cavanaugh, was a city cop, so the family had to live in Detroit because of the residency requirement. All his life, Danny had lived in the hardness of the inner city, in the heart of blackness. He knew all too well what he was talking about.

"So, you feel your anger comes from this sickness?" asked Gordon.

"Yeah. Only it's worse because of what I see in the mirror."

Danny grew up on the east side of Detroit, in a ghetto fortress bounded by Six Mile, Dequindre, Conant, and a hole that became the Davison Freeway. He was forced to accept the ways of black people. He learned the rhythm of life, the philosophy and attitudes of the people, which manifested themselves in everything from a discussion of global politics to the proper way to cook a slab of ribs.

Danny had caught a lot of shit for this early on. Black people thought he mocked them, trying to have the best of blackness without the terrible burden. Whites thought quite simply that he was crazy, a crazy-ass white boy trying to be something he wasn't. But over time, people noticed it less and less.

"You certainly don't sound like a white guy," said Gordon.

"Yeah," said Danny. "I hear that all the time. But I don't understand that shit. I sound how I sound, you know."

"So why do you think you had such a problem with your temper?" asked Gordon. "You think you have some kind of rage?"

"Not like the brothers have," said Danny. "I'm not mad because I've been treated like shit by a whole country."

Danny didn't think a guy like Gordon could understand how black people took their pain and pushed it into a deep place where it stayed just behind every thought, perception, hope, and fear. And how you did this until it became an inseparable part of you, like a psychological shadow cast by the cold, fucked-up light of the world. And there in the bosom of your deepest humanity, it became a fire, a power that propelled you over the obstacles of life and allowed you to find peace and joy even as you suffered. Gordon wouldn't understand how this was what it meant when they say black people have soul.

"How did you feel when all the other white families left your neighborhood?" asked Gordon.

"Didn't think much of it at first. Families came and went all the time. Then I realized that I was the only one left, the only white boy at everything. Man, I got chased, beat up, and teased."

"And what about your parents? Your father?"

"He was drinking a lot back then. Fighting with my mother and shit, you know."

"Did that make you upset?"

"Made me sad mostly," said Danny. "Sad that we couldn't have a normal life. But I had a good time as a kid. It wasn't always cool to be the only white guy, but after a while the kids didn't give a shit. See, there's this thing in the city where everybody recognizes that we're all fucked, so it don't matter if your daddy's black and out of work, or white and a drunk. Fucked is fucked."

"And yesterday when you approached the killer with the Uzi, were you angry then? Did you want to shoot him?"

"Yeah, I did," said Danny. "In the old days, I would have waited for him to move, then fired. But now, I'm . . ." Danny became quiet for a moment, looking for the right words. "I'm trying to be better."

"So how did your parents feel about living in that neighbor-hood?"

"My mother hated it. My old man, well, he thinks black people are strong. He wanted me to be strong, too, that's why he put me in that school."

"And your brother?" asked Gordon.

"Shoot, I'm sure he didn't care. He was pretty much out of the house by that time."

Gordon took a moment, thinking. Danny had already picked up on this move by the doctor. It meant he had a hard question to ask him and was looking for the right words.

"You do understand that you are not black?" asked Gordon.

"I understand that a man is more than his color," said Danny. "That it's what's in his heart that makes all the difference. See, every-body's always talkin' 'bout how we all the same underneath, love your brother and shit, but don't nobody really believe it, nobody but me."

Danny had evaded the question somewhat, but Gordon did not push. Danny noticed that Gordon never pressed the point. Danny was a complex man who had been hammered by stark cultural dif-ferences at an early age and was still trying to deal with what it all meant. He guessed that the doctor understood this.

"You're not alone," said Gordon. "A lot of young white males are heavily into black culture."

Danny snorted and leaned back in the chair. "I know what you mean, Doc," he said. "I ain't no wigger. I don't idolize black rappers and athletes. My love ain't tied to black men performing for me. These guys who ride around blasting rap music will be Republicans living behind a six-foot fence when they turn thirty. It's one thing to admire black people from across the street, it's another to have one as your best friend, the only person that you absolutely trust. To live with them, eat with them, and love and have sex with a black woman. And most of all, to see them as human, as people, and not what their image is in the world."

"I seem to have hit a sore spot with you," said Gordon.

"Sorry, Doc," said Danny. "But because of where I come from, I see everything about black and white people, all the truth, lies, secrets, and evil they each try to hide. Here in Detroit, there's a lot of that to go around."

"Then maybe your anger came from this truth, your truth," said Gordon, getting back to his point.

Danny thought about this for a moment. Gordon was frustrating, but he was smart. Danny knew that his upbringing, his father's alcoholism, and his family's hard times had had some effect on him.

"Maybe," said Danny. "The truth can be jacked up if you ain't ready for it."

"Do you have any white friends?" asked Gordon.

"Not really."

"Do you find that strange?"

"I stick to the people I'm used to, like everyone else," said Danny.

"But most black people have white friends," said Gordon. "Why not you?"

"I don't got a lot in common with them," said Danny.

"Do white cops try to hang out with you?"

"Yeah, but they want to go to them square-ass bars in the suburbs. The shit is so exclusionary. The brothers go to better places. All kinds of people there. Better music, better food, better everything."

Gordon took another moment and Danny could feel it coming again.

"Do you think you were scarred by being put in that black school?"

"Scarred? Like how?"

"Changed in a bad way," said Gordon.

"No," said Danny. "I was changed, but in a good way."

"But something like that can alter a child. Scars never heal, they just stop bleeding."

"I certainly would have been different if I had grown up somewhere else," said Danny, "somewhere white. But growing up in a black neighborhood didn't make me crazy or nothing."

Gordon took another moment, then: "Do you like white people, Danny?"

Danny waited a long time to answer. He was not afraid of the question. It was just that he didn't really know what the answer was. He resented the establishment, but any working stiff felt that way. He'd never really thought about it.

"I don't hate nobody, Doc," he said finally.

Gordon folded his fingers together for a second. Danny had the sense that Gordon didn't like his answer or didn't believe it.

"We'll resume here next time," said Gordon.

Danny got up, shook hands with Gordon, and left. He walked out of the professional building and hurried back to work. All the way, he thought about Gordon's terrible insinuated question as to whether or not he hated himself.

4

THE BADY BROTHERS

The clerk looked at the twenty-dollar bill he'd been handed and frowned. The money was covered with a big bloodstain. The blood had turned brown from age and cut off half of President Jackson's face.

The clerk checked out the kid who'd given it to him. He was about thirteen or so, and dressed in the normal style, baggy pants, big coat, and skull cap pulled low over his baby face. He'd come to the counter with a shitload of goods, mostly junk food. The clerk wanted to make the sale, but he didn't like the bloody money. It disturbed him. He'd seen defaced money before, but this was disrespectful.

"I can't take this," said the clerk, a black man about thirty-five named Deion.

"It's money, ain't it?" said the kid. His voice was high-pitched but coarse from smoking, a man's voice coming from a kid's face. It also had a Southern accent to it, which made him sound as if he were pulling the words from his throat.

"Come on, man, I got some place to be," said a skinny man behind the kid. He held two six-packs in his hands.

"Shut da fuck up," said the kid. "You wait till I'm finished up in here."

The kid turned and looked at the skinny man, who was about to say something but stopped when he saw the face of the kid, the angry snarl of his lips and emptiness of his eyes. That was a look he'd seen in the city before. It was a look you didn't mess with.

"This money's got blood on it," said Deion. "What am I supposed to do with it?" The clerk slipped the bill back under the bulletproof glass. "Give me another one."

The party store was one of the few black-owned stores in the inner city. Most of the black businessmen had sold their small businesses out to foreigners, moving on to the green pastures of the suburbs. But this store was owned and operated by blacks, servicing the neighborhood. Like all party stores, the prices were inflated and most of what was sold was alcoholic beverages, the staple of the hopeless.

"What kinda muthafuckin' bullshit you dealin' in, nigga?" asked the kid. "You better take dat money." The kid shoved the bill back under the glass.

"Who do you think you are?" asked Deion. "I'm supposed to be scared of you? A hundred bad-asses come in here every day."

"They ain't me," said the kid. "They ain't Akema Bady."

"Take the damned money, Deion!" said the skinny man to the clerk. "Don't be fuckin' around. I gosta go."

"Be cool, Keith," Deion said to the skinny man. To Akema, he said, "Just give me a different bill. I ain't got time for this shit."

Keith groaned. Now it was a dick-measuring contest and those could go on forever.

"Fuck it," said Akema. "I'll just take the shit then." Akema grabbed the goods and walked away from the counter, leaving the bloody bill on the tray. He grabbed the goods as best he could in his arms and headed to the door.

Deion cursed loudly and hit a big black button on the underside of the counter.

Akema had gotten to the door, when the distinct sound of a pump-action shotgun sounded behind him. Akema turned and saw the clerk standing next to a guard, who held the weapon.

"Put that shit down," said the clerk.

"Fuck!" said Keith. He moved out of the line of fire, going into an aisle with his beer.

Akema dropped the potato chips, soda pop, and other things he had on the floor. The plastic soda bottle bounced and popped open. The strawberry soda spilled, foaming red on the hardwood floor.

"You just bought that," said Deion.

"Get yo' ass out," said the guard. He motioned with the weapon.

Akema just stared at the barrel of the weapon, looking at it with a tiny smile playing around his lips.

"You want me to shoot yo' little ass?" asked the guard.

There was no sign of fear on Akema's face. The guard shifted his feet, unsettled by the kid's lack of fear. Suddenly, Akema opened the door and stepped out.

Deion sighed in relief, then moved forward to clean up the mess. "Damned fool," said Deion.

"Crazy," said the guard, who lowered his shotgun and walked toward Deion. On his way, he saw Keith, still cowering in the aisle next to his beer.

"You can come on out now," said the guard to Keith. "He gone."

"What you doin', man?" asked Keith. "There was more of them outside. I saw them—"

Akema burst through the door, knocking Deion back. Next to Akema was his brother, Rimba. Rimba was much bigger than Akema, his long dreadlocks swinging over his face. In his ears were headphones. The cord trailed off into his big jacket. Rimba recited the rap tune he was listening to.

". . . Niggas don't cry, niggas can't fly, niggas why? Niggas die . . ." Rimba rapped melodically. He had the same Southern lilt as his brother. Rimba's eyes darted to the men in the room as he rapped and scanned them at the same time.

Then Rimba coughed hard, a wet cough that bespoke a chest cold. He never took his eyes off Deion. He and Akema knocked Deion to the floor, and began to stomp on his face and kick him in the ribs. Deion yelled and tried to roll away, but Akema stomped on the bridge of Deion's nose, breaking it. Blood poured from his nostrils and through his covering fingers. Rimba rapped louder as he saw the blood and heard the screams.

The guard raised the big shotgun and took a step toward the attacking brothers. He was going to fire at Rimba, on whom he had the clearest shot. Suddenly, the guard sensed movement to his left side. Before he could turn his head, he felt the cold metal of a gun barrel being placed against his temple, and the last sound he heard on earth was the weapon's discharge.

The guard fell to the side, his body losing all of its coordination as the bullet tore through his brain. The gun in his big hands discharged, blowing up a shelf with breakfast cereal on it. Boxes lifted into the air and nuggets and flakes of cereal rained down on the scene. The guard's big body fell forward and landed with a resounding thud.

Akema locked the front door, turning the CLOSED sign outward. Then he ran quickly behind the counter and expertly emptied the cash register, also taking the security camera tape, which had recorded everything that had happened.

Rimba continued to rap to his tune and kick Deion, whose pleas fell on deaf ears. Deion's face and hands were covered in blood as he feebly tried to fight off the attack. Then Rimba stopped his attack. He quickly pulled out a small lead pipe and brought it down with all his might onto Deion's head. Deion's body jerked once, then he was still.

Keith shook uncontrollably as he kneeled next to his beer in the aisle. He'd wet himself, and the stain was still spreading on his gray pants. A shadow fell on him and he looked up at Muhammad Bady, the eldest brother, who had come in the back of the store and shot the guard.

Muhammad's face had several scars that had healed badly and were made more noticeable because of his shiny, bald head. He stood over Keith, who was crying and muttering something about how he should have left when he had the chance and how he hated Detroit.

The Bady brothers had reached their final destination. They'd been on a long and fateful journey since their mother was killed in Texas.

Sherindah Bady had been a good mother to the boys. She was a former black Muslim, a strong woman whose one weakness was the mind-altering effect of drugs. This failing was supported by her husband Herman, a petty criminal and part-time dealer.

The couple struggled with their addiction and codependency. Herman was a day-to-day dealer in crack, heroin, and anything else that would get you high. But he was a bad businessman. Herman used his own product, often owing thousands to his supplier. And he couldn't resist the advance of any young girl, so he was constantly fighting with Sherindah about his sexual indiscretions. It had always struck Muhammad as strange that their mother could shoot a speedball into her veins, but still cared if her good-for-nothing husband screwed some prostitute for a nickel bag.

When Akema was still in diapers, Rimba was about ten, and Muhammad was just starting to like girls, Herman murdered their mother. Sherindah had followed him out late one night and caught him with a girl in a local park. Muhammad would later hear that Sherindah waited until they were done, then confronted Herman, who beat her in a blind, drugged-out rage and dumped her body into a man-made lake. Sherindah was found a week later, dead, bloated, with all traces of evidence washed away. Herman had disappeared and was never seen again.

Muhammad and his brothers were split up and put into foster homes. The next years were hellish by all accounts. The brothers were beaten, abused, and shuffled from one uncaring home to another. And there in the midst of America's unwanted lives, they had all gone a little insane. Rimba turned to music as a refuge, shutting out the world. Akema was short-tempered and quick to violence, and

Muhammad was calculating and devoid of pity and remorse. This was what their father had made them, according to Muhammad, and it was nothing to be ashamed of.

Muhammad ended up in juvenile detention at fifteen. He'd cut up a rival gang member and copped to it to get a light sentence. He lost touch with Rimba and Akema for the first time and it drove him crazy not knowing what had become of his brothers. When Muhammad got out at eighteen, he took custody of his brothers. He could not afford to go through the proper channels, so he just tracked them down and took them out of whatever home they were in. The foster parents never objected.

From there, Muhammad took his reunited family from one crime to the next, careful not to leave a trail. They'd burglarize a home, then steal a car, rob at gunpoint, then carjack another, never leaving a witness or a clue. They did this while moving steadily north, on a mission that had been started by Muhammad in prison. They were going to find their father and kill him.

For the last ten years, Muhammad had been tracking Herman Bady through sources in prison and the criminal underworld. He'd spent a lot of money and favors, but he'd finally come to the conclusion that Herman was in Detroit under a new identity.

Muhammad was the only one with any memory of their father. He could barely remember his face. But if he was not using drugs anymore, he would have put on weight in the last ten years, aged a little. In that regard, he could be anybody.

Detroit might be their last, final destination, Muhammad thought, but it was as good a place as any to die. Maybe it was even better than most. So Muhammad was happy this day. They had finally stopped running.

During their crime spree, Muhammad had turned his brothers into the family he'd always wanted. They were close, loyal, and committed to their goal. All they had to do now was kill their father and they'd be whole again.

Muhammad knelt next to Keith, who was shaking with fear. "Not your day," he said to Keith in a voice that was soft and surprisingly pleasant.

"I didn't see nothin'," said Keith. "I swear."

"I know," said Muhammad.

"Deion is stupid!" cried Keith. "I told him to take the damned money. Nigga always tryin' to be tough."

Muhammad regarded the man cowering on the floor. He'd seen men like Keith many times. In prison, they were the first ones turned out by the bull fags and lifers. In life, they were turned out by the demands of responsibility and strength put on a man. Keith was here in the morning buying beer, setting up for another day of drinking, lying around, and pretending that his pathetic life was not his own fault.

"You gonna keep our little secret?" asked Muhammad.

"Hell yeah!" said Keith. "I ain't never gonna talk about this shit."

Muhammad asked Keith to get up, and as he did, Muhammad raised his gun to Keith's chest and fired. Keith flew back into the aisle, still holding a six-pack in one hand.

Rimba and Akema grabbed beer and food from the store as Muhammad walked over to them and kissed Akema on the head.

"Don't never take shit from nobody," he said to Akema. "I don't know what's wrong with these muthafuckas in Detroit. A man can't even buy a little food without some shit jumping off."

"Word," said Rimba, who never spoke much, a result of living in the homes of strangers. Rimba coughed loudly again as he continued his rapping.

Muhammad looked at his brother with concern. "Take some of that cold medicine, Rimba. You sound like shit."

Rimba went off dutifully and grabbed the medicine from the shelf as Muhammad looked after his brother, worried that he'd catch pneumonia or something awful.

Akema continued to plow through the store, knocking over boxes and cans and taking anything that looked good, then stuffing all of the items into a big plastic bag.

Muhammad glanced out of the store window for a moment.

Somewhere out there was the man he'd come for, the man who'd caused so much misery and pain. He'd find him and his death would be the worst thing they'd seen in this town in a hundred years. Then Muhammad casually walked over to the counter, took back his brother's bloodstained money, and shoved it into his pocket.

5

THIRTEEN HUNNET

Detroit police headquarters is located at 1300 Beaubien Street in Detroit. The building is called simply "thirteen hundred" by the city dwellers. In the proper vernacular, the correct pronunciation is "thirteen hunnet."

Danny worked on the sixth floor in the SCU, or Special Crimes Unit. It was called the Sewer, the place where all the shit goes. The worst crimes in the city ended up there. Danny didn't like to think about why he'd ended up there as well.

Danny did his best hunting and pecking as he completed the reports on the incident the night before. The papers were stacked in a thick pile on his desk as he struggled to complete them. Erik sat across from him reading the morning paper.

The Sewer was a cramped room full of furniture older than time. The air had a feel to it, heavy, like something just wasn't right. The desks were placed close together and facing each other so you could talk to your partner. In the far corner was the boss's office, with its door that was almost never closed.

The division was small, only about eight cops in all. The SCU used to be bigger, but it was downsized after a corruption scandal a few years back. There was Danny and Erik, Lisa Meadows, who had been the only woman in the unit until her partner, Gretchen Taylor, joined right before Danny. No one wanted them to partner, but they requested it. Danny guessed that neither of them wanted to deal with the shit you get from having a male partner. Brian Lane and Joe Canelli were veteran detectives, both survivors of a corruption probe, and Reuben Mitchell and his partner, a young black kid named Wendel Hamilton, rounded out the group.

The SCU leader was Inspector James Cole, an almost legendary cop, twenty-year man, commendations up the ass and the whole nine. Jim was a tall man, about the same height as Danny, only Jim had a face like a goddamned movie star. Jim's rep was that he was a ladies' man. Women were always making up excuses to come into the Sewer, and they wore the most revealing outfits when they did. But Cole took it in stride. He was all business and didn't like it when his men were distracted from their work.

When Danny arrived at the SCU, Jim had walked up to him and said, "I heard about you, since you was a rookie. I got just one rule— you don't fuck me, and I won't have to kill your ass." Then he smiled and shook Danny's hand. Danny knew what he meant. Danny had to behave himself, but Jim would back him up if he didn't, as long as Danny did things his way. Jim was a good boss, the kind who actually understands the job and knew how to be a leader.

Jim Cole was also best friends with the Deputy Chief, Tony Hill, the man who'd sworn in Danny as a detective. Hill had made some slick political moves, and had gotten Danny the assignment, and he wasn't complaining about it. He loved the job.

Hill had given Danny the single best piece of law enforcement advice he'd ever gotten. He'd told him that a good cop can find out what's in people's heads, but a great cop knows what in their hearts. Danny understood this to mean that he had to learn how to read people, to use his experiences on the street as a way to figure out what people were capable of. He always had notions about the people he saw and he was usually right. In police work that first instinct could solve a case or save your ass.

Danny sat at his ratty desk, opposite Erik's. He reached over for his little desk CD player and popped in the newest by DMX, a hardcore rapper who told stories of ghetto life, a world that was familiar to Danny.

When Danny came to the Sewer, he didn't want a partner. He worked alone, he wanted to tell them, but that was the kind of shit Clint Eastwood would hiss at his commanding officer in a movie. In the real world that will get your butt busted, so he took the partner and made the most of it.

When Erik and Danny met, Erik was taken aback a little by Danny's demeanor and tone of speech. He was seeing a white man but feeling a black one. He got over it quickly as most people did. All cops are race-sensitive, even if they're black, but Danny didn't want their relationship to be defined by all that nonsense. Danny could see that Erik was not the kind of guy to put anything before competency in his judgment of a person.

Danny grew to like Erik after that initial meeting but the real test would be how Erik was on the street. Danny knew Erik probably felt the same way about him. A cop can be the nicest guy in the world but if he was slow, dumb, or, God forbid, weak on the street, he would not make a good partner. Fortunately for Danny, Erik was a tough and smart cop on the street. He was savvy, had good connections, and was always watching his partner's back. Danny watched and learned from him. Erik tried to keep him in check. He wasn't always successful.

A few months back, they were investigating a murder on the west side around Livernois and Puritan, a nice enough area, but one that has grown increasingly bad in the last few years. Some woman had gone nuts with a gun. The short word was that drugs were involved. Normally the SCU would not have been called in on such a routine homicide, but Danny and Erik had been out in the area so they'd caught the case, at least for the time being.

When they got to the crime scene, there was a drugged-out woman holding a gun on the uniformed officers who'd gotten there first. How they'd let their guard down Danny didn't know.

Before Erik could say anything, Danny had his gun out. The standoff was tense, and Danny could sense that the bullets would fly at any moment.

Erik stood behind the other cops and assessed, trying to talk her down. Danny had a clear shot at her. Danny didn't know if she'd jerk and fire at one of the officers, but a hit from an unsteady hand was a better bet than what they faced at that moment. The odds were good.

Danny was about to take the shot, when Erik did something that Danny would never forget. He walked over to the lady with the gun, and snatched it from her hand. She fell in a heap and started to cry as she confessed to shooting her abusive husband.

Later, Danny asked Erik why in the hell he'd stepped into the firing line. Erik said, "She didn't seem like she was gonna do it. She just didn't look like the type."

That display of smarts, instinct, and bravery always reminded Danny that there was another way, an alternative to a violent solution, even if it meant he had to put himself in harm's way.

The SCU had gotten confessions from the three men on Tireman they'd arrested, and so Danny was feeling pretty good. The shooter was a hard case named Odace Watson. He had three warrants outstanding, and priors going back five years. He was ready for the long stretch. The other two men had sung their asses off about how Watson was the triggerman and they were just along for the ride.

"How about puttin' some music in that thing?" asked Erik. "Marvin Gaye, Aretha, hell, I'd even settle for Whitney Houston."

"Don't got none of that," said Danny. "What's wrong with my man, here?" He held up the DMX jewel box, showing the rapper covered in blood.

"He looks like we should be putting cuffs on his ass, that's what wrong with him," said Erik.

The other cops laughed. Danny and Erik had an ongoing feud about the former's choice of music. For Erik, there was only classic soul, anything else was noise.

"Don't listen to him," said Wendel Hamilton, the young black detective. "He's just old. Turn it up." Danny bumped up the sound a notch.

"That shit ain't music," said Erik. "And y'all know it. These rappers just recycling old soul tunes anyway. Damned thieves. Oh hey, Danny, Marsha wants you and Vinny to come over this weekend, to eat me out of house and home."

"Can't," said Danny. "Vinny's real busy with her law classes, and the rest of the time, she's got reserved for bitchin' at me."

Venice Shaw was Danny's live-in girlfriend and former partner. After she'd caught a bullet in a botched robbery, she had quit the force and enrolled in Wayne State Law School. Danny was happy at first, but the strain of her first year was taking a toll on the relationship. And it wasn't as if they didn't already have enough problems. Vinny was black and her family, a big loving bunch, had never warmed to her living in sin with a white man.

"Can't believe you got a fine piece of woman like that." Erik put the newspaper down. "And when she gets that law degree, she's gonna be making big bank, too. You ready for your woman to make more money than you?"

"It's all good, baby," said Danny. "Money's money, you know. But this law school shit has been makin' Vinny a real pain in the ass. I already had enough trouble from her damned family. They practically walk around with 'Fuck the White Boy' shirts on."

"That's what you get for messing around with black women," said Erik. "Safer to play with fire, or a tiger or something." He laughed and all the detectives within earshot did, too.

Erik was kidding, but he was more right than he knew. Danny had not expected the resentment he'd get for his love for Vinny. He'd always thought prejudice was the exclusive province of white people. But black people were prejudiced, too, and something worse, they had right on their side when they said you were not good enough. To them, it was not bias, it was truth, and they had a shitload of history to back it up.

"Brown and Cavanaugh!" yelled Jim Cole from his office. Danny and Erik dropped their conversation and went over to him.

"Yes, sir," they said almost in unison.

"Good work on those drug hits. City hall is happily wiping the sweat off their nuts. But we got us another situation. I want you two to come with me to a crime scene."

Jim put on his jacket and walked off. That was Jim, quick to the point, quicker to action and don't ask any unnecessary questions.

Danny and Erik looked at each other for a second then followed, grabbing their stuff. They were reading each other's thoughts. If Jim Cole was going to a crime scene, then something had happened that was more than murder.

6

KILLER SECRET

The big house on Seminole was crowded with police cruisers, medical examiner's vehicles, and forensic trucks. Danny always got a thrill when he pulled up to a crime scene, a rush that could best be described as happiness. That's when you knew you had it bad for the job, when you looked at the devastation of evil and saw only the beginning of adventure. In a sense, you became an observer of life, detached from the normal feelings of men. The crime scene was an oasis, a clearing in the clutter of life.

On the ride over, Jim had informed Eric and Danny that a couple had been murdered and that they were going to get the case. The victims were John and Lenora Baker, rich and well connected. The Bakers were millionaires who owned gas stations, McDonald's franchises, and lots of other shit. They were also close friends with Mayor Crawford and had helped bankroll his election campaign. That's why Jim had come along. Someone important was dead.

Danny snapped on plastic gloves as he stepped into the house. He was always worried about contaminating a crime scene. When he'd started as a detective, he used to literally shove his hands into his pockets to keep from touching anything accidentally. Today a single smudge or print could win a case, so he took no chances.

The forensic team swarmed around the room. There were twice the number of people as usual. They dusted, looked for samples, and tried to get shoe prints from the floor. They had cleared a path across the big living room. A sheet of plastic ran through the room and up the staircase like a malevolent yellow brick road. But this was not Oz or Kansas. It was a murder scene and somewhere in this former place of safety there were people whose lives had been taken.

Jim veered off to talk to the tech team leader. Danny and Eric walked into the back to check the point of entry. The killer had come in via the rear door, which led into a pantry. The alarm system on the adjacent wall had been neutralized.

"The bastard disabled the alarm like a pro," said Danny.

"Maybe he's one of them master burglars," said Erik.

"He didn't take anything," said Danny. "He came to kill."

"A lot of trouble just to pop somebody," said Erik.

"All depends on how important the killing is to you," said Danny. "Remember that lady last year who killed her husband because he was cheating on her with the woman's own sister? She waited until she got a business trip to China, took a two-day trip into the country to get a rare herb she'd read about. She slowly poisoned her husband for over a year before he died."

"I remember," said Erik. "She was cold-blooded. She'd've gotten away with the shit, too, but she was so fucked up with guilt that she confessed."

Danny and Eric watched the techs finish their work then decided to take the plastic road upstairs. When they got back into the living room, Danny saw that Jim had been joined by Tony Hill, the Deputy Chief of Police. Hill was an intense-looking man who was known to have an unfailing sense of duty. He'd killed the former Chief, Bill Fuller, in a shootout when Fuller had gone bad in a murder investigation. Hill and Cole stood next to each other in that way only partners can, like friends and much more.

Tony Hill caught sight of Danny and nodded. Danny acknowledged him and moved on upstairs.

Before he got to the room, Danny smelled it, the pungent odor of something that wafted out of the kill room. Danny and Erik put plastic bags on their feet and walked to the door.

In the master bedroom, forensic techs worked feverishly on the scene. Danny's eyes focused on what his nose had already confirmed.

The room had been covered in dirt.

The killer had brought a bag of potting soil from the downstairs and tossed it all around the room. He'd done this after the victims were dead, because the bodies had been covered in soil as well.

"What the fuck?" said Erik.

"I smelled it, but I didn't expect this," said Danny.

"Is he crazy?" asked Erik almost to himself.

"Maybe he's smart, making sure it's not easy for us."

Danny and Erik walked inside on a path that had been vacuumed through the dirt. All around the room, the techs worked and cleared the dirt at the same time. Danny could feel their frustration as he made his way to the bodies on the bed.

The bodies were still tied up, their hands placed on their chests. The dead couple was black and in their mid-fifties. Their faces were ashen and their bodies bloated and discolored. The wounds that had been inflicted were covered by thick electrical tape to stop the bleeding. There was some blood on the bed, which had seeped through the tape.

Erik scanned the place, taking it all in. He was methodical, and didn't like to rush into anything.

Danny saw a flash of white from the corner of his eyes. He turned and walked over to the forensic team leader, Fiona Walker, a woman whom he knew from several cases. Fiona was brilliant, dogged in her investigations, and a bit of a smart-ass. He liked her.

Fiona looked at Danny with her pale eyes, which were lodged inside even paler skin. Fiona was an albino, an affliction which she took in stride, but which usually shocked anyone who didn't know her. Fiona's albinism was extreme. Her skin was almost translucent, her hair a stark white, and her eyes a color that Danny had never seen. If he'd had to guess, he would have said they were a light gray. She wore tinted glasses because her eyes were light-sensitive, something she called photophobia.

But what Fiona lacked in pigment, she made up for in brilliance. She had solved several major cases in the last two years and had even been asked to consult on a joint task force with the Justice Department a few years ago.

"So what we got?" asked Danny.

"I see dead people," said Fiona, laughing.

"We noticed that," said Erik. "What's with the dirt?"

"Someone's making my life hell," said Fiona with anger. "Definitely intentional."

"Was it meant as a clue or something?" asked Danny.

"How the hell should I know?" said Fiona. "If I had to guess, I'd say all he wanted to do was taint the room before we got here. From my point of view, that's the scariest damned thing in here. This guy knows my business, the sonofabitch."

A young black kid in a lab coat started a vacuum and began to vacuum some of the dirt. He moved slowly, carefully, and checked the floor after each stroke.

"That's Jacob," said Fiona. "He's the newest genius who's come to take my job from me. It was his idea to vacuum all the dirt for analysis. This killer's already a pain in my ass."

Danny saw her point. The killer was smart enough to know that the cops would try to get forensic evidence, so he threw dirt all around the room to make it impossible to do so. If anything was found that led to the killer, he'd say it came from the taint.

"So, how'd they get it?" Danny asked.

"They got shot," said Fiona. "Looks like a small-caliber weapon, probably a .22. Then the sick fuck stopped the bleeding with this." Fiona showed where the bodies had been taped up over the wounds.

"Why the hell would he do that?" Erik asked, looking at the corpses with growing interest.

"They stayed alive longer," said Danny.

"Right," said Fiona. "A bullet tears through vessels and organs and causes bleeding. Body cavities fill up, and the victim drowns in his own fluids. It would take a while. And our boy was clean. No prints, not even foreign fibers as far as we can tell so far, but who the fuck can tell for sure in all this mess?"

Fiona kept talking as Danny tuned her out. He wanted to look at the murder scene and try to get a notion of what had happened. Danny had learned a long time ago that all crime comes from simple human motivations, and could be solved only by the same kind of elementary logic. If you assumed too much complexity in a crime, you could miss the obvious motive.

With this in mind, Danny looked at the faces of the victims. The killer had put gags on them, thick elastic bands with a plastic ball in the middle. But that was not what held his attention. On the sides of their faces, he saw a red mark where the gags had been, only it was wider than the band itself.

"How come these marks are so wide?" Danny asked, cutting off Fiona.

"What?" she said.

"These marks on the sides of their faces, the gags made them, but why are they so damned wide?"

"I'll be," said Fiona. "I didn't notice that. I'd've caught it later, though, Mr. Smarty Pants. Maybe they tried to get them off."

"How?" asked Erik, and pointed to their still bound hands.

"Jesus," said Fiona. "Don't be asking me questions, okay? I'm a scientist."

"Maybe he moved them," said Danny. But why? he thought to himself.

Danny and Erik left Fiona to her work, promising to call on her after she had some hard scientific data. They walked back down the plastic road to their boss, who was now alone. Jim saw them and waved them over.

"We don't have a lot of time," said Jim. "This thing's gonna hit the front page tomorrow, and the high-society types will be calling city hall trying to find out why these two were killed and if they should mourn or hop a plane to Barbados. We get anything from Fiona and her people?"

"No, sir," said Danny. "It's a straight-up whodunit so far."

"And some sick shit," Erik added. "This boy's got to be a psycho."

"I'm with you," said Jim, "and you can never predict what a sick fuck will do. Still we have to try to head this off as much as possible."

"Victims have any family?" asked Erik.

"We're checking it," said Jim. "Right now, I got a tip from the Deputy Chief that these two had some bad blood with some other high-enders just a few days ago. I need you two to check it out tomorrow." Jim gave Danny and Erik the names and an address.

"They know we comin'?" Danny asked.

"Yes," said Jim. "They're not suspects, but try to get a lead out of them." Jim walked off, pulling out his cell phone.

"Political shit," said Erik.

"Society shit," Danny added. "Five or six kids get smoked every day and I give a fuck about this?"

They walked out of the house carefully as the tech team kept at it. The plastic covering their shoes was cleared of the dirt they'd tracked, then put back into the room.

It was a fact that a killer always left something behind at the scene of the crime. In the age of microscopic evidence, that was more likely than not.

Danny wondered what the team would find in the mess left by the killer, and if it would lead to anything. Beyond his preliminary thoughts about the case, however, he was deeply troubled by the thought of a killer who was so determined to kill and had the knowledge and foresight to thwart a forensic investigation.

7

FIRST YEAR

Danny cruised down Six Mile on Detroit's west side. The sounds of Busta Rhymes pounded the inside of his car. He passed Greenfield and turned down his street, Forrer. Danny neared his house, a little place with a nice patch of lawn that he hated to mow every week. He paid a kid named Jyrell from around the way to do it for him. He did a lousy job, but it helped to keep the kid out of trouble.

The neighborhood was decent, though in recent years, the influence of crime was more and more obvious. Used to be at night, all you could see on Six Mile, the main road, was a few cars and buses on the street. The street itself had been lined with businesses, party stores, and restaurants. But eventually these nice little places were replaced by fast-food joints, gas stations, and empty storefronts.

In the city proper, a proliferation of fast-food places was the surest sign of despair. There were a lot of single-parent houses and a working mother couldn't always come home and fix a meal for her kids. The people who make burgers, chicken, and tacos know this, so they set up shop, allowing these families to get a hot meal quickly and cheaply. A newspaper reporter called it "lifestyle need," a nice term for a family who can't have a sit-down meal every day. It was really a tragedy, the stark evidence that the world did not always change for the better.

With the fast-food joints came shady brothers in big cars, kids without supervision, and young women with no particular place to go. Crime went up, and suddenly there were bars on windows in what was once a good place to live.

The local neighborhood organizations got together and put an end to most of the illegal activity. The cops came around a little more (thanks in part to Danny and a few well-placed calls) and soon the neighborhood got back to normal. But the fast food still got eaten and some of the night people were around. That always made Danny feel better. He didn't want to live in a place that was too clean.

Danny went inside his house and called out to his girlfriend, Vinny. Vinny was a dark beauty who was soft-spoken, strong, and fiercely independent.

Danny and Vinny had been partners for a whole year before they slept together. It was all he could do to keep from being all over her in that car. They'd shared the job and each other's lives, stealing looks, and disapproving of each other's dates. They used the partnership to feel each other out and test the waters, a sort of professional foreplay. In the end, it was Vinny who had made the first move. They'd gone to her place after work, and after some very weak denials, they'd slept together, making love until the wee hours.

This frenzied lovemaking went on for about a week, every day. It was a while before they took their time and made love the right way. They'd both been thinking about it too much, wanted it too much. In truth, they'd both had a feeling that it would never last and just wanted to enjoy themselves.

But it did last. They partnered three years without incident, if you didn't count Vinny's constant nagging about his overzealousness with the criminal element. They didn't put their affair on display, so the department didn't say anything about it. People knew, but as long as they didn't screw up, it was cool.

The relationship was fine until Vinny caught one in an attempted robbery and decided to call it quits and go to law school. Danny didn't protest. He thought Vinny was more cop than lawyer, but he'd learned a long time ago not to tell her how to manage her future. Most women in general didn't like that, but it particularly troubled a black woman when some man tried to control her.

Danny learned that there was an animosity between men and women in the black community that is different from the one in mainstream America. It's not so much a battle of the sexes as it is a war of souls. In a nutshell, black men dealt in a lot of bullshit, and the sisters were not having it. So when Vinny decided to make this major life change, he shut the hell up and let her do it.

But her decision had an effect on the relationship that he didn't see coming. The first year of law school is a trial by fire. The workload is heavy, and the professors challenge, intimidate, and belittle you in class.

Since she'd started, Vinny had been gone all day and studied all night. She was like a phantom roommate. When Danny's mother died, Vinny had been right there, like a rock, but when she was sure he was okay, she was off again. Danny didn't like it, but Vinny was going for a dream and he was not about to whine about not seeing her. They still loved each other, and for now, that was all he really needed.

"Vinny?" he called as he stepped into the living room.

"We're back here," he heard her voice call from another room.

He started toward the den, wondering about the *we* Vinny referred to. They lived alone, so she had to have company. Vinny came from a big family, ten kids, so it could be any one of them. He hoped it wasn't Renitta, her big sister. Danny disliked her and knew the feeling was quite mutual.

Danny dropped his coat and moved closer to the den. He was

hoping he could unload a little of his day on her, but Vinny didn't much like to talk about police work anymore. So as much as he wanted to talk about the elusive killer, he decided not say anything.

Danny entered the den to find Vinny at a table covered with books and papers. She looked up and smiled. He scanned past her to the black man who sat next to her, smiling like an old friend.

"Hey," said Vinny. She came over and put a kiss on his cheek.

"Wha'sup?" asked Danny casually. He was still looking at the man, wondering how long it would be before Vinny told him who he was.

"This is Clarence Stanton, my study partner," Vinny said finally.

Danny shook Clarence's hand. His grip was firm, hard even, as though he wanted Danny to know he was a real man. Danny squeezed back just as hard.

"Nice to meet you," said Clarence.

Clarence was of medium build. He was a good-looking guy, one of those men who cared a little too much about just how handsome he was.

"We got anything to eat?" asked Danny

"We got that chicken from yesterday," said Vinny.

"Cool. I'm gonna have a beer. Anybody want one?"

"No, thanks. I don't drink," said Clarence quickly.

"I'll take one," said Vinny.

Danny got two beers and walked back to Vinny. Clarence was still sitting next to her, but he'd moved farther away.

Danny handed Vinny the beer and gave Clarence a quick smile. He went back into the kitchen and ate his chicken cold. If this was a typical night, Vinny would be up until midnight with her nose in some book, so he didn't count on any companionship.

Danny finished his meal and watched TV, trying to ignore the occasional laughter that came from the den. He didn't like Clarence and the implication of "study partner" was not good. But this was why he was seeing Gordon. The old Danny would have been in Clarence's face, giving him shit just for being close to his woman. But now he would wait it out.

He spent some time going over Fiona's preliminary report. Then he decided to go to bed. He said good night to Vinny and Clarence and hit the sack at ten-thirty. He and Erik had to run down a lead tomorrow, and the boss would want to know right away if they'd made any progress.

Danny tried to sleep but it didn't come for a long time. And when he finally drifted off it was restless, filled with images of the Bakers being murdered, the killer taping up their wounds as they bloated and bled to death in ungodly pain. Then he was awakened by a noise in the room.

"What time is it?" Danny said, searching for the clock.

"Sorry. It's one A.M.," she said. "I didn't want to wake you."

Vinny took off her top and wiggled out of her jeans. Danny took in her form and was aware that they had not been intimate in a long while. School was putting a damper on that, too.

"You know what class is kicking my ass?" asked Vinny. "Criminal law. Can you imagine that? A cop who can't hang in that subject. All the shit us cops think we know about law, it's just that, shit." She took off her bra.

Vinny slipped on a T-shirt and got into bed. He moved closer to her and slipped his hand under her shirt. In the age before law school, Vinny's hand would have been moving, too, but tonight nothing happened. He felt her hand move to his and gently tap it.

"I'm tired, Danny. I'm all stressed out."

"You know what's good for that?" said Danny. "Sex."

"Stop it."

Danny persisted in the foreplay, partly because he was a man but mostly because their sex life had taken a backseat to her new life and that pissed him off. He kept it up until she pushed away from him.

"Come on, Danny. Life ain't about sex, you know." Her words were a little sharp.

"Yes, it is," said Danny, and he saw her face take on an "explain that shit" look. "People make love because it feels good, and because they care for each other. It's human, Vinny. It's easy to say a man just wants to get his rocks off, like it's some selfish shit, but you know it's more than that with me."

Vinny shifted in the bed and for a second, Danny thought she was going to get up and walk out, but she didn't.

"All you ever talk about is school," Danny continued. He didn't see any reason not to go for the whole ball of wax now. "And I care because it's you." He was quiet for a moment, then, "I caught a murder today, but all I can think about is us."

Vinny was silent and he got ready for it. They'd never really argued about her school endeavors. They'd only had tense discussions, which usually ended with them apologizing and going to sleep. But he had thrown down a challenge just now, one she couldn't simply ignore.

"I'm glad to find out how important sex is to you." She propped herself up on one elbow. "I wouldn't want your heart to give out because you didn't get some tonight."

"Truth is truth." He smiled at her, knowing that she had already changed her mind. The only thing better than getting it was winning it, he thought.

"Who got killed?" she asked.

"Some rich people. They had big connections, so everybody's got their drawers in a bunch."

"How did they die?"

"Shot with a small-caliber gun and the wounds were taped up so that they bled internally."

"Damn," said Vinny. "Any leads?"

"None, so far, but you know what I always say. Everybody dies for a reason. Now, we just have to find it."

He felt her move closer and drape one of her legs over his hip. She kissed his shoulder, and despite the fact that he was still pissed of, he got excited. He thought for a second of not responding, but that thought didn't last long.

Danny rolled over and kissed her, letting his hand fall to her behind. Her hand slipped quickly down between his legs and she took in a deep breath.

They engaged in their familiar foreplay, and the routine made Danny feel better. He needed to be with her to remind him that he *was* with her. His mind filled with intense pleasure from this woman he adored, chasing out his newly discovered killer.

8

GROSSE POINTE

Grosse Pointe was one of those towns you grew up hating if you weren't lucky enough to live there. It was the historical home to many of the richest people in the metropolitan area and the country. They even had the nerve to separate it into little kingdoms: Grosse Pointe Farms, Grosse Pointe Woods, Grosse Pointe Shores. Some wondered why they just didn't call it Mount Olympus.

The Pointe was also just minutes outside of Detroit. A few miles in distance but a million in affluence, comfort, and power. Danny always felt one city mocked the other, like an old friend who has turned out more successful.

Danny and Erik zipped up Jefferson Avenue, watching the city fade from downtown's urban renewal, into urban decay, then burst back into the affluence of the suburb.

Danny was playing a tune by a rapper named Trick Daddy. Erik turned it off and replaced it with the oldies station, which was belting out "Call Me" by Al Green.

"See," said Erik. "Now, that's music."

As they left Detroit, Danny felt the city slip out of him. It was like someone peeling off a layer of skin. A city is like an extra set of cells in your body: heavy, and laden with dark forces. Going into the suburbs made you feel lighter, more human as it were, and Danny didn't like that one bit. He was used to the heaviness of Detroit. It fit him like a suit of armor.

Soon, they were driving down a long, private road toward a large house that had a big circular driveway with several cars in it.

"Jesus, look at this place," said Erik.

"Yeah," said Danny. "I'm living the wrong life."

"Looks like someone's throwing a party."

"Then we're right on time."

Danny felt himself tense as he thought about their upcoming interview. Danny always thought that anyone with too much money had to fuck somebody else out of it. That was the basic rule of American economics: the rich fed off the poor. This big house was built out of the lives of a million poor people who'd be shot on sight if they came here after dark. Or maybe he was just pissed because he dodged bullets for a living and couldn't afford the sports package on cable.

Danny and Erik went up to the house and rang the doorbell. An elderly Latino man in a nice suit came to the door soon after. He had that pseudo-military gait that let you know he was a servant and proud of it.

"I'm Carlos," he said. "You from the police?"

"Yes," said Danny. "We need to speak to Mr. and Mrs. Long."

"Follow me," said Carlos. "I'll let them know you're here."

Danny and Erik followed Carlos into the opulent mansion. Danny had a bad feeling inside. The smell of jasmine and floor cleaner filled his lungs. Clean, he thought. The place was clean, too clean. The only reason for this much clean is to hide the dirt, he mused.

They walked into a huge alcove with marble floors. The walls were covered with paintings, and there were sculptures and tapestries all around them.

Carlos led them into a living room area and Danny could hear voices from the party not far off. He readied himself.

Paul and Inez Long were the soul of affluence and they knew it. Mr. Long was tall, about six three, and Inez looked him right in the eyes in her heels. They were elegant and graceful and had that air about them that never let you forget they were loaded.

"Is this about the Bakers?" asked Paul. His voice was surprisingly high and feminine. For some reason, this made Erik smile a little.

"Yes," Danny said. "We just need to ask you a few questions."

"Terrible thing," said Inez. "They were good people."

"Please, we're entertaining right now," said Paul. "Let's go into another room."

Danny was about to ask about their guests and why they needed to be away from them, when one of them walked in. Danny looked over and saw a black man of medium build wearing a nicely tailored suit. He looked familiar, but he could not place him directly.

"Anything wrong?" asked the man. His voice was smooth and rich with bass.

"Hamilton," said Paul. "These men are here about the Bakers."

At the mention of the name "Hamilton" Danny knew who he was looking at. Hamilton Grace, the president of the NOAA, a large group of black political organizations. Danny had seen him in the papers and on TV. Now he knew why Paul Long was so nervous. Hamilton Grace meant power. Not the kind of guest you wanted to know that the cops had come calling about a corpse.

"Hamilton Grace," he introduced himself. "You're the police, I assume."

"Yes, sir," said Danny. "I'm Detective Cavanaugh and this is my partner, Erik Brown."

"Detectives," said Hamilton. "This is tragic. The Bakers were good friends of mine. If there's anything I can do, please let me know."

"We will, sir," said Erik.

Danny detected a respect in his partner that had not been present with the Longs.

Hamilton whispered something urgently to the Longs, then excused himself and walked off.

"Hamilton and his sons were visiting," said Paul. "They live close by. We wanted his sons to meet our daughter, Amy, but she flew the coop. Can't blame her actually. Maybe parents shouldn't meddle."

Hamilton came back to the foyer with two young black men. One was well groomed and dressed in an elegant suit. The other was scraggly-looking and dressed in hip-hop gear: baggy pants, big shirt, and boots. He also had a stud in the side of his nose.

"We'll come back soon," said Hamilton. "Thank you for having us."

"Thanks so much," said the son in the suit, "and give my best to Amy."

"Peace," said the scraggly son, and he walked off. He was all attitude, Danny thought.

Paul followed Hamilton to the door, practically kissing his butt out of the house.

"Those are his sons?" asked Erik. "They don't look anything alike."

"Jordan's adopted," said Inez. "And he's an exemplary young man. Logan is another story."

Danny understood that Logan, the natural son, was the hip-hop kid. The adopted kid was the one in the suit.

"I'd be exemplary, too," said Paul, "if my father was loaded like Hamilton." His tone was very gossipy.

"Any reason you know of that someone would want the Bakers dead?" asked Danny, trying to get back to business.

"No," said Paul quickly.

"We understand that you had recently had some bad business dealings with the Bakers," said Erik.

"Surely, you don't mean to suggest that we had anything to do with this?" said Mrs. Long.

"We just need to know the nature of the business in question," said Danny. He didn't want to digress.

"I don't like this inquiry, Detective," said Paul. "I'll refer you to my lawyer."

"You're not under arrest," said Danny. "And you don't have to talk to us if you don't want to. But people will wonder why. I know I would."

"We had a fight," said Paul with a sigh. Mrs. Long was about to say something, but he cut her off with a look. "We met the Bakers at a society function. Inez and I are originally from Atlanta. We moved here because Detroit's coming back to life, and there are a lot of business opportunities. We hit it off with the Bakers and got into business together on an Internet deal."

"What kind of Internet deal?" asked Erik.

"It was a company called New Nubia.com. It was a Web site that dealt in Afrocentric goods, art, books, everything. It went up a few years ago and posted strong sales. The Bakers got a lot of us in on the ground floor based on sales. We all bought equity in the company and were looking forward to an IPO next year. We were going to sell shares, cash out, and get a thousand times our investment. It looked like we were going to make millions."

"But it didn't turn out that way, did it?" asked Danny.

"No," said Paul. "The company's IPO was less than stellar."

"It was a disaster," added Inez angrily. "We lost a fortune."

"Inez," said Paul in a cautioning tone.

"There's no sense in hiding it," said Inez. "We got taken and they're going to find out sooner or later."

Danny and Erik kept quiet, each knowing to let the argument proceed naturally so they could get more information. When the Longs calmed down, Danny broke in.

"How much did you lose?" he asked.

Paul looked embarrassed for a second. It was obvious that he had pushed for the deal. Paul had fear in his eyes. He unconsciously shifted on his feet, looking down for a moment. "A couple of hundred thousand or so," he said.

"Four hundred thousand," corrected Inez.

Danny and Erik hid their shock at the number. It was lot of money even for people like the Longs.

"Were you angry about losing that kind of money?" asked Danny.

"Sure," said Paul. "Who wouldn't be? But when you check, you'll see that there are people who lost a lot more. Millions ran through that company."

"So where did the cash go?" asked Erik.

"We don't know what they did with it, but it didn't go into the company," said Inez.

"Mr. Baker have any bad habits?" asked Danny. "Gambling, drugs, anything?"

"No," said Inez quickly.

Paul was quiet and looked away from the detectives for a second.

"Something you wanna say, Mr. Long?" asked Danny, noticing his demeanor.

"No," said Paul.

Danny and Erik caught his evasiveness and wanted to push him, but if they gave him too much time to think about it, he'd dig in and find an avenue around the information he was so obviously hiding.

"We can ask you to join us downtown, if you like," said Danny.

"I told you all I know," said Paul.

"Okay," said Danny. "We'll tell our boss what you've told us and he'll say 'go back.' And we'll come back here again and again until everyone around you thinks there's some kinda bad shit going on. So, if you know anything, you'd better tell us, or the investigation will start to focus on you and that could get ugly."

Paul looked even more upset now. Danny didn't know a lot about rich folks, but he was sure that no one liked his friends to think ill of them. And Paul seemed like the twitchy type, the kind of man who'd wear a gas mask on the toilet, so he'd never know that his shit did in fact stink.

Erik caught Danny's eye and gave him that look, that partner look that said, "Good job." Danny smiled a little. Erik's approval meant a lot to him.

Paul's face showed defeat, but he had a smile on his lips. It stayed there for only a second, then it vanished into a flat line.

"He had a thing on the side," said Paul.

"Mr. Baker had a lover?" asked Danny.

"I wouldn't call it that," said Paul. "She was a whore." He said the word with more than a trace of disgust.

"Do you know her name?" Erik asked.

"Most certainly not," said Mrs. Long.

"Xena," said Paul without hesitation. This got him a look of shock, then pure evil from his wife.

"Like the TV show," said Danny.

"TV show?" asked Paul.

"Never mind," Danny said as Erik chuckled softly behind him. "Was she a call girl from a service?"

"No," said Paul with a sly smile. "She was some girl he found on the street. Imagine that." Paul straightened his back a bit, enjoying his gossip.

"And just how do you know John's whore?" asked Mrs. Long. She had turned her body toward Paul and raised her hands to her hips.

"Inez, it was male talk," said Paul.

"John told you the name of his hooker girlfriend? Some street tramp? I don't think so."

"He didn't tell me. Charles Eastergoode told me, and I don't know how he found out."

"Judge Eastergoode?" asked Erik, recognizing the name.

Before Paul could answer, his wife was in his face. "And you never shared that with me? Why?" Inez raised an accusing finger in his direction.

"Yes, it was the judge," said Paul, then he looked back at his wife.

The couple was headed for a nasty argument, and as much as Danny and Erik wanted to watch it, they had to get back to the job. They had business with the forensic lab.

"Thanks for the information," said Danny. The Longs stopped arguing and looked at the detectives as if they had just walked up.

The couple turned back into congenial hosts and quickly had Carlos escort Danny and Erik out of paradise and to their car. They drove out of the private road, leaving the mansion behind.

"So, what do you think?" asked Erik.

"I think I need to play the lotto tonight," said Danny. "This company, the New Nubia, had to have records. We get them, and I say we got us a list of suspects."

"Yeah, if I lost that kinda cash, I might have killed their asses, too."

"Or paid someone to do it," Danny added.

"Right," said Erik. "These kinda folks don't get their hands dirty."

Danny glanced out at the Detroit River rushing by them as they headed back into the city. Soon the river would disappear and only the urban sprawl would be in their view.

"Man, a lot of times I wonder what it feels like to be rich," said Erik. "You know, you see some shit, you want it, you just buy it and not once even think of how much it cost. Me, I buy a Tic Tac, and I automatically deduct from my retirement."

"It's probably not a lot different from being poor."

"Bull—shit," said Erik, taking a pause between the words. "You been watching too much TV where they want you to think rich folks are all sad and fucked up, crying and shit. 'Poor me I got so much money and it's killin' me,' " he mimicked crying. "In real life, they're happy, drunk, fuckin', and laughing at your poor ass."

Danny laughed at Erik's assessment. He had a way of reducing things to their common denominators that was amazingly fast and always right. In his head, Danny saw the Longs laughing, screwing, and drinking from large bottles of liquor.

Just as quickly, Erik was back to business. "Those people, the Longs," he said. "They suspect something, but I don't think they even know what it is."

"Yeah, I got that," said Danny. "But it could be they're just two scared-ass people. I'm sure this kind of thing don't happen a lot in their lives. I just wonder what kind of person did it."

"What kind?" Erik sounded curious.

"Well, the Bakers had money, so let's say someone hired a man to kill them. Your average killer for hire comes in two basic types. The lowlife muthafucka who'll whack you over the head for a high, and the pro who'll cap your ass with a silenced pistol, then make it look like a burglary. Our murderer was neither. He was angry, but he was also clean and planned out. Maybe he's crazy, but he's not a fool."

"And what about this alleged ho Mr. Baker was seeing?" asked Erik.

"Shouldn't be hard to find her, although the name Xena is obviously fake. All the girls use them."

"You seem to know a lot of hos, my brother," said Erik with a smile.

"I know a few, professional and not." Danny laughed.

"I got a boy in Vice," said Erik. "I'll get him on it. Shoot, he knows every hooker from here to Argentina."

They drove out of Grosse Pointe back into Detroit via Jefferson Avenue. As the brightness of the suburb gave way to Detroit, Danny could feel the hardness of the city slowly creep back into him, filling him up.

9

TRIPLE THREAT

Fiona sipped coffee from an enormous mug while she stood over the Bakers' dead bodies. Forensic science was fascinating, but it was complicated. Danny had learned that to think like a forensic cop, you had to think of a world you could not see, a place where every molecule told a story. He didn't know what the hell that meant exactly, but he knew Fiona was good at her job and he trusted her.

Fiona's lab was one of those white, sterile rooms where you had to wear latex gloves and paper on your shoes. It was cold as hell, and Danny got a chill every time he came here. The place was creepy, filled with bloody solutions and dead bodies. Not the kind of place for a street cop.

And what was worse, the room reminded Danny that his mother's body had been in one of these rooms not long ago, on a slab being examined by a doctor. He'd tried to stop the procedure, but it was routine in such cases. It was ruled death by accident.

"Well, I thought this was going to be some boring shit, but I was wrong," said Fiona as she put down her mug and grabbed a clipboard. "Our boy is a sadistic bastard and very smart."

Danny looked at Fiona with her all-white skin, wearing a white lab coat against the white walls of the room. If he blinked hard enough, he'd lose her in the whiteness.

"Give me the sadistic part first," said Danny.

"He knocked them out with chloroform. Since the wounds show that the victims moved, the asshole waited for them to wake up. Then he shot them with a .22. Only like a million of those in the city, right? And we got slugs, but they've been doctored. Check this shit out."

Fiona grabbed a pan. About seven lead slugs rolled inside. She put one under a projector and an image jumped onto a screen.

"What in the fuck is that?" asked Erik.

"That's what killed your victims," said Fiona.

"That ain't no ordinary bullet," said Danny. "It looks like a jagged rock."

The picture on the screen showed a dark shape with peaks and valleys cut into it.

"Yes," said Fiona. "Our killer filed the tips of the little bullets, so they would be sharp and jagged after they fired. That way, after the bullet entered the body, it would hurt you three times. Once when it went in, again as it tore through tissue and organs, then the third time when you moved—it would move and do even more damage."

Fiona took another swig of coffee and Danny wondered how long it had taken her to be able to consume food around dead people. She put down her mug, and Danny noticed the faded picture of a ballerina on it. He remembered that Fiona had trained as a dancer in her younger days.

"The male victim was shot four times—in the heart, liver, and spleen areas," she continued. "Our killer knew that these areas would do the most damage. The body filled up with bile, blood, and other fluids and he drowned in them."

"But it would take time, right?" asked Danny. "How much time?"

"Depends on the person, the shot, and other factors," said Fiona. "I'd guess it took them a half hour or so before they were pretty much goners. Now, the woman was shot in the same manner, but one of the slugs is still in her. It impacted some bone."

"Okay, so what else did our boy leave at the crime scene?" asked Danny.

"Not much," said Fiona. "We found some fibers that didn't match anything in the bedroom, but they are so common, they could belong to anyone. We found powder residue used in the making of surgical gloves, so we know why there were no fingerprints at the scene."

"Hair, skin, blood?" asked Danny. Even he could hear the desperation in his voice.

"*Nada*," said Fiona. "That's the smart part. Our boy is no dummy. He knows enough about forensics that he was not going to get sloppy." Fiona smiled at them. "Fellas, you got yourself a goddamned dilly of a murderer."

"How many sweeps did you do of the house?" asked Erik.

"Two," said Fiona.

"Do another one," said Erik.

"Okay, but we won't find anything," Fiona said. "I've seen a lot of sick bastards in this town, and I'm telling you, this guy's gonna be on my top ten. You know, these stiffs, the Bakers, had one helluva bad week. We found dog hairs in the house, but no dog, right? Turns out their dog died."

"How?" asked Danny.

"I know what you thinking," said Fiona. "It wasn't shot. We found the records from a vet. The mutt died of old age."

Fiona finished up her report then Danny and Erik left. Danny felt his body warm as soon as he stepped into the hallway. Erik looked pissed about something. He walked along, his steps falling a little harder than normal.

"What's up?" asked Danny.

"I had some downtime coming," he said. "But now it's not gonna happen."

"Probably not. The boss will want us on this full time."

"Marsha and me were going to Mackinaw. Boating, fishing, fucking. I had it all planned," said Erik.

"If it's that important, we can ask Jim to let you off," said Danny.

"You'd like that, wouldn't you? Solve this case by yourself and get a promotion?"

"Did I say that?"

"No, but you were thinking it," said Erik. "I know you."

"Then you know I was just trying to be nice. I don't want your ass to go anywhere while this guy's out there. There ain't nobody in the squad who can cover my back the way I work."

They walked out of the forensic area not saying another word. Danny was sure that Erik was thinking about how he was going to tell his wife that she'd be stuck in Detroit for the rest of the spring. Danny was thinking that if the killer had a plan, it was mysterious and so elaborate that he'd invented a unique and terrible new way to kill.

10

THE LOCKE

The Locke watched the abandoned house as the last of the men went inside. He was one street over looking through the vacant lot. The weeds had grown big, so he had to look over them to see, but there was no doubt that these were the men he wanted.

They had no idea what Detroit was about or they would have left town right after they'd robbed his store. Perhaps they were as crazy as he'd heard. His street sources told him that the three brothers were from out of town, from the South somewhere. When he was done today, they'd wish they had stayed there.

The Locke, as he was called, waited until the men had been inside the little dilapidated home for a few minutes; let them settle in. When he was sure it was time, he signaled his men to get ready.

In the back of the SUV, Dapp, a muscular black who sported a gold stud in the side of his flat nose, and Grease, a kid with a bald head and a Tiger's cap pulled down tightly over his brow, took out their guns and checked them.

Desandias Locke was that rarest of criminals, the successful one. When he was just a kid, the Locke was double promoted in grade school, after his distraction in class was found not to be a learning disorder, but boredom. He had dazzled the teachers with his mastery of math and science and his remarkable memory. In junior high, he had skipped another grade as he exceeded his teachers' already high expectations. He'd graduated from Northern High School at fifteen.

He should have gone on to college then some good job somewhere, escaping the nightmare of the ghetto. But the long arm of the hood was longer than anyone knew. The Locke's parents were both alcoholics. Codependent and hopeless, they took little interest in their brilliant boy and so when the Locke started running numbers for a man named HiLo, all they cared about was how much money the boy was going to make.

The Locke took the job and excelled. He "kept book" as they called it, for HiLo, mentally marking all monies owed and owing. HiLo loved this because there were no written records to use against him if the cops caught on. But the Locke was more than just this one useful function. He thought up new ways to make money for his boss. The Locke invented a game that was tied to the sum of all the points scored by Detroit's professional teams in one day, another was a card game that traveled in a small mobile camper. He was so good that when HiLo was killed by his girlfriend the Locke took over the game at the ripe old age of eighteen without so much as a ripple in the transition.

The numbers game got old after the lottery caught on big, so the Locke moved into drug trafficking. The money was great, and he'd set up middle men, mostly juveniles, to do the dirty work. He never got so much as arrested.

When the Union drug wars started, the Locke got out of narcotics. The organization of all the independent drug groups was a violent undertaking that closed off the avenues for profit. Either you joined, or they killed you. Locke saw this as a sign to move on. He got into all manner of nonviolent sin. If it was stolen, he had it, if you wanted sex, he could arrange it, and if you wanted to bet on anything, he was your man.

The Locke made peace with the drug dealers and hired enforcers to keep the random criminals away from his deals and businesses. He kept several small legitimate enterprises and paid taxes, so the IRS would look the other way. He greased the palms of the local community activists so they'd do the same.

The Locke loved "the life," as they call it, so he always kept close to the action, financing a buy, setting up a pyramid scam or a robbery. Lately, he was doing a lot of auto arson. He'd torch a car for the insurance. With a burned-up car, you could inflate the value. He took 10 percent of the nut. Good money and no one ever resisted because everyone hated insurance companies. The Locke even sold information to the cops if it was safe to do so. He liked the ladies and ran a few girls, taking a modest cut of the earnings. They were a pain in the ass, but he got to sample the girls for free.

The Locke was a big man. He was only five nine or so, but he weighed in at almost three hundred pounds. He had a large, roundish head covered with thick hair that he never combed. His eyes were deep-set and seemed to be tiny circles of brown in the fleshy folds of his face.

So the Locke maintained a lifestyle devoid of criminal stench. To the public, he was a man with a small party store and a gas station. Things were good, that is, until someone robbed his store and killed two of his men. They had come into the store and robbed it, making sure to take the surveillance video. Only serious, hard-ass pros did that. But the video theft didn't stop him from finding out who they were. The Locke had many street connections, and so he quickly discovered who the killers were. The three brothers were from out of town. They were young, ruthless, and were described as crazy more than once.

The Locke had withheld this information from the cops when they came to investigate the murders. He wanted these men. No one on the street could think that he would not avenge a thing like this. The clerk was a friend of the Locke and also one of the best forgers in the business, a valuable asset gone.

The Locke popped some M&M's into his mouth as he checked on his hitters. "Y'all ready?" he asked.

"We up," said Dapp.

"Hit 'em hard," said the Locke. "If they got any of my money, get it back."

Dapp and Grease opened the door to the SUV and rushed toward the house. The Locke turned on the engine and watched. He had faith in his men, but if there was any sign of trouble, he'd get his ass out of there in a hurry. He watched as Grease and Dapp disappeared. He was excited. Sometimes, he did miss the violence.

Muhammad Bady casually read a newspaper account of the hit on the party store. He was never a good reader and struggled with the long sentences. He also liked to read in front of his brothers because they never read and it made Muhammad feel like a father to them, the man who had all the answers.

The news account of the robbery was the usual shit, "unknown robbers," "no witnesses," and the like. But the thing that bothered him was that the owner of the store's name was not used and he wasn't quoted as saying anything. They'd done more than their share of robberies, and if there was a story, the owner always said something, usually how the world was going to hell in a handbasket. But this owner was silent, almost as if he didn't want anybody to know he owned the joint. That bothered him a little, though he didn't know why.

The house they were in had been recently occupied by a crew of drug dealers who'd been taken down by the cops. They'd boarded up the place, but that was easily remedied. Muhammad also knew the utilities would be easy to turn back on.

Detroit was a wonderful place for them to end up. There were many abandoned houses in forgotten neighborhoods that could be easily lived in with little work. And the people in the hood were nice and stayed out of your business. The brothers took advantage of this as they always needed cheap living space, and free was as cheap as you could get.

The place was still very cluttered, but that didn't bother the brothers. They didn't plan to be there very long. Muhammad had tips on where to find their missing father.

Rimba was still nursing his cold and was sprawled out on a old sofa in a corner. He had his headphones on and he muttered a rap by Nelly.

Muhammad made sure his brother took it easy. Rimba was an energetic person who'd only make the sickness worse by his natural tendency to run around. And if he wasn't careful, Rimba would give the cold to Akema, then they'd both be sick. They did need looking after, he thought.

Suddenly, there was a loud pounding sound from above them. Akema bounded down the stairs, jumping down the last two.

"Men comin'," said Akema. "One in the front, one sneaking round the back way. They got guns."

Muhammad cursed then pulled out a gun and yelled to Rimba, who ripped himself from his slumber and grabbed his coat off the floor. Out of the inside pocket, he took a big knife.

"Go to the back," said Muhammad. Akema and Rimba rushed to the rear of the house. Akema pulled out a small pistol and waited by the door.

Dapp kicked in the flimsy front door and raised his gun. He saw no one in the room. He entered slowly, waiting for any sound or movement. He moved out of the living room toward the small den to the right of the front door. Quickly, Dapp approached a closet whose door was ajar, flinging it open, pointing the gun inside. He fired a shot inside the darkness, but soon saw that the closet was empty.

From across the room, Muhammad rose from behind the old sofa and fired a shot at the man facing the empty closet. The shot caught him in the back of the head. Dapp flew forward, disappearing into the closet. Muhammad kept firing into the closet as he walked across the room.

In the rear of the house, Grease heard the shots and kicked open the back door. It was sturdier than the one in front and he had to kick it twice before it flew open. He started firing as soon as the door was open. He saw the two people in front of him for only a second before the big knife hit him in the throat. He jerked from the impact and fired off a round. He was shocked at the speed of the attack. His mouth popped open as he tried to make a sound, but none came out.

Akema's shot flew right into Grease's open mouth and out of the back of his head. Grease's errant shot just missed Akema's left arm. Both attacks had come right on the heels of one another. Grease faintly heard his gun fire, and saw the blurry images of his killers as he fell on the dirty floor, dead.

A moment later, Muhammad walked in holding his gun and the one he'd taken off Dapp's dead body. He moved over to a window and looked out. A street over, through a lot, he saw a white Cadillac Escalade parked on the street. Exhaust came out of the tailpipe, signaling that the engine was running. The vehicle was much too nice to be in a place like this, thought Muhammad. The windows were darkly tinted and he could not see who was in the driver's seat.

Muhammad went out of the back door so the driver could see him and know that his men had failed. The Cadillac quickly sped away, burning rubber. Muhammad frowned as the SUV rolled off. He walked back inside.

"We got us an enemy," said Muhammad.

"Who?" asked Rimba.

"Probably the man whose store that was," said Muhammad. He now knew why the owner hadn't wanted his name used and made no comment. He was a player, a criminal, and he wanted revenge. "Akema, put your hat back on," he said with a little anger.

Akema's hat had fallen off, and with it gone you could see what the hat was designed to hide. Akema was a girl. The baby face she tried so hard to make look tough was now clearly the face of an adolescent girl. Akema stuffed her hair back under the hat, feeling embarrassed. Her brothers didn't like to think of her as a girl. Years of abuse in the foster care system had turned Akema away from her God-given sexuality and into the one she felt gave her the most security. She was neither female or male. She was tough and that was what it took to be left alone.

"Get all your shit," said Muhammad. "We got to go."

The Badys gathered their meager belongings and started to vacate the house. They would leave their car and steal another. Muhammad was too smart to keep using the same car now that they had a formidable enemy. This was not good, he thought. They had business and this enemy would be a distraction. But all it meant to Muhammad was that they had to get down to business of finding their father that much quicker.

Muhammad instructed his brothers to pull the bodies together in one room. They did, dragging them into the center of the floor. Then Muhammad picked up their belongings, started a fire, and left as the house burned to the ground.

11

CANDIDATE

Danny dropped the last page of Fiona's report on his desk. He'd spent two hours that morning reading it with *Police Forensics* by Lance Kimbrough at his side. It was the detective's guide to the subject written in plain English. Fiona liked to use the technical terms in her written work, and Danny sometimes needed translation.

He could barely keep his focus on what he was reading. Thoughts of his mother's death had wrecked his mind since he'd started the case. There was nothing to compare to the loss of a family member, he thought. It was awful when someone who had formed the foundation of your life was suddenly taken away. You were left to determine who you were without them, afloat without explanation or reason for the pain. The sadness and horror of it had left a stinging pit in his gut and peeked at him around every image in his head.

Focus, Danny thought to himself. The report was thorough, but it contained nothing of use. The killer had taken his victims from this earth and left not one clue. The analysis of the dirt had not yielded anything. All of the slugs had been studied and other than the doctoring on the tips, they were just ordinary pieces of lead. The SCU's routine check uncovered thousands of .22 caliber handguns in the tri-county area. The gun would not be the clue to catch the killer.

The Bakers had dined on steak, potatoes, Caesar salad, and red wine. For dessert, they'd packed away a chocolate soufflé. A great meal. Sounded as if they knew they were going to die, Danny thought to himself. Mrs. Baker had not been sexually assaulted, and Fiona, always the pro, noted that neither had Mr. Baker. He knew everything, which told him nothing.

Erik was fresh from the property room of thirteen hundred, where, with an expert from Fraud, he'd looked over the Bakers' records for New Nubia, the Internet company. He sat down opposite Danny with a smile on his face.

"I hope you got news," said Danny, "because Fiona's report ain't givin' me shit."

"The list of investors in that company is a who's who of Detroit's big-money players," said Erik. "And the Longs were small-timers in terms of their losses on the deal." He pushed the thick file across the desk to Danny.

"Was it on the real?" asked Danny. "Or some kinda scam?"

"The Fraud guy says the company was real, but the way they ran it was bogus. All we know is the thing went belly-up and a shitload of money disappeared.

"Where did it go?" asked Danny.

"A lot of it was spent by the Bakers. They were living pretty large, according to the records, but that doesn't seem to cover all of it. There's about two million unaccounted for."

New Nubia.com had fallen apart and lost all of its value. The investors had gone down for more than twenty million dollars. People brought in by the Bakers were drawn to the enterprise by the booming tech stocks and the big money being made in the market. Danny imagined someone with dreams of cashing in big and coming out with more money than God, then seeing those hopes dashed. In his experience, that was more than enough for murder.

"Maybe someone really wants that two million," said Danny. "More than enough money to kill for. Let's start with whoever went down the hardest," said Danny.

He was silent a moment, thinking about how money drove men to desperate means. If a crackhead would kill for a dollar, two million could drive a desperate person to do almost anything.

"I'd like to find that hooker," said Danny finally. "See what other skeletons my man had in his closet. One of them might point us in the right direction."

"You read my mind," said Erik. "Maybe Mr. Baker's little sins caused him to lose that money."

Danny and Erik reported their findings to their boss, who appreciated knowing that they were about to interrogate some of the most powerful and connected people in the city. Jim suggested that they get the lowdown on each of the people on the list as they didn't want to go in unprepared. Many of these people were powerful, rich, and very intelligent. They would be way ahead of the normal questioning.

Danny and Erik contacted city hall and the local papers and got all the information they could on the affluent people on their list. Danny left the Sewer thinking that if he found the the missing New Nubia money, the killer would not be far from it.

Virginia Stallworth was regaling a small crowd with a story as Danny and Erik walked into her garden party. She was entertaining, and there was a large crowd of mostly black people in her spacious dining hall. On the far wall was a banner that read: STALLWORTH FOR NOAA PRESIDENT!

Danny didn't like the idea of interrupting a party, but Virginia Stallworth and her family had been number one on the list of money losers in New Nubia.com. By making her entire family investors, she had lost more than three million dollars.

Danny and Erik inquired as to which of the women was Virginia, then made their way through the crowd of well-heeled people.

The party was a political rally for Virginia, who was running for president of the National Organization of African Americans, which was composed of several civil rights groups. The NOAA was powerful, prestigious, and doing well these days, thanks to powerful allies in Washington.

The president of the organization was a coveted job. In many ways, he or she was the de facto black president of the United States. His picture was in every major newspaper, his words were quoted as gospel, and he wielded considerable political power. The president of the NOAA also went all over the world meeting with heads of state and was on the A-list of every political party.

So it was no surprise that the NOAA's current president, Hamilton Grace, was conspicuously missing from the party. He was Virginia's opponent in the race and there was no love lost between the two. Hamilton was annoyed at being challenged and even more angry that the competition had come from within his own backyard.

Danny approached Virginia Stallworth in a corner of the room, a regal-looking black woman. She was in her fifties, but she looked ten years younger than that. Virginia had a head of full, silky dark hair with gray streaks, which cascaded over her shoulders. Her eyes were gray and jumped out at you because she was dressed in an outfit that matched. And if Danny hadn't known she was black, he might have mistaken her for a white woman as she was very light in complexion.

Virginia held a flute of champagne as she finished her story. Then she, along with a tall woman, broke off from the crowd. Danny and Erik took the cue and intercepted them before they could get lost in the party.

"Ms. Stallworth?" asked Danny.

"Yes," said Virginia. "May I help you?"

"I'm Detective Cavanaugh and this is Detective Brown. We need to speak with you."

Virginia reacted with surprise to the statement. Danny didn't know if it was the cadence of his voice or the word *detective* that elicited the response. He suspected a little of both.

"Police?" said Virginia. "You picked a terrible time to come around."

The tall, black woman with Virginia was stunningly beautiful and about thirty or so. Since Danny and Erik had walked up, Virginia's companion had not taken her eyes off Danny. In her heels, she looked Danny right in the eyes. After a moment, the tall woman cleared her throat and looked at Virginia.

"Oh, I'm sorry," said Virginia. "Gentlemen, this is Olittah Reese."

Danny and Erik turned and nodded to Olittah. Danny was surprised to find her thrusting out her hand toward him. Instinctively, Danny shook it. Olittah's grip was firm and she lingered on it a bit too long. She smiled beautifully at him. For his part, Danny was looking at the big wedding ring on her left hand.

"Nice to meet you," she said.

"Same here," said Danny.

Olittah took a second then turned to Erik and said a very businesslike hello.

Danny ignored the flirtation, but Erik was already smiling like a snake.

"Ms. Stallworth, is there some place we can speak in private?" asked Danny.

"Sure," said Virginia. "Olittah, we'll finish up later, okay?"

"Sure," said Olittah. She took another lingering glance at Danny then walked away.

Danny, Erik, and Virginia moved in the opposite direction. Danny didn't want to look after Olittah, but he let himself sneak a peek at her. When he did, he saw her long legs carrying her away. He also saw her turn and look back at him over her shoulder. Embarrassed, he smiled awkwardly and turned to find Erik looking at him with a smile.

Virginia led Danny and Erik out of the dining hall into an adjacent room. Inside, they found a group of young black people, all in their twenties.

"Gwen, we need the room," said Virginia.

The room emptied on command, and Danny couldn't tell to whom Virginia had spoken.

"I suppose you're here about the Bakers," said Virginia.

"Yes," said Danny. "We got a few question for you if you don't mind."

"I surmised that. My family will be here shortly."

"We'd rather just talk to you and your husband," said Erik.

"Anything you say will be said to us as a group," said Virginia. "We all invested in the Bakers' company."

"Your call," Danny replied.

The many pictures on the walls caught Danny's eye. One in particular drew his attention. He walked over to it. It showed a group of black people gathered outside for a barbecue. The title below the photo read: CASTLE PICNIC—DETROIT 1943.

Danny noticed there were policemen in 1940s uniforms. They were all white cops who were watching the gathering from a distance. There was a woman in the photo who looked a lot like the one in the room with him.

"Your mother?" Danny asked.

"Yes," said Virginia. "She lives in Florida now."

"Was this a family picnic?" asked Danny.

"No, it was a society event," said Virginia. Then she casually walked over to Danny and stepped in front of the photo he was looking at. "I wasn't alive when that one was taken," she said. "Here I am with my mother some years later." She pointed to another picture of the same woman, ten years older, holding a little girl of five or so.

Danny was about to ask Virginia why there were white cops watching a black family picnic in the 1940s. The races were not very friendly back then.

Before he could speak, the rest of the Stallworth family filed in. Oscar Stallworth, Virginia's husband, entered first. He was sixty and looked every year of it. He was a smallish man and slightly overweight. His head was balding, and he sported a graying beard. He was just a little darker than Virginia, but not much. Oscar followed by a tall young man who looked a lot like Virginia, and two young women. One of the women was thin, pretty, and wore glasses. The other was tall and full-bodied, not fat, but shapely. This one fixed her gaze on Danny as if he had insulted her.

"I heard the police were here," said Oscar in a tone that suggested he was not happy about it.

"Yes, they are," said Virginia. "Detectives, this is my family. Gwen, Cal, and Felecia."

Danny and Erik nodded. Danny stared at Gwen. She held his attention because she was many shades darker than the rest of the family. If she hadn't been introduced as family, he would not have guessed.

"My people told me you had two sons," said Danny. "Where's the other one?"

There was a brief silence at this and Danny felt a tension rise. Cal shifted on his feet, and Felecia shot Danny a look of annoyance. Oscar stepped forward with the same look on his face.

"Are you trying to mock me talking like that?" Oscar asked Danny.

"Ain't nobody mocking you," said Danny. "This is the way I talk."

Oscar looked at Erik as if to ask: "Is he for real, brother?" Erik just returned Oscar's gaze, unsmiling. Danny caught this exchange and grew irritated. This was the last thing he needed right now.

Oscar relaxed a bit. "Our oldest son is dead, Detective," said Oscar. "Whatever it is you want, get on with it. As you saw, we have guests."

"I'm sorry," said Danny. "We need some information about your dealings with New Nubia.com."

Virginia let out an exasperated sound. "That bogus company was over a long time ago—"

"Just a moment," said Oscar, cutting her off. "Cal, you and the girls leave now."

"Why?" asked Cal in a voice that sounded a lot like his father's. "This concerns us, too."

Oscar went to his son and whispered something to him. Cal's expression turned embarrassed, then he took the girls and left the room.

"Okay, Detectives," began Oscar after his children were gone. "I'm an attorney in case you didn't know, so I know what you're doing here. The Bakers lost a lot of our money. Therefore, you see that as a motive for their deaths."

Virginia's face expressed shock at this and Danny couldn't tell if it was staged or genuine. She just looked at her husband and absently covered her mouth.

"We hated them for deceiving us, Detectives," said Virginia, "but we are not—"

"No, Virginia," said Oscar. "We are under no obligation to say anything."

"Okay, Mr. Stallworth," said Danny. "Since you want to cut to the chase, can you account for your whereabouts on the night of the murder? The seventh?"

Virginia and Oscar looked at each other for a second, and something passed between them. Virginia shook her head ever so slightly and Oscar turned to Danny.

"We were together that evening. We had guests. My children were all at home with us."

Danny took down the response, not surprised that they had an alibi. The Stallworths were not the kind to go lurking with a gun looking for revenge.

"Did you argue with the Bakers about the company?" asked Danny.

"Yes, we did," said Oscar. "But it was not a big deal."

"Dear, don't say that," said Virginia. She placed a hand on her husband's arm as if on cue, and again Danny had the feeling that it was planned that way. "We had a terrible series of confrontations," said Virginia. "They escalated into a shoving match at a party a month ago. You would have found out about this sooner or later."

Now Danny was impressed. Virginia was giving up incriminating information and making it look as if it had come from a sense of honesty by second-guessing her husband. Danny noticed that Oscar did not seem upset that she had just about called him a liar.

"And were any threats made?" asked Erik.

"No," said Virginia.

Erik had been looking at Oscar when he asked the question, but the answer had come from Virginia.

Now Danny's pulse quickened just a little. There was definitely something going with these two. First Oscar was doing all the talking, but after the alibi was mentioned, Virginia was taking the lead. They were hiding something. He decided to try to shake loose a clue by shocking them.

"When New Nubia was taken public, were there questions about Mr. Stallworth's past?" asked Danny.

The Stallworths both expressed anger at this. Oscar's eyes expressed shock and his nostrils flared. Virginia was about to say something when Oscar cut her off with a look.

"Ancient history, Detective," said Oscar. "All of it is a matter of public record.

"You were suspended as a lawyer and did some jail time," said Danny.

"Yes, and it's all a matter of public record," said Oscar. "I was a kid back then."

"You were forty or so," said Erik. "That's not a kid."

Oscar Stallworth had been arrested along with several organized crime figures for running a fraud racket. They had gotten bogus companies to get public contracts for supplying goods and services to county hospitals. Money was funneled off, and the goods and services either were way below what was promised, or nonexistent. The county oversight officer who exposed the fraud had disappeared and was never found. He was presumed dead.

"You were hooked up with Leonardo Castellana. A man was killed," said Danny.

"Leo and I were in business, and no death was never proven," said Oscar quickly.

"No body was ever found," said Erik.

"Look," said Oscar. He was clearly getting angrier. "What I did was wrong, but we didn't kill anyone. I did some time, but I eventually got my law license back. Took me years to do it, too. I'm a legitimate businessman now, and I don't need the past coming back on me."

"But don't you still hang out with Mr. Castellana?" asked Danny, who noticed that Oscar had referred to Castellana as "Leo."

"Of course not," said Virginia. "Oscar is a lawyer. He knows that wouldn't be—" She stopped when she saw the look on her husband's face. Oscar's expression had shifted from anger to fear.

"I'm afraid this interview is over," said Oscar.

"You took the fraud rap for him, and he stayed out of jail," Danny said. "Where I come from, that means he owed you a favor."

"A big favor," added Erik.

"This is very compelling, Detective," said Virginia. "But you have no proof of what you are so obviously accusing us of."

"No murder is perfect," said Danny. "Mistakes are always made."

"And why would I have killed the Bakers?" said Oscar. "I needed them alive so I could sue their asses."

"New Nubia was going to file bankruptcy," said Erik. "You wouldn't have gotten a dime."

"But with them dead," said Danny, "the Bakers' assets, including the insurance on their lives, is available if you can get to it. One well-placed lawsuit would get some of your money back. Am I right?"

Oscar's head started to turn to look at Virginia, but he stopped himself. His eyes burned as he glared at Danny, who did not break the gaze.

"You have it all figured out, I see," said Oscar. "The only problem is, it's all bullshit speculation."

"That's how all cases start," said Erik. "It would be better for everyone concerned if you came clean."

"Came clean?" said Virginia. "There's nothing to come clean about."

"I think it's time for you to leave," said Oscar.

"We may be back to talk more," said Danny.

"Do it through proper channels next time," Oscar snapped.

"We have friends in the department," added Virginia. "We'll be talking to them about you."

Danny didn't answer. He and Erik left the room, saying the briefest of good-byes.

"So, what did you think of her?" asked Erik.

"She's a stone-cold player," said Danny. "A manipulator, and I wasn't buying that shocked shit when she found out she was under suspicion."

"Not Ms. Stallworth," said Erik. "That good-looking sister who was all over you."

Danny blushed at this statement ever so slightly, but that feeling was short-lived. "What can I say? The woman has good taste," said Danny.

"I'm sure she was using you to get to me," said Erik.

"Well, I was glued on that big-ass wedding ring on her finger. Did you see it?"

"No, my eyes were filled with legs," said Erik. "Man, sometimes I wish I wasn't married."

Danny thought about Vinny and their growing problems at home. He couldn't stop himself from wondering where she was and what she would do if some man hit on her.

"Let's get out of here," said Danny.

They walked out of the party and headed to the next interview. Erik was thinking about the Stallworths' connections to people who could have done violence to the Bakers. Danny had this on his mind, too, but he also kept seeing the photo from the forties that Virginia had so clumsily tried to divert his attention from. And strangely he thought about the Stallworths' daughter Gwen, who was so much darker than the rest of her family.

12

GRACELAND, HOLYLAND

Hamilton Grace was not a hard man to find. Danny and Erik had placed a call to him after getting his private number from the mayor's office. He invited them to his home, which was in Grosse Pointe, not far from the Longs.

Grace had a lot of money, and he wasn't trying to hide it. His house was more like two of the Longs' mansion. It was a massive structure, with manicured lawns and shrubbery, marble sculptures, and fountains that looked as if they'd been lifted from an Italian villa. It was one of those houses you see in a magazine or on TV, a place that had a name.

Hamilton Grace had lost almost as much money as the Stallworths, more when you considered that he'd brought in other people on smaller deals. He was known to be an astute businessman, but New Nubia.com had embarrassed him.

Danny and Erik were silent as a young black woman in a dowdy suit led them to Hamilton, who was on the phone by his pool. He looked to Danny to be very casual for a man involved in a murder investigation.

". . . no, Mr. Speaker," said Grace on the phone. "I can't take that position so close to the convention. . . . I know what they've done for us and we appreciate it but my mind is made up. . . . Yes, sir, I will."

Hamilton hung up the phone, and Danny saw a look of anger on his face. It was soon replaced with the practiced look of a politician.

"Detectives," he said. "I've been expecting you."

"We're here about the Bakers," said Danny.

"I know," said Hamilton. "I was called by the mayor and told you'd be coming."

Danny noticed that he said the last part with just a little more emphasis, as if he wanted them to know he was holding all the cards.

"How may I be of assistance?" asked Grace.

"We just need to know a few things about your involvement with New Nubia.com," said Danny.

Grace thought a moment and Danny could see something cross his mind. His brow furrowed and he took on a somber tone. "Yes," he said. "Well, I lost a lot of money on that deal, and I use the word deal very loosely. I don't know if the Bakers ever expected to make any money."

"So, you were upset about the whole thing?" said Erik.

Grace straightened his back, a kind of offensive gesture that seemed to make him stand taller.

"I won't waste your time," said Grace. "I didn't like the Bakers in the end. I'm sorry they were killed, but people like them usually get what's coming to them."

"And what kind of people is that?" asked Danny.

"Niggers," said Grace.

Danny and Erik were both a little shocked to hear that word coming out of Grace's mouth. He was a national black leader who himself had railed against the use of the word in the media, and now here he was slapping down two dead people with it.

"Wanna tell us what you mean by that?" asked Danny.

"I know it's surprising, but if you know anything about me, you know that I do not tolerate black people who deal in worthlessness, crime, drugs, or foolishness. The Bakers were educated, refined, sophisticated niggers." He raised a finger like a lecturer does when he's making a significant point. "They started that company to make money and stole the confidence of all of us, playing not on our greed, but our nobility as black people. Did you know that a portion of the profits were supposed to go to college scholarships at black colleges in our names? That's the kind of thing they did to lure us in. And all the while they were living like kings. Private jets, new cars, big salaries. They even bought matching gold Rolexes on the company. Nigger shit."

Grace's expression was filled with anger at the memory. Something about the case had triggered his ire and he was not going to just let it slide away, not until he made his point.

"I've dedicated my life to uplifting our people," said Grace. "Sometimes in a fight like that you can lose your perspective, let your guard down. I did. You know, in the old days, a black person who stole from his own people would have been taken out and whipped in public. It was how we used to keep principle."

Danny wasn't getting too excited about Grace's outburst. He hadn't incriminated himself by anything he'd just said. He was too smart for that. It wasn't a crime to be pissed off.

"We're going to have to ask you where you were the night they died, sir," said Danny.

"Here at my home asleep," said Grace without missing a beat. "My wife was with me."

A servant entered carrying a tray of ice tea. She was followed by a young, pretty black woman and Jordan, the preppy son. They were dressed in boating outfits. Jordan wore a captain's hat that made him look silly.

"Thank you, Moira," said Grace to the servant. "Detectives, this is my wife, Kelly, and you remember Jordan."

They all greeted each other and Danny noticed that Kelly was not much older than Jordan, who looked to be about twenty-five or so. Danny surmised that Kelly was wife number two.

"We're going to the club," said Kelly. "We wanted to know if you'd come."

"Can't," said Grace. "I need to talk to these men, then a news crew is coming. The convention is almost upon us, you know. I have to do PR."

"May I stay and help?" said Jordan eagerly. "It will look good to have family around you."

"No, you've done enough this week, Jordan," Grace replied.

"It would be no problem, sir," said Jordan. "I'll stand in the background."

"No," said Grace with more authority. "Go see if my son wants to go with you."

Jordan almost recoiled from this statement, as if he'd been slapped in the face.

Danny realized what had just happened. Grace had referred to Jordan by his first name, but to the other sibling as "son." The picture could not have been more clear.

"Of course," said Kelly dutifully, trying to ease the moment.

Kelly and Jordan moved off toward the guest house. Danny noticed that Jordan was big, powerfully built, and walked in an ordered, almost military manner.

Hamilton turned back to Danny and Erik and offered ice tea, which they both refused. Hamilton took a glass and sat in a chair. Erik and Danny sat also.

"Anything else, Detectives?" asked Hamilton. "I do have that news crew."

"I wondered why there's someone else running for president of your group, the NOAA," said Danny.

"It's a free country," said Grace. "Virginia has a right to run if she wants. It's no big secret that she's challenging me for the presidency, and it's causing a bitter divide within the organization."

"And the Bakers?" asked Erik. "Where did they stand?"

Grace took a sip of ice tea, but not before Danny saw his lip curl in an expression of disgust that quickly faded.

"They were with Virginia," said Grace. "Although they pledged loyalty to me, they were working for her behind my back." There was a tone of challenge in his voice, daring Danny to make the obvious connection.

"It seems like someone is trying to get rid of your enemies," said Danny with the same note of challenge.

"It was politics, not life," said Hamilton. "I know it's your job to come here and make your little incriminating remarks, Detective, so I won't be offended. But don't ever think that I'm not catching them."

"You said the Bakers embarrassed you when the company failed," said Danny, not responding to Grace's arrogance. "Why did you care so much?"

"My reputation is all I have, Detective," said Grace. "And there is an election for president at the convention in Detroit this year." He put down his drink. "I have been married twice, once to my son Logan's mother, Erica, and now to Kelly, whom you just met. I have an adopted son, Jordan, who is actually my biological son born out of wedlock to another woman named Carin Wilson. Jordan and Logan are the same age, hence the first divorce. When all this came out, I did the right thing and took Jordan in. I made some mistakes in the past and they cost me. People punish you for being human. Ask Bill Clinton. That's why I cared about being deceived."

"Were the Bakers spreading stories of your past around?" asked Danny.

"I wouldn't know," said Grace. "I try to stay above pettiness."

"Wasn't there concern about the way you've handled the organization's finances?" asked Erik.

"I wouldn't call it concern," said Grace with definite scorn. "We had a bad year. Some money was lost."

"How much money?" asked Danny.

Hamilton set his drink down and his eyes narrowed a little. Erik had obviously gotten to a sore spot with this powerful man.

"The organization lost five million on a bad investment I recommended," said Hamilton.

"So, when you add New Nubia to that," said Danny, "didn't some people doubt your ability to lead the organization? I mean, the Bakers made you look like a man who's foolish with money."

"I'd be careful in the way you phrase things with me, Detective," said Hamilton.

"Like you said, we have to ask these questions," said Danny. "We have people to answer to."

"Yes, and I know them all," said Hamilton. "They're good friends of mine."

Danny and Erik both got the gist of this statement. Don't mess with me because your bosses know how powerful I am and I'll get your ass. Grace was obviously happy to see the Bakers dead. It helped him in many ways, the money, his reputation, and it was one less political enemy between him and reelection.

The servant came back looking worried. "Sir," she broke in, "the news crew is here."

"Okay, Moira," said Grace. "Detectives, Moira here will show you out. If you don't mind, I need you to avoid the news crew."

Grace stood up and extended his hand, signaling that the interview was over whether they liked it or not. Danny and Erik checked with each other. They had as much as they needed for now. He had given them a lot of words, but precious few clues as to how he could have engineered the death. And the thing that bothered Danny the most was Grace didn't seem upset about the interrogation. It was almost as if he'd been expecting it. Either he was the coolest customer on the planet or he was innocent.

Moira walked briskly around the back of the house with the detectives in tow. Danny was acutely aware of being sneaked out like some kind of mutated relation they kept in the basement.

There was a news van outside, but no sign of the crew, which had already been taken into the house by someone else.

"Good day, gentlemen," said Moira. She turned quickly and walked off.

"He played us," said Danny. "He talked a lot, but he didn't say a damned thing."

"You know, that man has done a lot for our people," said Erik. "You think he's a killer?"

"Somebody did it," said Danny. "That means somebody ain't what they seem. I'm not taking him off my list. Not yet."

Erik cut Danny a hard look They stared at each other for a moment. They didn't disagree a lot, but Erik had his limits on all things and he didn't care if Danny agreed or not. Danny could see that Erik admired Hamilton Grace.

A loud voice broke the silence and Danny and Erik turned toward the driveway and garage. They saw Kelly and Jordan standing next to a Range Rover with Logan, the hip-hop son.

"Fuck that," said Logan.

"No need to swear," said Jordan.

"Really, Logan," said Kelly. "You don't have to go. Your father wants you to."

"You just be sure to tell him that it was your choice," said Jordan.

"Look, I got some shit to do," said Logan. "Y'all can go do that white people shit by yo'self." Logan walked away, got into a little BMW roadster, and pulled off.

Kelly and Jordan saw the detectives looking at them, and quickly got into their car.

"Interesting family," said Erik, forgetting his anger at Danny.

"Looks like the real son don't like the rich lifestyle," said Danny. "He's probably rollin' hard with some brothers from the hood."

"I know the type," said Erik. "Trying to prove something about being black."

Erik's statement made Danny think about his last session with Dr. Gordon for a moment. Then his mind shifted back to the family. They were screwed up, but that much was obvious. What he wondered was how far Jordan would go to protect his father from those who would harm him. Conversely, he wondered what the other son would do to prove just how tough he was.

The Range Rover rolled by the detectives, and Danny could vaguely see Jordan's face obscured by the dark tinted glass.

The Holyland Survival of Ministry stood regally against the blue sky as Danny and Erik got out of their car. Danny remembered when the building was called St. Michael's Cathedral. It had been a Catholic church for fifty years until the city turned black. Then the church did, too. The archdiocese participated in the "white flight" of the sixties and seventies and sold the church, building a new one in the suburbs. Danny remembered going to the church, taking Communion, and hearing adults talk about the changes going on in the city. The memory was vivid. People stood in God's house talking about how men were ignoring his word.

"This place brings back the memories," Danny said to Erik as they walked toward the big wooden doors of the church. "I used to go here when it was a Catholic church."

"Please, don't tell me you were an altar boy," said Erik. "I couldn't live with that image."

"No," said Danny. "My mother wanted me to, but I was more interested in baseball."

On their way to Holyland, Danny and Erik had noticed there were many properties for sale in the neighborhood near the church. Pale blue and white signs dotted the landscape. Danny knew that many black churches liked to buy up land around them for commercial purposes. What he didn't know was why someone was selling these lots.

They stepped into the building and Danny saw that the place had not changed much. They'd kept all the stained-glass windows and the pews were still as he remembered. But the confessionals were gone, replaced by more pews that didn't match the others.

The Holyland Survival Ministry had lost close to a million dollars in New Nubia.com. A lot of money for a church. Holyland was widely viewed as a fundamentalist cult because of its extreme views and practices. Danny was thinking that a disgruntled true believer might have done harm to the Bakers. It wouldn't be the first time someone had killed in the name of religion.

A heavyset black man walked into the sanctuary followed by two other black men. They moved quickly to Danny and Erik, who met them halfway across the expansive room.

"Can we help you?" asked the heavyset man. Danny noticed that all three men wore blazers that had HSM embroidered on the front pocket. They were hard-looking men, not the kind you'd expect to see in a house of worship.

"We're detectives from Special Crimes," said Danny as he flashed his badge. "We need to speak to the reverend."

"About what?" asked the heavyset man. Now his voice had an edge of irritation in it.

"The reverend will know," said Erik.

The heavyset man thought about this for a second, then led Danny and Erik through the church into an annex. They moved quickly into the office of the pastor. It was a nice office, the kind a businessman might have, only it was filled with religious decorations. Crucifixes, portraits of Jesus (black and white), framed passages of the Bible on colorful velvet. It was enough to save your soul just stepping inside.

"Cops here to see you, Rev," said the heavyset man as Danny and Erik entered.

A tall, well-built man with sharp features stood up from behind the desk. He was dressed in an expensive suit. He looked more banker than minister.

"Thank you, Carl," said the reverend. The three young men moved to the back of the room and stood, watching.

The reverend smiled at Danny and Erik and motioned them to sit, which they did. Danny preferred to conduct his interviews standing, but there was something commanding about the church, and he couldn't fight it.

Reverend Rashus Boltman was an all-state basketball player in the South during the seventies. He was a fearsome power forward who was known for hard play and harder living off the field. He graduated from high school and took a scholarship to a college. But when he flunked out of school, he was thrown back into ghetto life without any hope of ever getting out again.

Boltman quickly found the drug crews and that life replaced his lost fame on the court. He lived pretty high for a while, but a bloody gang war killed all of his friends and sent him to prison for ten years. In prison, he found God and a new purpose in life. When he got out, the Reverend Bolt, as he was now called, dedicated himself to his new vocation and started a small storefront church, in the South which grew into a large one. His success lead him to Detroit, where ministers were power brokers and community heroes.

"So, what can I do for you gentlemen?" asked Reverend Bolt.

"Unfortunately, we're here on business," said Danny.

Reverend Bolt smiled at Danny. "You one of us, I see. I got two white members just out of the joint sound just like you."

Danny didn't know whether this was a compliment or not. He decided the smile on Bolt's face meant it was.

"So, one of my congregation in trouble again?" asked Reverent Bolt.

"No, sir," said Erik. "This is about the Bakers."

Reverend Bolt's face showed no change in expression. He sat down and leaned back in his leather chair, taking just a second to look up at the ceiling.

"My heart is still heavy for the loss of John and his wife," Reverend Bolt said finally. "I understand that there is an investigation, a tracking of the killer."

"Yes," said Danny. "We believe the Internet company New Nubia was somehow involved. We understand that losses incurred by the church's investment resulted in some hardship."

"Yes," said the reverend. "We lost some funding—"

"Those people were devils!" said Carl loudly from the back of the room.

"Blasphemers!" the other two young men said.

"That's enough, Carl," said Reverend Bolt, holding up a hand. The men quieted down obediently. Reverent Bolt turned back to Danny and Erik, pleased with his control over the men. "Excuse them, Detectives. They're full of the holy spirit."

Danny thought about Reverend Bolt's rise to power and how it was not unlike the rise of a businessman, a politician, or a criminal. No one got to the top of his game by being a nice guy. He wondered what a man of God had to do to reach his pinnacle.

"New Nubia only listed how much money you invested, Reverend," said Erik. "We need to know what that investment capital came from. So we'll need to see all of your records on the deal if you don't mind."

"Actually, I do mind," said Reverend Bolt. "My financial deals are kept strictly private. It's a church rule."

"But don't you make the rules?" asked Danny.

"God makes the rules," said Reverend Bolt. The other men in the room clapped at this. "I just do what's necessary to carry them out."

"We respect that, Reverend," said Danny, "but everyone else involved is cooperating. I wouldn't want your refusal to raise suspicion."

"My ministry has taken its lumps," said Reverend Bolt. "The righteous are always set upon, but God watches over this house, and that's all there is to it."

Danny realized that he was up against more than a suspect. Reverend Bolt's life was his vocation. The black church's power in the community was legendary and formidable. It was the salvation of blacks from the time they arrived in the country and had produced almost all of its great leaders. The reverend was obviously unwilling to allow anyone to see just how much the Bakers had hurt his institution. He was not going to open up his church to the cops, the IRS, and the newspapers. To that end, he was standing behind God himself.

"If you change your mind, sir, you can call us," said Danny. He had to tread softly with a man of God. Nothing was frowned upon more in Detroit that harassing a black minister.

"We won't be changing our mind," said Reverend Bolt. "What's done is done."

As they started to go, Danny had one more thing to ask.

"I notice a lot of your neighbors are leaving, selling their homes," said Danny.

"We own those lots," said Carl. Then he stopped suddenly as the reverend shot him a look.

"We haven't gotten around to removing the signs yet," said Bolt casually. "This way, Detectives."

Danny and Erik were not so much shown out as they were dismissed. Danny wasn't sure what the reverend's last statement meant. Were they buying up houses or trying to sell them?

Danny knew that Reverend Bolt had been giving a sermon on the night of the murder, but he still had deep suspicions. Bolt was a man who was not too far removed from the violent tendencies of his past. But he was no fool, and so Danny was more interested in where the three true believers in the back of the room were the night the Bakers were killed.

13

RED DAM

Cameron Cole hated Detroit. It was a sick, diseased pile of shit, a depraved animal that ate itself, populated by people who were less than human. And he knew this because he was one of those people, a ruthless, violent parasite who feasted on weakness and the good intentions of normal people; then again, this was his occupation and a man had to make a living.

Cameron collected the money from the young girl. She shoved the crumpled green paper into his hands impatiently. The newer bills made that beautiful crackling noise as he grasped them. Cameron counted the money quickly then sent the girl and her date into a back room. The couple smiled behind their wet, druggie eyes and staggered off, using each other for support.

"Wait," Cameron called to them.

The couple stopped in their tracks, almost tumbling over in the process.

"Here, use this," said Cameron as he shoved a condom at them.

"Thanks," said the young girl, grabbing the small package. Then she continued her staggered walk into the back room.

Cameron checked his supply of condoms. He was getting low. He'd bought an economy box of fifty just two days ago and now he was down to ten. He made a mental note to go out and get more. Cameron didn't much care if they had safe sex, he just didn't like cleaning up when they didn't.

Cameron walked through his rented home. It was a large, boxy place with high ceilings and crown moldings that had terrible cracks in the corners. He rented the place from an old Jewish couple who lived in the suburbs. Cameron always paid in cash, on time, and they never bothered him.

As he moved through the house, he heard the moans and cursing attendant to people having sex. Even though he was disgusted by his street clientele, he was still turned on by the sound, and he wasn't above peeking through a door when he needed to.

Cameron ran a sort of motel for local drug-using women. The girls traded sex for drugs, but they needed a safe place to make the exchange. For a small fee, Cameron let them use his place. Business was good. It seemed the only thing people liked more than drugs was sex. And he had witnessed every kind of deviance and depravity you could think of. He even had a trick die in bed with a girl once. It was messy affair that had him dumping the body in an alley at three in the morning.

Cameron was a tall, thin man who had just turned fifty-three a few days ago. His hair was thinning badly and he was fond of jeans and T-shirts with logos. Today, he was wearing one that read BACK THAT ASS UP.

He was from what most people would call a good family. His father was a trucker and his mother, a postal worker. Cameron and his three siblings enjoyed a nice, peaceful, blue-collar family life. But Cameron, the eldest, was not satisfied with that life. He had shunned his parents encouragement to go to college and taken up with one street crew after another. Inevitably, he ended up in jail at fifteen. After that, he'd spent most of his life in prisons of one kind or another, his hope fading with his morality.

Cameron halted at a room just off the living room. He heard a particularly loud couple inside. He stopped to listen, and realized that it sounded like two men. He grew angry. He knew what that meant.

Cameron opened the door, which he told his girls never to lock. He looked inside and saw two men about twenty or so going at it with a girl who looked to be no more than sixteen. She was bent over by one man and had the other in her mouth. The men were loud and high-fived with each other over the girl's back.

Cameron slammed the door shut and the threesome stopped their activity. The girl pulled the man from her mouth and turned her face away.

"What the fuck is this?" demanded Cameron. "You know this freaky shit is extra."

"Yo, man, we fuckin' in here," said the man on the back end of the girl.

"I don't give a shit if you playing poker with Jesus, muthafucka," said Cameron. "One of y'all snuck in here and that cost extra."

Cameron waited as one of the men gave him some money. He counted it, then walked out of the room, ignoring the faint curses he heard behind him.

Cameron smiled a little as he went into the big bedroom at the front of the house. This was his room, his sanctuary. He was going to close up for a while, take a break. Setting his own hours was one of the few things about being in this business he liked. He shoved his money into this pocket as he walked inside.

"What the fuck—" said Cameron as he entered and saw the three young men in his room.

Cameron reached for his gun, a 9 mm he kept in his waistband. But before he could get to it, Rimba Bady's knife sailed into his shoulder.

Akema then kicked Cameron in the face and he fell to the floor. Cameron felt hands over his body, searching, hitting. Finally, a foot crashed into the side of his face. He felt a rag being stuffed into his mouth as his hands were bound in front of him and he was sat upright on the floor.

"Wha'sup?" said Muhammad. "We need to talk to you."

Muhammad motioned Akema to get a wastebasket that was

across the room. Rimba turned on a boom box and blasted out a song by the Ruff Ryders. Muhammad got closer to Cameron so he could hear him.

"Herman Bady is our father," said Muhammad.

Cameron's face contorted at the sound of the name. Whatever memories he had of Herman were not good.

"You was his cell mate in Texas," said Muhammad. "You used to pull jobs together after you both got out, only he'd changed his name by then. You was his boy, probably had sex with him in the joint."

Cameron shook his head vigorously at this statement.

"No?" said Muhammad. "Well, whatever. I know you keep in touch with him. Where is he?"

Cameron shook his head again. Muhammad sighed, then took off Cameron's belt and wrapped it around his left arm. He then placed Cameron's belted arm over the wastebasket. Cameron began to struggle and shake, acknowledging that he knew what this meant.

Muhammad took Rimba's knife from Cameron's shoulder and cut a deep gash in Cameron's forearm. Cameron winced and grunted under his gag. Blood poured out of the cut, running and twisting in evil patterns through the hair on his arm. The coppery smell of it filled Muhammad's nostrils. The blood stopped as Muhammad pulled on the belt tighter.

"You remember this from the joint, don't you?" said Muhammad. "The red dam? Tell me where he is or I'll let you bleed."

Cameron's eyes got bigger as he realized that they meant to kill him. He nodded his head vigorously as Muhammad took off the gag.

"He's here . . . in Detroit," said Cameron.

"We know that, nigga," said Muhammad. "Where?" He loosened the belt and more blood flowed.

"I don't know!" yelled Cameron. His eyes rolled and Muhammad stopped the flow of blood. "Herman sent me a letter when I was locked up in Kentucky," said Cameron. "Said he had a scam running here in the city or something like that. It came from some place in Detroit. . . ." Cameron fell silent trying to remember.

Muhammad pressed on Cameron's wounded arm making it bleed faster and causing pain. Cameron yelled loudly and twisted his body.

"What place?" asked Muhammad through gritted teeth.

"Damn," said Cameron. "It started with an O—Oasis! That's it. It came from a place called Oasis."

"Where's the letter?" asked Muhammad.

"I didn't keep the shit," said Cameron. "It was just a letter from an ex-con."

"Oasis," Muhammad said softly. "Is that all?"

"Yeah, yeah," said Cameron. "I swear, that's all I know, man."

Muhammad pulled the belt tighter until all of the bleeding stopped. He then put the loose end into Cameron's other hand. Cameron held it tightly and expelled a big breath.

Muhammad stood and held out his hand. Cameron raised his bound hands, thinking Muhammad meant to help him up from the floor. Instead, Rimba handed him Cameron's gun. Cameron's eyes grew wider at the sight of the weapon. Rimba turned the music up full blast as Muhammad aimed the gun at Cameron's forehead and fired.

14

MARSHALL

When Danny and Erik got back to the SCU, things had become hot concerning the case. The Longs had called Jim Cole directly to complain. Oscar Stallworth had threatened legal action, while Virginia had phoned the mayor's wife. Ever the politician, Hamilton Grace had contacted Tony Hill, the Deputy Chief, to "just say hello." Reverend Bolt had not made a peep.

Danny and Erik had a brief meeting with their boss, who was pleased with their work. When people complained, it meant buttons were being pushed. Still, they had very little to work with. The murders had been committed with a common weapon, and the killer's efforts to ruin the crime scene had apparently succeeded.

They were about to call it a night. Most of the other cops were already gone. Danny said good-bye to Erik and sat for a while looking at the case file. He listed all of the big losers in the Internet company, and even though none of them seemed like killers themselves, they all had ties to those who could have done the deed. He'd learned a long time ago that no matter how wealthy a person was, he was one cousin, one friend, one relationship away from the underbelly of life.

"What are you doin' up here, man?" asked a familiar voice.

Danny looked up into the face of Marshall Jackson, his best friend. Marshall was a tall, good-looking man who had been Danny's friend since they were kids. The two had been through hell and back investigating the assassination of Justice Farrel Douglas. Since Danny had been promoted to detective, they'd made a regular date to have a drink once a week, not wanting the demands of their jobs to become an excuse for losing contact with each other.

"Hey, man," said Danny. "I'm sorry. I forgot."

"Big-time detective ain't got time for his boy, huh?" said Marshall.

"Who the hell you callin' boy," said Danny laughing.

Danny stood and Marshall slapped him on the back. They walked out of the SCU and outside into the evening.

"How's that damned new job of yours?" asked Danny.

"Fine," said Marshall. "And don't say it like that. You know I couldn't stay at the U.S. Attorney's office, not after what happened. Private practice is more lucrative anyway. I'm making some serious money now. And I need it with the two kids."

"Defending criminals," said Danny. "I still don't believe it."

"The law doesn't have good and bad guys, Danny. Get over that shit."

"Well, if you ever have to cross-examine me, be nice." Danny laughed a little.

They walked over to Fishbones, their favorite bar and eatery in Greektown. Danny barely listened as his friend talked about a recent case involving insurance fraud and a prosecutor named Jesse, who was all over him on the matter.

"You okay, man?" asked Marshall, noticing Danny's distracted look. "You still thinking about your mother?"

"Yes, but it's more than that."

"Look, man," said Marshall. His voice was tense. "Your father didn't cause her to die."

"I know," said Danny. "I just have to get it out of my head. You know how I get."

"I know. You get stuck on something like this and you obsess. Let it go." Marshall looked upset with himself, then added, "Look, I'm sorry, man."

"Don't be. I'm working my way through it. Anyway, that's not my only problem. I caught a bad case. The Baker murders. We're interviewing suspects, wealthy black suspects."

"Uh-oh," said Marshall. "Touching the untouchables."

"They all seem to be hiding something. The day ended with me getting my ass tossed out of a church."

"Holyland?" asked Marshall.

"How did you know?" asked Danny.

"The Reverend Bolt is the only minister I know who would do something like that."

"His helpers look like a goddamned drug crew," said Danny.

"They might have been," said Marshall. "Reverend Bolt's prison ministry is still going strong. He gets them while they're in the joint then gets them back on their feet when they get out. You know people suspect some of them in a killing."

Danny perked up at this statement. He'd been suspicious of Bolt's assistants, but it was normal cop prejudice concerning the way they carried themselves.

Danny and Marshall ordered a pitcher of beer and some of the restaurant's famous alligator voodoo.

"What's the story?" asked Danny.

"Well," said Marshall, "when Reverend Bolt still had a storefront church, it got ripped off by some locals. The cops got a tip where to find the stuff, which they did, but they also found two dead bodies."

"And you think it was Bolt's prison ministers?" asked Danny.

"Nothing was ever proven. But have you ever read the stuff Bolt gives out to his people? It's like a damned cult. He talks about being the hand of God, and the Old Testament being the way."

"An eye for an eye," said Danny almost to himself.

"Exactly," said Marshall. "But don't get me wrong. I think Reverend Bolt has a good heart, it's just that he's a hard man and the people who follow him are loyal and not too smart."

Marshall was always right about these things, Danny thought, so he would have to do some more checking on the reverend and his people. He was happy to know he might have been right about Bolt's men. The real question was just how dangerous they were.

"Thanks," said Danny. "That was good shit. You need to get back with the good guys."

Marshall laughed off the joke. "So how's Erik doing?"

"Good. Still gettin' used to me, though."

"You still seeing the shrink?"

"Yeah, he's into my head about the black thing."

"Oh, fuck that," said Marshall. "You're one of us, and it's too late to change that." Marshall took a moment then, "So how's Vinny?"

Danny sighed heavily. "She's so into school that we're starting to have problems about the shit."

"Dammit," said Marshall. "I had a feeling this was coming." Marshall looked guilty for a second then, "Vinny's been calling me."

Danny was shocked, but didn't say anything. His head filled with the usual stuff, like why didn't Marshall tell him, and what the hell did they talk about. But Danny knew Marshall had more to say, so he didn't want to jump all over him.

The bartender, who was familiar with Danny and Marshall, brought the pitcher and the food. He smiled, said hello, then left.

"At first, she had a lot of law questions," said Marshall. "Nothing big, the normal stuff. But then she started asking about people I knew, lawyers, judges, and groups she should join. That's when I got suspicious."

"Why would that make you suspicious?" asked Danny.

"Because I know Vinny. She's never been interested in social climbing, and all of a sudden, she's into that legal world shit." He sounded angry, as if he thought he could have stopped her.

"Well, she's all into it now," said Danny. "And I got a feeling that I don't fit into whatever she's seeing for a lot of reasons."

Marshall took another drink of his beer. "Vinny's long past caring that you're white."

"But the world cares," said Danny quickly, as if the response had been in his head all night. "It's just another thing to keep us apart."

"Damn, I should have said something to her." Marshall jerked his hand a little, as though he wanted to hit himself on the head.

"Don't blame yourself. You were just being a friend."

Marshall sighed, a frustrated sound that mirrored what Danny was feeling. "Well, as you know, I have experience with women trouble. I mean, I thought my loving wife had killed a girl over my little indiscretion."

"Man, you don't even need to be thinking about that situation," said Danny. "Let it die."

It was typical of the pair that they sacrificed for each other. Each not caring about his own pain, he tried to ease that of his friend. They'd been doing it since they were kids and neither man even noticed it anymore.

"All I can say," said Marshall, "is nobody understands women, especially black women. Vinny is strong like my wife, Chemin, and she's got to work through this thing. You remember how it was when I went to law school? I was into the social step up, the parties, the idea that I was lifting myself out of my situation."

"But you didn't stop hanging out with me, did you?" asked Danny pointedly.

"But I could have. See, it's different for a man. I can have any kind of friend, but a woman likes to think that her man is going in the same direction as she is. She always wants him to be a little older, a little taller, a little *more*, you know what I'm saying?"

"Fuck if I understand that," said Danny with a tinge of frustration. "A person is what he is, you know. You can change the job, and the kind of clothes you wear to work, but that's all."

Marshall looked at his friend, saw the face of the kid he used to be, and smiled. "You just don't understand prejudice, do you, Danny? I guess you never did. Man, I wish you could teach that to a lot of other people I know."

"You remember my first day of school?" asked Danny. "Over at Davison, the old school?"

"Never forget it. A playground full of black kids and there you were, sitting in a corner looking scared as hell."

"You were playing basketball with some other kids," said Danny, taking up the tale. "I was sitting there about to shit in my pants and you came up to me and said, 'So, you playin' or what?' I said yes."

"And I yelled out, 'Yo, we got the white boy!' "

The two men laughed at the memory. They eased a little now and each of them remembered why they made it a point to be together every week. A friend can get lost in the big bad world of working, striving, and living. You had to make sure you had your peace.

"Anyway," said Marshall, "Vinny has to work through this thing herself, and no one can do it for her. If you try to help her, she'll accuse you of treating her like a kid. If you don't help, she may think you don't give a shit."

"I know exactly what you mean," said Danny. "Women are a muthafucka. So I can't win, can I?"

"I like to think that you can't lose. Either she wants you, or she doesn't, and in the end, whatever she chooses will at least end the shit."

Danny sat there looking down at the wooden bar, knowing that this was the only person that he could be so open and vulnerable with. Everyone had to do it sometimes, and although he thought of it as a weakness, Danny knew it was also a necessity, and he felt better just being able to show how fucked up he was by all this.

"Okay," said Danny almost to myself. "I'll back off of Vinny. I got my work, you know. That'll keep my mind occupied."

"I'm not finished yet," said Marshall with a sternness in his voice that reminded Danny of his father. "You've always loved Vinny because she was a lot like you, and it made your life easier."

"Oh, that's bullshit, man," said Danny, but even as the words came out, he knew what Marshall said was true.

"You don't like complicated relationships," said Marshall. "Our relationship is about as complex as you've ever had. So, what I'm saying is don't be afraid. I may not understand everything about women, but I do know that when a woman grows, things change, and you have to deal with it. They make you work at being better and sometimes you can't see it. And us men, we don't like being told how to act, because it makes us feel like less of a man. It's the way it has to be. Men have been going through this shit since they were living in caves and eating wild animals for dinner. Let it be, man. And you'll be better off for it."

Danny nodded, although he admitted to himself he didn't understand all of it. Marshall was the kind of man who spoke in simple words, but they carried depth, nonetheless. No one knew Danny better than this man, so he would heed his words because he knew they came from the heart.

The two friends hoisted another round and told more stories about their coming of age together. Better days, thought Danny. The old days always seemed like better ones for some reason.

Danny let go of his concerns about Vinny, but those thoughts were soon replaced by images of all the people who had good reason to kill the Bakers.

15

FLOATER

The Sewer was loud with laughter as Danny walked in. He'd just come from Vice, where he'd been trying to get some info on John Baker's hooker friend. The Vice cops helped narrow it down to a couple of dozen girls who frequented the part of town that Baker lived in. They promised to put the word out on the street. Danny had figured that it wouldn't be easy to find the girl. The woman was probably smart enough to know that her man had been killed, and if that was the case, she might have gotten spooked and gone to another state by now.

The laughter he heard came from some of the cops who were assembled and listening as Lisa Meadows told a story. Some clerical people were there as well as a couple of uniformed cops. Danny drifted over to see what was going on.

"Wha'sup?" Danny asked Erik.

"You missed it," said Erik.

"Tell it again, Lis," said Joe Canelli, a husky Italian cop. He was still laughing when he asked her.

"You do it this time, Gretch," said Lisa to her partner, Gretchen Taylor. Lisa's Brooklyn accent was still detectable even after years of living in the Midwest.

"Okay," said Gretchen. "Lisa and me got a call that someone had a tip on that serial rapist working the west side, right? So, we go to this house and we hear a man screaming and something hitting the walls like this—" Gretchen rocked a desk. " 'Go, go, go!' he screamed."

The other officers who had heard the story laughed a little at this, knowing where it was going.

"So we kick in the door, pull out our guns, and identify ourselves as cops," said Gretchen. "Well, what should we see but a man bent over a chair with his wife . . ."

"His two-hundred-pound wife," added Lisa.

". . . fucking this guy in the ass with one of them plastic strap-on dicks!"

Danny and Erik laughed along with the other officers at the visual image in their heads.

Gretchen waved everyone to quiet down then, "So they just look at us for a second in shock that we caught them, right?" Gretchen continued. "Then the man says 'Latasha, we gotta talk to them. Take yo' dick outta my ass.' "

They all laughed again at the punch line. Danny leaned on Erik and burst into laughter once more as Joe Canelli bent over and Gretchen demonstrated on him, smacking his backside and yelping like a cowboy.

The laughter stopped when Jim Cole's door burst opened. He thundered out of his office.

Jim made a beeline for Erik and Danny, and hardly stopped as he headed for the door. "Got another body," he said. "In the river. We think it's your man again."

The Detroit River was choppy and tossed the big Coast Guard cutter up and down. The boat floated by the body, which was just off the Detroit shoreline. The corpse had actually been found on the Canadian side of the river, but it was a U.S. citizen, so they'd brought it over here. The Ontario police were present, but they were not doing much. The Canadians, just a mile from Detroit, had not had a murder in their city for several years and were eager to push the floater off on Detroit.

Fiona and her crew were already on the scene, and their preliminary investigation had lead to a call to the SCU. The dead woman, though found in the river, had not drowned. She'd been shot several times with a small-caliber weapon.

It appeared that the body had been rolled into the water close to a construction site. The body was tangled in some debris, and had been hit by some kids in a boat.

The corpse was down a low grade by the shore. Danny motioned to Erik and walked down. Erik stayed behind talking to Jim Cole.

As Danny made his descent down the grade, he heard a helicopter overhead, then saw a big black sedan pull up. He knew the police brass had to be inside. The killer was now a multiple murderer, and that meant political control would be put on the case. Detroit was making an economic comeback and nothing was worse than a case like this. The press was being kept away from the scene, and all the detectives and uniforms had been told not to talk to anybody about the case.

Fiona and her team worked on the dead woman's body, which was slimy and discolored. It was hard to tell what had caused the lack of color, the river or the method of death.

Danny regarded the body and suddenly it turned into his mother's corpse lying there twisted and broken, a lifeless vessel. He was aware that he had stopped breathing in that instant. He calmed himself. No one could see him react this way. It was not professional.

"You okay?" asked Fiona.

"Yeah," said Danny. "Who is she?" He had to speak up because he'd stopped a good distance away from the forensic crew.

"Don't know," said Fiona. "She had ID on her, but the smart guys took it away." Smart guys was Fiona's word for Danny's police superiors.

"Is it our man?"

"It's our boy all right. Looks like he used the same weapon, a .22, and same kind of tape on the wounds. At least he didn't cover the scene with dirt. He let the river do it for him this time. Smart bastard."

"Why would he try to hide this one and not the Bakers?" Danny asked himself. "Why dump her like this?"

"Don't know," said Fiona. "Who can figure out a sick fuck like this?" Her voice had a note of defeat in it.

Jacob, the new kid, barged into the conversation and before Fiona could stop him he was talking to Danny. "You know, it's a miracle we ever found her," he said. "The undertow in the river is strong."

"Jacob, what are you doing?" asked Fiona. "Get back over there with the others and check the shore."

"But there's nothing there," he said like a petulant kid in grade school.

Fiona just glared at him and soon he walked off. "Eager fuckin' beaver," she said. "But he was right. The undertow should have carted her off to the Eastern seaboard, but see this big gash here." Fiona pointed to an unsightly wound on the woman's back. "Our boy didn't do that. We think her back got caught on something down there and it held her. Then the joyriders hit her." Fiona turned suddenly and admonished one of her workers.

"Fiona, I'm gonna need all your genius on this, baby. I want to know everything. If our man is trying to throw us off the trail, then we gotta stick to it that much more."

"You got it, Danny, and I like that 'baby' thing. Sexy."

Danny moved back up the grade and saw that Erik and Jim were in a crowd now. With them were Tony Hill, the Deputy Chief, and Chief of Police Vernon Noble. Erik stood a few paces off from the big shots and said nothing. Danny did the same as he joined them.

"The mayor wants this shit wrapped tight, fellas," said Chief Noble. "We need a lid on this and anyone who talks is ass out."

"Impossible," said Tony. "We got a crew of seven down there, six uniforms, not including the Canadians, and three detectives already, not to mention the reporters with their fancy camera lenses." Tony pointed to the helicopter hovering over the scene. "So, it's gonna get out. Tell the mayor that he has to beat the press to it and release a statement ASAP."

Noble nodded and pulled out a cell phone. Tony and Jim shared a quick smile. Everyone knew that Noble was just warming the Chief's seat for Tony. Tony was running the department and every officer understood that if you had a real problem, he was the man to see. Tony motioned Danny and Erik to come closer.

"Okay, fellas, you caught the case," said Tony. "So you're gonna to be the men on this. You're gonna hear some shit about how Jim and I are personally taking this case, but don't believe it. This is yours, and we'll need you to act like it." Tony looked over to Jim.

"The floater is Olittah Reese, one of the mayor's chief aides," said Jim.

Danny thought for a second, then he remembered the name. It was the flirtatious woman he'd met at Virginia Stallworth's fund-raising party. Instinctively, Danny looked back at the body, remembering how pretty she was. He saw her walking away from him, the subtle sway of her hips, the elegant way her long legs stepped, and the smoothness of her neck as she turned to look back at him. A sadness washed over him. He looked at Erik, who had the same emotion written on his face.

"If this murder is related to the first," said Jim Cole, "then we've got two killings linked to the mayor."

"I assume his security is going to be beefed up," said Erik.

"Already done," said Tony. "So you can see the greater implications of this."

Tony said nothing, but Danny knew he was referring to Harris Yancy, the former mayor who'd been murdered in office. It was a nasty affair, one that no one had forgotten.

Noble came back and shoved the cell phone at Tony. He took it and stepped away with the Chief.

"We'll establish a team of men to assist you," said Jim. "From this moment, the case is your top priority. Got anything that looks like a lead?"

Before Erik could answer, Danny said, "Yes, sir, we got a hooker who had a little booty thing with Mr. Baker."

"A hooker?" said Jim with interest. Danny knew that Jim was making the same sordid connections in his head that he had. "Where do you think she is?"

"She's a local girl, so we're going to shake some trees," said Danny.

Erik dummied up. Danny knew he'd get it as soon as this conversation was over. But Danny didn't like to tell his boss that he had nothing.

"Good," said Jim. "When you get her, I'm your first call."

"Yes, sir."

Jim walked away, and at the same time, Erik tapped Danny on the shoulder.

"What the fuck, man?" said Erik.

"You know Jim," said Danny. "If we had said we had nothing, what would he say?"

"Get your asses out and find something."

"There you go. We got the same pressure, only he's not pissed at us."

"I won't argue," said Erik. "We'll be waiting forever on Vice to find her. So, let's go find us a hooker."

"I think we should split up, ask around. We'll cover more ground, and if we go together, people will think we're looking to bag her. She'll get tipped off and scatter."

Erik agreed. If they went together, it would look like an official investigation to the folks in the hood. People would be less likely to give up info. And if the girl was connected to a murder, everyone on the street would know it.

The other reason Danny wanted to separate was that he liked to work alone when he went into the neighborhoods. Each time he went back, it was like opening a door to his past, a past where danger was always a word, thought, or mistake away. Danny was already excited about the prospect, his mind running lists of contacts and things he might have to do.

"You takin' the east side, I guess," said Erik.

"Yeah," said Danny. "I got a couple of people who might have something."

"I'm gonna do the same on the west side," said Erik.

They walked back to their car, and Danny could see the line of uniforms holding several TV crews at bay not far off. Absently, Danny thought about Vinny, and how this case would now consume him, and that might make things worse between them. Danny turned and looked back at Fiona and her crew. They were lifting the body and placing it into a long, black bag.

16

SISTER'S KEEPER

Danny got home late that night. The department was buzzing with the news of the second killing, and he knew the newspapers would both carry front-page stories. He'd done some checking on the property around Holyland, and just as he'd thought, there had been a renovation planned.

Reverend Bolt had wanted to start something called Holyland Gardens, a low-rent housing project for members of his order. He was set to break ground when funding fell through. It was around the same time the New Nubia.com scam was uncovered. So, it appeared that the Bakers had ruined his plans to build a little religious city in his own backyard. And who had solicited Bolt at one of her parties? None other than Olittah Reese.

Danny expected the house to be empty, or Vinny to be passed out on the sofa with some thick book in her hands. What he found instead was Vinny in the living room talking with her big sister, Renitta.

Vinny was from a family of ten kids. In order, they were, Renitta, Juan (pronounced *jew-wan*), Ivory and Ivanna (the twins), DeWayne, Easter, Teyron, Devinna, and Marcus, who was named after his father.

All of the kids were a year apart or so in age, and so Renitta was only thirteen years older than her little sister, Vinny. But those years made all the difference. Renitta had practically raised the younger kids. It broke her heart when Vinny enrolled in the police academy, and it killed her when she started dating a white man. Renitta hated Danny as she did most white people, and the feeling was mutual.

Danny felt the room go cold as he stepped inside and said hello. Renitta shifted her big frame on the sofa. She was overweight, but carried it in that regal manner that black women do. She was comfortable with her size, and didn't give a shit if you had a problem with it.

Danny walked toward Vinny and waited for her to greet him. She didn't. She just smiled and looked at him, so he bent over and kissed her. He could feel Renitta's butt tightening as their lips met.

"Anything to eat?" asked Danny.

"No. I ate down at the school," said Vinny.

"You can cook something. I'm kinda hungry," said Renitta. Her voice was full and loud, just like the woman herself. Her statement held contempt in it. She was suggesting that Vinny did not exist to serve a man. Renitta smiled and gave Danny a sly look.

"I got a couple of pork chops in there," said Danny. "You can have one if you want."

"One pork chop?" said Renitta. "That ain't gonna fill me up."

"How do you know if you've never stopped at just one?" said Danny.

It was a silly game they played, but it was better than saying the things that were really in their hearts.

"I'll pass," said Renitta, ignoring Danny's cut on her. Danny was sure that in her mind, she was being bigger than he.

"Hey," said a voice from out of Danny's vision.

He turned to see Ivory, one of the twins. She'd been in the bathroom and was just coming out. Danny said hello and then thought it best to get out of there. Ivory disliked him, too, more than Renitta if that was possible. Ivory was a gorgeous, free-spirited girl. She was the opposite of her bookish identical twin Ivanna, who was a teacher and who liked Danny just fine.

Danny knew that if Renitta and Ivory were here, something was up. He didn't stay around to find out. He went into the kitchen, cooked his dinner, and had a beer.

When he was done, Renitta walked into the kitchen and sat down at the table with him.

"We need to talk," said Renitta.

"About what?" asked Danny. "You and me got an understanding about things, don't we?"

"Yeah, I guess we do, but some things change."

"So, you love me now?" Danny smiled.

Renitta reacted to this statement with a mixture of shock and mild revulsion. Danny wondered what particular thing had made her come to hate white people so much. Then on second thought, he decided that he didn't want to know.

"Did you know that I can't have children?" she said. She checked to make sure Danny had heard her correctly. "The doctors don't really know why, but let's just say I wasn't born with all the necessary equipment."

Danny was shocked. First by the nature of the statement, then by whatever it was that had made her share this intimacy with him.

"But you have a daughter, Serena," he said.

"Adopted. Actually, she's the daughter of my cousin from Alabama. My cousin is a drug addict, and the family thought it was best to give the girl up."

"Vinny never told me that." He felt a little sorry for Renitta, which he guessed was her plan all along.

"It wasn't Vinny's secret to tell," said Renitta. She sat up straight, taking on the proud look she liked so much. "I'm telling you this because my little brothers and sisters are like my kids. I take pride in their accomplishments. Marcus is in the University of Michigan, Easter is in dental school, and Teyron and Devinna have a little computer company. The older kids are doing good, too, but that's not my doing."

"And Vinny's here stuck with me. Is that your point?" asked Danny.

"No, that's just part of it. Vinny's now in law school, where she always belonged. You getting her shot was actually a good thing. It woke her up."

"I didn't get her shot," Danny said angrily "It was a robbery and we tried to stop it."

"You'd better watch that temper," said Renitta. "It's gonna be the end of you yet."

Danny calmed down. He thought about Gordon and their talks about anger and his self-image. He eased in his chair ashamed that she'd pushed his buttons so easily. Renitta smiled and he knew she was happy she'd gotten a rise out of him.

"The bottom line is, she got shot and you got a promotion out of it. But you know what? Vinny got promoted, too. She's back where I wanted her to be, on the road to being a professional black woman."

"But that ain't yo point either, is it?" Danny sensed that something more was coming.

"Let my sister go," she said. He was sure she didn't mean to sound like Charlton Heston in that movie, but she did.

"We've been through all this, Renitta. You know my answer to that."

"This time it's different. I'm trying to help you."

"How is your prejudice against me helping anything?"

"Black people can't be prejudiced," said Renitta in a matter-of-fact tone. "Your people invented that shit. I'm just telling the truth. Vinny is on a journey that you don't understand. She's about to enter a world filled with lawyers, judges, doctors, and all kinds of high-class people. How do you think your world of guns, murder, and beer is going to look to her after that?"

"Vinny doesn't want my world, she wants me." He meant the words to sound defiant, but they ended up sounding defensive.

Renitta smiled, sensing a crack in Danny's armor. "She won't separate the two. I think the only reason she's still here is because your mother died."

Danny felt himself tense all over. Only Renitta would be so evil as to bring up the pain of his loss in such an insulting manner. But he would not lose his temper. Not just because Vinny would be angry, but also because he had to learn to live beyond his mother's death.

"I think Vinny would disagree with that," he finally said calmly.

"I know you believe you got a black man's heart," Renitta continued. "Hell, sometimes when you talk, I almost forget myself. Vinny may have been fooled by your so-called soulfulness, but not me. I know that deep down inside, you just like all the other white folks. Against us. And now that Vinny's eyes are opened, she'll see that to make it here in Detroit, where blacks have power, she'll have to get away from you." Renitta smiled at Danny. "You know, it's funny, the world will do what I couldn't."

Danny didn't say anything. Renitta would have liked nothing better than for him to get mad at her. So he was silent as she pushed herself out of the chair and walked back into the living room, where Vinny and Ivory chattered noisily. But before she left, he did manage to say the one thing he heard echoing in his head.

"You're wrong."

Danny cleaned up the kitchen and waited for the evil sisters to leave. He went into the den and read over the file on the killer again as he tried to deny Renitta's vile words.

After about an hour, Vinny entered holding an overnight bag. She stood in the doorway wearing a pair of jeans and a jacket that was too big for her. She never looked better to him. He wanted to grab her and kiss her, refuting all that he'd just heard from her sister.

"Going somewhere?" asked Danny.

"To stay with Ivory," said Vinny. "I have a big test tomorrow morning and a mixer tomorrow night. Ivory lives closer to campus, so it'll be easier for me to just crash there. I'll be able to study in the morning."

He looked into her eyes and imagined everything Renitta had said. He saw Vinny in the company of her fellow students and professors, discussing all kinds of smart people shit. Then he saw himself, standing over the bodies of the Bakers covered in dirt and rolling Olittah

Resse out of the river, dead as you can get. Then finally, he saw his mother tumbling to her doom.

"I'll get up early and we can go down together," Danny said.

"Won't you have to report early at the SCU?"

"Yes, but—"

"But what, Danny? I know how it goes. You got a hot one, and you have to take the lead on it. So do it."

"What about this mixer thing tomorrow? I'll come to that then." He was grasping now and hated himself for it.

"Oh, you wouldn't like that," said Vinny. "A lot of stuffy people talking about school. I'm just going to make contacts. I don't really want to go myself."

He started to say something, to keep the discussion going, but he didn't want to argue anymore. He knew their relationship. They would both dig in, it would get ugly, and she'd leave anyway. So, he kissed her, said a quick good-bye, and declared victory.

Danny watched Vinny and her sisters walk to the curb. As they moved away, he was strangely reminded of the kids at his elementary school and how they had all shunned him in those first days.

Scars never heal, they just stop bleeding. He heard Gordon's voice in his head.

The three sisters got into their cars and drove off. Danny couldn't help but think that for all of Renitta's terrible feelings for him, she had tried to do him a favor. But he didn't think she was right. He didn't think the world could take Vinny away from him.

17

JURISDICTION

Danny and Erik arrived at work early, thinking that they'd get a preliminary from Fiona on the Reese murder. Danny had had a restless night. He tortured himself thinking about the new murder and the fact that Vinny had walked out on him. And for the life of him, he couldn't figure out which bothered him the most.

The SCU was alive with activity. A couple of detectives from Fraud had been transferred to their unit temporarily and several uniformed officers had been assigned as well. The already cramped office was made even more so with all the new bodies stuffed into it. Danny was painfully aware that he and Erik were at the center of all this new activity. No matter how many people were on the case, it was theirs to win or lose.

Jim Cole opened the door to his office and asked Danny and Erik to come inside. He'd been holed up in there all morning, with the door closed, which was unlike him.

In the office, they were greeted by two federal types, straight and clean in their nondescript suits. The man was an FBI agent named Chip Unger. Danny knew him from a couple of joint investigations. Chip was white, about forty-five or so, and bald as an eagle. He stood like a soldier at attention, and Danny recalled that Chip had also been in the marines. Chip was all spit and polish.

The woman was black and thirtyish. Her face was pretty, but not overly so. Her skin was light brown, her eyes were about the same color, and her lips were nice and full. She hid this under some old, schoolteacher-type glasses. Her hair was pulled back and wrapped tight, completing the matronly package.

"Detectives," said Chip, "this is Janis Cates. She's from Quantico."

Danny and Erik shook Janis's hand, said hellos, then looked back to Chip, who just smiled.

"Did Jim tell you what's going on here?" asked Chip.

"No," said Erik.

Danny didn't say anything. He was watching Janis, who was looking at him strangely. It was that look a defense attorney gives you when he moves in for cross-examination. "What do you mean my client raised the weapon?" Danny imagined Janis saying. He didn't know what to make of the look, then it dawned on him that she was *reading* him. The way he read suspects and situations. He couldn't resist a smile. At this, she cocked a eyebrow.

"Sorry," said Jim. His voice cut the look between Janis and Danny.

"No problem," said Chip. "We can all get acquainted."

"Good," said Jim. "Brown, Cavanaugh, the FBI has come in on your murder case."

Before Danny and Erik could say a word, Jim held up a hand.

"You can be pissed later," said Jim, "but it's already done. Olittah Resse was found in international waters."

"The Detroit River?" asked Erik.

"The Canadians found her," Chip corrected. "They reported it to the Justice Department. It's routine. Look, guys, I know you don't like this kind of thing, but we do have jurisdiction here. However, we haven't come to take over the case. We've come bearing gifts."

"What?" asked Danny a little too hard.

"Janis here," said Chip. He raised a hand in her direction.

"Ms. Cates is a behavioral psychologist from FBI headquarters," said Jim, grabbing some papers with FBI letterhead. "She's been assigned to help us do a case study and any analysis we need on serial murder."

"Serial killer?" said Danny with surprise. "No one said nothing about that."

"He's killed in the same manner more than once," said Janis in a very official tone. "That's textbook. I'm interested in this particularly because there has never been a black serial killer proven to satisfaction in America. As far as the science is concerned, it is the exclusive province of white males."

"What about that brother in Atlanta?" asked Erik.

"Wayne Williams," added Jim. He seemed to be interested in where Janis was going.

"Many people believe that Wayne Williams is innocent," said Janis. "He was convicted on circumstantial evidence, carpet fibers, and in the end, he was only connected on two of the killings. As I said, there hasn't been a black serial killer proven to satisfaction and the advent of one must be treated in more than just a casual manner."

Silence hung for a moment as all the detectives got used to the idea of working with each other as well as referring to the murderer as a serial killer, something Danny and Erik didn't like one damned bit.

"There have only been two murder scenes," said Danny. "How did you catch on to the case?"

"I was wondering about that, too," said Jim.

Chip looked at Janis, who took a step forward as if she had been called on in a class.

"All of the homicides in the country are run through a national database. Eventually, they all come through our office's computers. I told the workers in data to keep on the look out for particular kind of murders." She paused and had everyone's attention. "I was looking for multiple murders where the victims were black and the perpetrator was also."

"And what makes you so sure he's black?" Danny said in a challenging tone.

Sensing what was in his voice, Janis turned to Danny.

"A serial killer preys within his own race or subgroup. All of our victims are black, that means the killer is also."

"Jeffrey Dahmer killed black men, but he was white," said Danny.

"Dahmer was a homosexual, and so he was within his subgroup," said Janis. "Race was irrelevant to him. He was motivated by sexual preference."

"And what about male killers who murder women of different races?" said Danny. "Are they within their subgroup?"

Janis looked irritated. The conversation had suddenly been turned into a debate between them. Chip looked upset about this; obviously he'd be charged with making the transition happen smoothly. Erik seemed amused and Jim even more so. He was openly smiling.

"In the case of women, the male killers usually have a sexual psychosis, impotence, or gender confusion. Therefore, he is still within his subgroup."

"That sounds thin to me," said Danny.

"Neither here nor there, Mr. Cavanaugh," said Janis.

They locked eyes for a second, but it was not anger that ran between them. It was respect. Janis was a tough woman and she wanted the men to know it. Danny could see in her eyes the most important thing of all. She wanted to nail the killer as much as they did.

It didn't take long for Danny to know what he thought of a person. Janis had a cop's heart, but she was horning in on his case, and he didn't like it. Still, he knew that if he gave her a hard time he'd be kicked off the case, and that wouldn't benefit anyone. There was more good than bad in Janis, so he decided right then and there that he didn't hate her.

"So, if our boy is black," said Danny, "how does that help us?"

Janis's eyes showed that she was claiming victory over Danny, but she was good enough not to make a big deal out of it.

"It's one more piece of information we have where before we knew nothing," she said. "My job will be to build a profile of this person, trait by trait, to narrow down the suspects."

"Janis has authored several papers on the subject," said Chip. "She's top flight on this." He was unmistakably proud.

"How will you build the profile?" asked Jim.

"The normal ways," said Janis. "Review of all violent crimes and reporting of all unusual or weird offenses since the killings started. Serial killers are often motivated by bizarre emotions, cravings, or desires. Like in Vermont, there was man who thought his pig was telling him to kill people. He broke into a toy store and stole a collection of piggy banks to put in his room at home."

They all laughed at this story, and it seemed to put Janis more at ease. Danny laughed, too, but he was still skeptical of the woman. Feds were arrogant and pushy, and so far she hadn't acted differently.

"So, will you need to review the case file?" asked Jim.

"I already looked at the Bakers' file," Janis said.

"And what did you determine?" Danny asked.

"Well," said Janis, adjusting her glasses, "he didn't pick the Bakers at random, he chose them for a reason. The ease with which he gained entry tells us that he may have been in the house before or cased it prior to the killing. He used a simple weapon and had a purpose for using it, so it would kill the victims slowly. He removed their gags and put them back in intervals. This leads me to believe that he wanted them to die slowly so he could question them about something, probably related to his psychosis."

Danny was impressed. The business with the gags had confused everyone and she made it seem so simple. The killer was talking to them. It was likely she was right.

"Of course this is all speculation," said Chip, again with pride.

"So, whatever we can do to help," said Jim.

"I'll need an office," said Janis. "And I want to talk to the forensic team leader, ASAP."

"I can get you to Fiona today," said Jim. "But it'll take seven years to get you that office."

Erik and Danny laughed along with Jim. Chip laughed, too. Janis, who was left out of the joke, looked confused and mildly upset, as if the men had just engaged in some secret, antiwoman joke.

"Only Jim has an office in the SCU," said Danny. "You can share desk space with me and Erik."

"Oh," said Janis. "I didn't notice. Excuse me."

Danny, Erik, and Janis left Jim and Chip to talk about the details. Erik stopped at the door, but Danny walked out ahead of her.

"Don't believe in chivalry?" Danny heard Janis say from behind him.

It took Danny a second to remember what the hell that word meant. "Yes, but we're all cops in here."

"I like that," she said. She smiled for the first time.

"You can sit here by me," Erik said. "We'll move our crap and clear a space and you can take part of both of our desks."

Janis thanked Erik and started dropping her things at the end of the desks. She took off her jacket, and Danny saw that what he thought was extra weight was actually a bad suit over a very shapely body. It's hard to hide a well-endowed chest and hips, but she was doing a good job. He could see Janis telling herself not to project a sexual image to the men, so she could be taken seriously. The SCU's own two female detectives never wore dresses, even when going to court to testify, and they generally maintained a demeanor that was not close to being feminine.

Danny saw a couple of the other guys give Janis a look and he felt uncomfortable with his thoughts. He didn't want to add to her problems, so he pretended not to notice.

Janis settled in and Danny got used to the idea of working with her. He got the file on Olittah Reese and gave it to Janis, who seemed genuinely happy to be reading about yet another murder. She was weird, but she seemed to love her job, and that would make them get along just fine, he thought.

Danny turned on his boom box and out came a tune by Mos Def.

"Why you wanna torture the woman on her first day?" asked Erik.

"Quiet, old man," said Danny. "You like this, right, Janis?"

"It doesn't bother me," said Janis. "Personally, I prefer jazz."

Danny smiled at Erik victoriously and turned up the music a little.

Janis pulled something from the files, then went to the bulletin board next to the desks. She grabbed several pins and tacked something to the board. She stepped aside revealing the faces of the three victims.

Mr. Baker smiled in a tux from a blown-up copy of a photo they'd taken from the murder scene. In another photo, Mrs. Baker was in gardening clothes, and Olittah Reese looked serious in her smart business suit in a publicity photo taken in the mayor's office.

"It helps to see the faces of the victim as they were," said Janis. "We'll be reminded of their cause every day we come in here."

Janis sat back down and Erik walked up to the board. He stood at the end of the pictures spread across the middle of the board and then turned to walk back.

Suddenly, something hit Danny. There was a marked difference between the living man and the dead people in the pictures. And in that moment he wanted to slap himself for not seeing it earlier. All of the victims were very light-skinned blacks. Erik's darker skin highlighted the clue.

Danny looked at the Bakers and Olittah Reese and none of them were even brown or light brown in complexion. They were very light in complexion, as close to white as you could get.

Erik was about to come back to the desk, when Danny asked him to stop, not to move.

"Why?" he asked.

Danny walked to the board, but stood on the other end, in front of the pictures, to show the spectrum.

"Janis," said Danny. "Look."

Janis turned and looked at the picture Danny had set up. She took a moment to get it, then, "I see," she said. "I never even thought about that."

"What?" asked Erik. His tone was impatient.

"All of the killer's victims are light-skinned blacks," said Danny.

Erik looked at the photos, then turned back to Danny. His face took on an odd look, an expression that Danny could make out, then he quickly washed it away.

"Do you think that's significant?" asked Janis. She had the same look on her face as Erik, only on her it lingered a while longer before disappearing.

"I should be asking you that," said Danny. "You're the psycho expert."

Janis frowned at the use of the word *psycho*, then she turned back to the board and looked at it again.

"It may be significant," she said finally. "Since our killer is black, he may have some kind of color fixation."

"I'd call three murders more than a fixation," said Danny.

Erik and Danny went back to their desks and sat down.

"Fascinating," said Janis. "This opens up a myriad of possibilities. And it means I'm right. Our boy is black and he's preying within his subgroup." To Danny, she said, "Good catch, Detective. Perhaps it took a nonblack person to see that so clearly."

Janis started to write notes furiously on a pad. Then Jim stopped by and he and Janis started talking about the process of gathering information on odd crimes in the city.

Danny sat down at his desk not knowing to make of her last statement. He didn't feel that he saw color any more or less than anyone else. But this observation was intraracial, he thought, color within color.

Danny was suddenly filled with a sense of dread. The killer had already proven to be deadly and elusive. Janis's words and observations only enhanced this fact in his mind. They scratched at the edges of his thinking, bringing clouds of menace into his normally focused mind. And somehow he knew that if he existed, a black serial killer was a more terrible force than a white one.

PART TWO

Vision of Justice

A killer always leaves a receipt.

—DANNY CAVANAUGH

18

THIRD PARTNER

Danny drove the car with Erik riding shotgun. Janis sat in the back, taking in the scenery. It was strange to Danny having another cop in the car, and he tried not to think of her as an intruder. The FBI had a long and distinguished history of working with the Detroit police, so any objections he had wouldn't matter.

They were headed to the Bakers' house, then to see Fiona. Janis wanted to examine the crime scene. She wanted to get the feel of the place. From just being there, she would get a sense of what their killer might be like. Danny didn't know what that meant, but he was going along with it. Since Olittah Reese was found in the river, Janis would have to be satisfied with whatever Fiona had for them.

"I didn't see the Bakers' blood work," said Janis.

"That was my bad," said Danny. "I forgot to include it. I'll get it to you."

"Your bad?" asked Janis in a very formal tone.

"Yeah," said Danny. "My mistake. I screwed up."

"Oh, right," said Janis. "I hear the young kids say that on TV." There was mild derision in her tone.

"This is Detroit," said Erik. "You got to be cool to make it here."

He laughed and Danny joined him. Janis said nothing as she looked out the window.

No one had said anything about the skin color of the victims since it had come up, but Danny was thinking about it. Blacks had long made differences among one another based on skin color within the race. It was something of an embarrassment, and no one liked to talk about it much. But whereas Erik and Janis might have been slow to make a big deal out of it because they had learned not to, Danny wasn't. And of all the things he knew about black people, this was the one thing he knew the least about. After all, he was always the outsider in every room growing up.

Danny had heard people making conversation about it, but they always seemed to stop when he came around as if they were afraid to air dirty laundry in front of a white person, even one who was a friend.

He didn't want to force Erik and Janis into a discussion of skin color just now. If the killer was motivated by the differences in the color of his black victims, Danny had to know everything about it.

"Is this your first time in Detroit?" Danny asked Janis.

"Yes," said Janis, her tone muted.

"Why do you say it like that?" asked Erik. "Like you just stepped into hell."

"Well, no offense, but the city isn't much to look at," she said.

"You haven't seen much of it," said Danny.

"I've seen enough," she said quickly. "Aside from the development downtown, the city is in pretty bad shape. And this casino thing will never work. It ruined Atlantic City and they had more resources." She made the last statement as if she had thought about it for a long time.

"Tell us how you really feel," said Danny.

"They're building new houses in the city," said Erik. "New jobs are coming, how about that for ruining the city?"

"That's right," said Danny. "The shit's been bad for a while, but Detroit is back, baby."

"You stay here awhile and you'll never wanna leave," Erik added.

"I know. I can't get outta this muthafucka," said Danny. Erik laughed with him.

"Have you always sounded like that?" Janis asked Danny in her best head-shrinker's voice.

"Yes," said Danny, not making a big deal out of it.

"The shit used to trip me out, too," said Erik. "It's like one of them movies where they change a guy's voice."

"I'm not shocked," said Janis. "Just interested. So, Danny, where did it come from?" She spoke these words as if he were her patient. Erik chuckled softly.

"I don't know," said Danny. "I just talked like the kids I knew growing up."

"But your parents didn't speak that way at home," Janis said quickly. "Cavanaugh, that's Irish, right?"

That irritated Danny a little, but he didn't let it show. Her question brought back a flood of memories about his family and his deceased mother. Danny glanced at Erik, who knew Janis had unknowingly hit a sore spot. His sympathetic look was comforting.

"Yes," said Danny, "but my friends were more of an influence. Like any kid, I wanted to fit in. You know how it is."

"I know?" said Janis.

"Yeah," said Danny. "If I didn't know you were black, I'd think you was white by the way you talk all proper and shit. So, you must have come up around white folks."

Erik turned and gave Danny a look that suggested that he'd insulted Janis. Danny heard her shift her weight in the backseat.

"I did," she said. "Well, I grew up in an affluent neighborhood, black and white, if that's what you mean."

"Yeah, I guess that's what I mean," said Danny.

"Some black people would consider that an insult," said Janis. "To say they speak like a white person."

"I know I would," said Erik. His laugh broke the tension that had built.

"And it's a compliment to say I talk like a black person?" asked Danny.

"White people aspire to blackness," said Janis. "It's like being thought of as cool. Black people aspire to the accouterments of the ruling class, but we don't like to think we haven't maintained our culture."

"You mean keepin' it real?" said Danny.

"What does that mean?" asked Janis. "I hear it all the time."

"Means the same as all that shit you just said," said Erik, and he and Danny laughed again.

Danny checked the rearview mirror and saw that Janis was not laughing. No sense of humor, he thought, all goddamned business.

"Speaking of affluence," said Janis, changing the subject, "I've been thinking about the victims. They were all high society."

"So does that mean our killer is some crazy-ass millionaire?" asked Danny.

"Could be," said Janis. "That could explain how he knew the Bakers' house so well and how he got close to Olittah Reese."

"So, when you say things about the killer like that, you're just speculating, right?" asked Erik.

"Yes and no," said Janis. "I don't know if it's ultimately true, but in the theory I'm building it is, so I treat it like a proven fact."

"We'll get him," Danny said. "All these guys fuck up and when he does, I'll be on his ass."

"Serial killers are the craftiest of all criminals," said Janis. "Twice as smart and more cautious. This guy's not going to just leave a receipt somewhere with his name and address on it."

"Not like that," said Danny. "But all scumbags are created equal and they all screw up. It'll just take the right kind of man to know how to read it."

"And that would be you, of course," said Janis.

"Damn skippy," said Danny. "Reading the street and its people is what I do best. It's like you see things and associate the shit with behavior then bam, you got the answer."

"And you've acquired this special power by being raised black?"

"Something like that," said Danny.

"He ain't lyin'," said Erik. "I've seen this man walk into a situation and know everything that was going on. The shit is spooky as hell."

Danny smiled at Janis proudly, as if Erik's endorsement was a validation to his statement.

"Don't be too proud, Detective," said Janis. "Sherlock Holmes invented your special skill a hundred and fifty years ago."

"Yeah, but Sherlock Holmes would get his skinny white ass capped on Mack and Van Dyke," said Danny.

Erik and Danny laughed and again Janis remained stone-faced.

"I won't argue with that," said Janis. "But you would do well to familiarize yourself with the material I brought on serial killers. These are dangerous men. They are driven by a compulsion to kill, deriving from repressed emotional trauma at a young age. Their rage is a deviant response to pain. So they would do anything, risk anything, to keep on killing."

"I feel the same way about stopping them," said Danny.

Janis had an annoyed look on her face, like a teacher whose student is too thick to get the day's lesson. It made Danny feel a little dumb, but he wasn't going to hold it against her.

"One thing I don't understand," said Janis. "Most multiple murderers take trophies from their victims, body parts, or personal items. Our guy didn't take anything."

"He's not a complete sick fuck, so what?" asked Erik.

"They need to relive the expunging of their pain by looking at the trophies and fantasizing about their kill," she said. "How is our guy doing that, if he doesn't take trophies?"

They rode in silence for a while as they all thought about Janis's inquiries. She did seem to understand these bastards, Danny thought. Danny wondered what the killer was taking from his victims. Maybe information. They thought he was asking questions of his victims, at least he did to the Bakers. Maybe their answers were what he needed. It didn't seem plausible though, so he didn't bring it up. He felt it was time to broach the taboo subject on his mind.

"What about skin color?" Danny asked. "How does that fit into the killer's psyche?"

"It probably doesn't," said Janis. "It probably just means he's part of that group."

"Group?" asked Danny. "The light-skinned group?"

"Yes," said Janis. Her voice was ever so slightly lower as if she was sorry she had said it.

They arrived at the Bakers' house, which was still covered in crime-scene tape. They'd gotten a lot of calls from the rich neighbors to take it down, but they ignored them. The police needed the place designated until they were done with it.

Janis asked to go in alone and Danny and Erik didn't argue. Every cop has his process, so they left Janis to hers. They saw Janis pass by a window talking into a recorder and gesturing with her hands as if holding a conversation with some unseen ghost.

When she was safely inside, Erik turned to Danny, still with an amused look on his face.

"Why don't you two just do it right now," he said.

"Do what?" asked Danny.

"What do you think? The way you two fight, I can almost see the clothes flying off. And don't even deny the shit. I'm way too smart to be thrown off the track."

"She's smart. And I kinda like fighting with her," said Danny.

"And I suppose them titties and that nice ass of hers don't affect you none, huh?"

"Yeah, she's fine, but I'm trying not to make a big deal out of it. I think she's gotten a lot of shit for it."

"Like how?" said Erik.

"Like another cop she's riding with talking about her titties and ass," Danny said pointedly.

"It's just a little man talk," said Erik with absolutely no guilt in his voice. "I respect the woman. Hell, she's a doctor, a Ph.D. Doctor of psychology. And I think you're her next case subject, my brotha."

"She's just wondering how some big, dumb white guy sounds like a big, dumb black one, that's all," said Danny.

"Well, I'd be careful, Danny; you got a bad habit of ending up in bed with your partners."

Danny didn't respond. He knew Erik meant it as a caution, not a joke at his expense. The truth was, Janis's interest in Danny was the last thing on his mind. He was more concerned with the killer and what he was planning next. And they didn't have any clues except the hooker and the color of the victims. One they couldn't find, and the other was, so far, meaningless.

"Why is this skin color thing making you so upset?" Danny asked Erik.

"Most blacks have some white blood in them," Erik said. "Only some of us are more white than others, and it makes a difference. The shit runs deep, you know, like nobody likes to talk about it." Then without missing a beat, he started a story. "When I was fifteen, there was this girl whose mama wouldn't let me go out with her because I was too dark." Erik's face took on an angry and hurt expression, then he went on. "I was all fucked up about it, you know, then I said forget it, it's just a girl, but it wasn't, you know, it was my own people not being my own people, and I felt like nothing."

Erik grew silent after this. He was not a particularly private man, but the things he kept to himself he considered sacred, and Danny had learned to respect that turf.

This story was obviously an important moment in Erik's life. Danny felt special that he'd shared it with him. Still, it sounded like more of a confession than a revelation, as if he was still ashamed of how he'd been mistreated, or maybe he was ashamed that it had happened at all, that his people were mired in some unhealthy consideration of color within their own race. Whatever it was, it had humbled this normally funny and outspoken man.

"Do you think we should take Janis with us to look for that hooker?" asked Erik in an effort to change the subject.

"No," said Danny. "We're doing it off-duty, and she don't seem like the kind to approve of that."

"Just wanted to hear you say it." said Erik. "I think we should go tonight."

"I'm down with that," said Danny.

They watched Janis in the murder house and didn't speak for a long while. Danny was thinking that Janis would be of great assistance to them but the key to the case was still somewhere on the streets of Detroit.

19

THE DARK HOUSE

Night was falling as Danny stepped out of his car on Mack Avenue near Van Dyke. Mr. Baker lived in Indian Village, so his hooker friend was probably from this area. Chances were that he wouldn't have wanted to venture far away from home when looking for his piece of ass.

Danny was wearing a big army jacket, jeans, and boots. He didn't want to look like a cop. It wouldn't help what was going to be an already risky situation.

Danny went to a couple of street guys he knew, trying to get the info he wanted. They were two brothers who worked the southeast side of the city, selling a little weed, nothing serious. He struck out. They didn't know anything.

Danny was disappointed partly because he didn't get the information, and partly because he'd hoped he wouldn't have to go to the place he was now headed.

Danny parked his car, then walked up Van Dyke and turned down a side street. He had a ways to go because he didn't want the people he was going to see to know for sure that he was alone.

Soon, he could see the house he wanted. It was nestled on a nice-looking street on a block with only one vacant lot, which had been turned into a garden. All around was blight, but this street could have been in any suburb in the metro area.

It was protected.

Danny walked up to the two-story house that was painted white with blue trim. Flower boxes had been freshly dug and planted and there was an old-fashioned bench swing on the left side of the porch. If he hadn't known better, he would have thought some nice old church mama lived there.

Danny was carrying both his weapons. Since this was not official, he went back to his old ways, feeling more comfortable with the revolver and the Glock.

He walked up the cracked sidewalk and was met by a kid about seventeen or so before he got to the house. The kid moved quickly toward Danny. He didn't appear to be armed, but Danny was not taking that for granted. Behind him were one man in front of the house and two others on the porch. The other men were all in their twenties. These men, Danny knew, were armed.

"Whatcha want, white man?" asked the boy.

Without missing a beat, Danny said, "I want you to respect who the fuck you talkin' to. Now take your narrow ass back and talk to King over there and ask him who I am."

Danny pointed to one of the men on the porch, a gangly kid who knew Danny and had helped him when he needed to recover an antique watch that had been boosted from a retired judge. Danny was told that no one knew anything about the watch, then it magically turned up on his desk the next day.

The little kid looked up at Danny, searching his face for some sign that he was not to be taken seriously. Danny just stared at him with that look he'd learned so long ago, that glare that said he didn't want trouble but he would start some if he had to.

"Hold up," said the kid, then ran back to King, who waved Danny up to the house. Danny walked past the first guard to King and another man, who was shorter, with a bald head. The kid ran off after cutting Danny a nasty look.

"Man's busy tonight," said King.

"If I'm here," said Danny, "you know I don't care about that. I got to see him right now."

"Is this muthafucka fo' real?" asked the bald man. King cut him off with a look.

"You can see him, but I gotta ask you to give them yo shit," said King.

"Not happenin'," said Danny.

"Then you gotta bounce," said King. "Man's nervous about white men with guns." The bald man moved one hand behind him, ready to pull a weapon.

"He ain't never been like that before," said Danny. "Why now?"

"I don't ask him why," said King. "He pays, I do. That's how it be and you know that."

"You know I ain't giving up my piece," said Danny. "So we got us a situation here."

"Then raise the fuck up outta here," said the bald man as he produced a gun from behind him.

"No!" yelled King.

Danny leaned quickly toward King, so that the bald man would have to aim in his direction. He hesitated long enough for Danny to shoot out an arm and knock away his gun hand. A shot fired, rocking the still night. Danny twisted the bald man's wrist. His hand opened up, and Danny easily took the weapon from him. Two other men walked up with their weapons drawn.

Danny held the gun a moment as all three men looked at one another. Danny turned the bald man's gun around, then he handed it to King.

"Only responsible people should have these," said Danny.

"Roe, what the fuck is your problem?" said King to the bald man. "He's a damned cop!"

King motioned the other men to lower their guns. They did. "Proody, go see if that shot hit anythang." The kid ran off. King turned back to Danny, who was smiling.

"See? I'm harmless." said Danny.

"Come on, man," said King. He walked toward the front door and Danny followed.

"What about my gun?" asked Roe.

"Shut your ass up," said King.

King took Danny inside and pointed to the den. Danny walked into the room and saw the Locke's massive back as he fed some tropical fish in a large tank against one wall.

The Locke talked to them like a parent does a toddler, in baby talk. He made kissing noises and smiled at the fish dumbly as if they knew he was happy with them.

Danny didn't like him, but he respected his position. Since the Locke was out of violent crime, he was no longer a concern of the police. The Locke flirted with both sides of the law, and a man like that could occasionally be an asset.

"Well, well," said the Locke. "The white man who ain't white, and the black man who ain't black. I heard the shot. I guess that would be your calling card."

"Your man tripped," said Danny. "I reacted."

"Roe," said the Locke knowingly. "He's a hothead. He'll be dead or in jail in the next year," He made the last statement in a matter-of-fact tone. "Sad, but that's the way the shit goes, you know."

The Locke walked over to a table with a chess set on it. The board was in midgame as if someone was playing. He studied it then made a move. Suddenly, he laughed.

"I'll have these fools beat in another three moves," he said. "I play against five of my guys. It takes all of them to even come close to being qualified," he said proudly. "You play, Detective?"

"I need some information," said Danny, not wanting to get engaged in small talk.

"Where was you when them muthafuckas ripped off my store?" asked the Locke. "I pay a lot of taxes and I got cops askin' me for shit." He took a deep breath then, "What is it?"

"I'm looking for a hooker who's using the name Xena."

The Locke popped some candy into his mouth and let his head roll upward. Danny saw his eyes flash for a second, the way they do when you recall a long-lost memory.

"Lotta hos use made-up names," he said finally.

"But you know who I'm talkin' about, right?"

The Locke walked back over to the fish tank, turning his back on Danny. He sprinkled in some more food, then tapped the side of the tank, making more baby talk. He turned back, grabbed a Squirrel Nut Chew, and ate it noisily.

"I know her, but I need something from you."

Danny had feared it would come to this. The Locke was an operator, and would not give up information without getting something in return. "What do you want?"

"I need you to smoke somebody," he said casually.

"Fuck you," said Danny.

"Just seeing where the limits are," said the Locke, laughing. "Let's say you owe me one, a get-out-of-jail-free card."

"And fuck you again," said Danny.

"Hard man. Then I guess I got nothing to say."

Danny moved closer to the Locke. "I'm not leaving without the information." Danny pulled his gun and pointed it at the fish tank. "You decide how I'm gonna get it."

The Locke's face expressed fear. He moved over to the fish tank. "Ain't no need for that shit."

"I mean it," said Danny. "I'll pop their fishy asses."

The Locke searched Danny's eyes the same way the kid outside had. He saw the same thing.

"Hard-ass white boy, huh?" he laughed. "I heard you almost got kicked off the police force for some shit you did."

"Ancient history," said Danny, putting his weapon away. "But old habits can be hard to break, if you know what I mean."

"The bitch stays over by Gratiot and Seven Mile," the Locke said. He blurted it out, like it was pent up inside. "She's a shooter, heroin, so she's got a lot of hard work to do to support that kinda habit. She probably been fucking her way all over the east side."

"Her real name?" asked Danny.

"Bellva, or at least that's what she said."

"She work for you?"

"For a minute, then she went indy a year ago. I don't hold on to them when they make that choice. They either come back, or they end up dead. You'd better move on her fast, because she's in the last category."

Danny left, not wanting to stay any longer than he had to. He walked off the porch past King and his men, who hustled back to their posts.

Danny went to his car, thinking of the Locke's comment about the hooker. When he said a person would probably end up dead, not only did he mean it, he was probably right. Danny moved a little faster and hoped that he wasn't already too late.

Danny drove over to the area that the Locke had told him about, a nasty little stretch near Seven Mile and Van Dyke. He nosed around, but he didn't ask about Xena or Bellva. He asked where a person might go if he wanted to get high. This led him to an abandoned house on the near east side. It was one of those old pre–World War II houses with an attic and a deep basement.

Danny went inside. The walls were covered with graffiti and stains, which could have been composed of anything. The floor was littered with trash and semiconscious addicts. Danny could smell the pungent odor of human waste with each breath.

It wasn't a drug house. Most of the dealers had long stopped people from using in their places. They'd sell you the shit, then send your ass packing. Too many of them had been popped by the police when heads gave their places up.

Suddenly he stopped. On the floor propped up against a wall was something that made his heart leap. A hand cut off at the wrist and covered in grime lay there.

"Jesus," said Danny.

He knelt down to take a closer look. He took out a pen and poked the hand a few times. It fell over, making a hollow sound.

"Shit," Danny said, picking it up. "Fuckin' plastic." He threw it back down in the floor and moved on.

Danny heard a noise and walked toward a room in the back of the first floor. He was stopped by a skinny man who was obviously a crackhead. He wobbled a little in front of Danny, doing that crackhead dance, which was really just their equilibrium being all fucked up.

"Yo, my man, whassup?" said the crackhead. "You don't wanna go in there, brutha," he said in a voice suddenly different from his crackhead one. It had a familiar tone to it. He was scared.

Danny waited. He'd learned never to ignore that tone when he heard it. "What going on back there?"

"You know, some brothers caught this bitch who was dealin' some bad shit, and you know, they takin' care of her."

Danny heard the distinct sound of someone being hit, the cold smack of flesh against flesh and he ran into the room which was a kitchen. There he saw three men, two black, one white. One of the black guys held a young black woman by both arms. The salt-and-pepper pair stood in front of her. Mr. Pepper had his fists clenched, and Danny assumed this was the one who had administered the blow. They heard Danny and all four people looked toward the doorway.

A quick glance told Danny they were all drug users of some type. They were thin and sick-looking, and had that gaze of not quite being in this world.

"Get the fuck out of here, white boy," said the hitter.

"Who's the girl?" Danny asked calmly.

"None of yo' muthafuckin' bid'ness," said the hitter.

"It is if it's the woman I'm lookin' for," said Danny, coming all the way into the kitchen.

The hitter and the white guy next to him turned toward Danny. The white guy was already shaking a little, like he was sick, and Danny could tell he wanted no part of a fight. Not knowing what any of them was packing, Danny decided to put a quick end to this.

Danny grabbed the hitter and slammed him into the wall. He crumpled, letting out an ill-sounding grunt, then passed out.

The man holding the girl released her without asking, then he and the white guy ran out of the kitchen.

Danny went to the girl and took her by the arm. He could see that she'd been pretty before she got into drugs. Her body was thin, ravaged by drug use. Her face was covered with fresh bruises, and one of her fingers was bent inward, having been broken but not attended to medically. Worse than all this was that she looked to be no more than seventeen or so.

"Bellva?" asked Danny.

"Huh?" she said in a thin, needy voice. She was still getting her bearings and she held on to his arm, which looked massive in her grasp.

"Are you Bellva, or Xena?"

"No, I'm Lilly . . ." She took a moment, for what reason he didn't know. "Them muthafuckas . . . They said I gave them some bad shit. I got it from this guy I fucked. I didn't know what that shit was, man."

"They're gone now. Do you know Bellva?" Danny had to get her back on the subject.

"Oh . . . Bellie? She's in the basement. You her man?"

"Yeah, I'm lookin' for her. She ran out on me, and I need to get her back home. Get her well."

"Oh, she'll be glad for that," said the girl. "She been real scared lately. I had to help that girl find a vein."

"Well, all that's over now. Show me where she is."

The girl took him into the basement. They descended the stairs. Danny always had an ominous feeling walking into the cellars of these drug houses. You never know what you'd find. A bunch of junk or a bunch of bodies.

The basement was dim and dank. It took his eyes a moment to focus, but soon Danny could see the people crowded on the floor and leaning against the walls. It was like a sick room, filled with foul human odors undercut with a sad medicinal smell.

"Bellva!" Danny yelled out.

The crowd murmured and a man said, "Whatchoo wont, honey?" followed by hoarse laughter and a stagnant cough. Danny moved farther into the room and felt Lilly fall off his arm. She moved over to a man whom he guessed she knew because she rammed her tongue into his mouth.

Danny called out for Bellva again and a man lumbered over to him.

"She upstairs, in da front. Now, stop all that yellin', man."

Danny ran back upstairs and scanned the bodies on the living room floor. There were ten people in the room and four of them were women. He called out the name suddenly and saw one of the women, a thin girl with a cascade of unkempt braids, jerk her head slightly, then just as quicky turn back. Danny moved over to her and knelt down to where she was sitting.

"I need to talk to you," said Danny.

"I don't know what you talkin' 'bout, man," she said in a voice that was decidedly unhealthy.

"John Baker is dead, and whoever did it might be looking for you." This was a lie, but Danny was hoping that she wouldn't recognize that. To make his point, he showed her his badge.

She reacted, scared, then stared into Danny's eyes, a gaze that was unusual for a drug addict. In her eyes, he saw the familiar look of devastation behind her fear.

"Johnny's dead?" she asked in an innocent voice. "I didn't have nothing to do with all that. Johnny was just a job, you know."

"Come on, I can't talk here."

Danny lifted her off the floor and walked her out of the building. He stuffed her into his car and drove away from the godforsaken place.

"You wouldn't be doing all this just to get me to do you a little favor, woulda?" She leaned toward him, trying to look pretty.

In the light, Danny could see that she was as young as Lilly but not as bad off. Bellva was still on the pretty side of her addiction. The drugs had not yet robbed her of all her beauty.

"No," he said. "I want to know what you know about John Baker."

"Hey, where we goin'?" she asked as Danny gunned the car toward the freeway.

"To meet a friend."

Bellva put another sugar into the black coffee at a McDonald's which faced the I-75 service drive at Warren Avenue.

On the way over, Danny had grilled the girl about her associates, and as far as he could tell, she wasn't hooked up with a pimp or some jealous boyfriend who could have killed the Bakers.

Danny and Erik watched the girl fill her Styrofoam cup with sweetness. Not like a hit of heroin, but it would have to do.

Erik had been happy when Danny called him with the news that he had the girl. Erik was over on the west side in the middle of some nasty shit with a snitch when Danny phoned. Erik was glad to get away from the snitch, who apparently had recently lost one of his hands in a dispute.

"Y'all gon' take me down the thirteen hunnet?" asked Bellva.

"No," said Erik. "Not unless you make us."

"Cool, cool," said Bellva, smiling. "I don't need that shit in my life. Thirteen hunnet Beaubien. Hey, did y'all know Beaubien was a French word? Beaubien, *B-e-a-u-b-i-e-n*," she spelled in a proper voice. "I'm good at spellin'. I won my junior high spelling bee when I was eleven," she said proudly. And for a moment she wasn't a drug addict, she was an innocent, a noble young girl with a special talent.

"That's cool," said Danny, trying to make her feel more comfortable.

"Yeah, it was in the newspaper and everythang," said Bellva. "I can still do it, too. Like you," she said, pointing to Danny. "Yo' name sounds easy, but it ain't. Cavanaugh, *C-a-v-a-n-a-u-g-h*. See, a dumbass would say *C-a-v-a-n-a*. But you got what you call silent letters in that shit."

She smiled again, proud of this singular knowledge in her ravaged mind. Her smile brightened her face, and for an instant she was cute. One of the saddest things about a drug addict is that you always see flashes of them as kids, Danny thought, and you know life must be some sick-ass shit to have turned anyone's baby into that.

There was a loud commotion on the other side of the restaurant. Danny and Erik immediately turned to check it out. The noise had come from the table with two loud young brothers of about twenty or so. They were layered in gold and wore expensive leather jackets. They had a mountain of food on the table. Dealers, thought Danny.

Erik cut them a nasty look. The dealers only laughed even though they had made out Danny and Erik as cops. Gone were the days when a lowlife was scared of the police. Now they were defiant, arrogant even. Not until you had the goods on them did they recognize that you had any special power.

Bellva saw the dealers and smiled at them, flirting. They nodded, then laughed, pounding their fists together at some comment.

"So, how long were you with Mr. Baker?" asked Danny, wanting to get back to business with Bellva.

"Me and Johnny was kickin' it about three months or so." She took a long swig of the coffee.

"And what did y'all do?" asked Danny.

"Sex," she said. "Damn, whassup with you?"

She didn't use the word Danny expected to hear, the *F* word. When a hooker didn't say that word, it meant she was up to something other than copulation. This made Danny suspicious.

"What kind of sex?" asked Danny, and he said *sex* with emphasis.

Bellva leaned back in her seat, and took on a frightened, then embarrassed look. "Well, we never did it the normal way, you know," she whispered, leaning in toward Danny and Erik. "He was scared. I don't know why. I never share needles, and I don't fuck them switch hitters. He let me get him off with my hand. He was gonna pay me a grip to do it with a girl, but I couldn't find one in time." Bella leaned

back, then a smile spread across her face. "Hey, I got one for you—
that street, Gratiot." She pronounced it *gra-shit*. "*G-r-a-t-i-o-t*, that's
French, too, you know, hard as hell to spell that one."

"Ever do it in his house?" asked Erik, trying to keep her focused.

"No," she said forcefully. "He'd never let me get close to his place.
He was scared as hell of his wife."

"Was he ever afraid of anything or anybody else?" asked Danny.

"No, Johnny wasn't scared of nothing, not like we think about
being scared."

"Then how?" asked Erik. There was some impatience in his voice.

"He was always worried about something called Castle," said Bellva.

"Castle what?" asked Danny.

"I don't know," said Bellva. "He wouldn't ever say a lot. One time
he'd had a few drinks in him and he started talkin' all proper and
shit, he say 'Fear stalks the Castle,' " she intoned in a deeper voice.
"It was like something out of one of them old scary movies."

"The Castle Society?" asked Erik.

"Ring a bell?" asked Danny.

"Yeah. It's a group, I mean *was* a group, but it don't exist anymore," said Erik.

Then it clicked for Danny. Castle was the name printed beneath
the picture at Virginia Stallworth's home.

"When Mr. Baker talked about the Castle, was it about history,
what it used to be?" asked Erik.

"Hell no," said Bellva. "He was talkin' 'bout right now."

"Did Mr. Baker say anything at all that would make you think he
was in danger from anyone in particular?" asked Danny.

"Naw, not really," said Bellva, "but this one time, I was doing
Johnny, had him in my hand nice and stiff, you know, and, he
started talking about that Castle thing, and he just went limp, lost
it, like he didn't care anymore. Only scary shit makes a man lose his
hard-on, baby."

"Did Mr. Baker ever mention a company that he started, New
Nubia?" asked Erik.

"Naw," said Bellva. "Johnny never liked to talk about bid'ness with me. Probably thought I wouldn't understand it."

"Did he ever talk about having a lot of money, or leaving town?" asked Danny. It was a long shot, but he had to ask.

"No," said Bellva. "If he was gonna skip town, he woulda asked me to go with him. Damn, I need another coffee. Do they do refills here?"

Danny and Erik questioned Bellva a little while longer, then sent her on her way in a cab. Danny felt sorry for her. She was just a periodic good time for the deceased Mr. Baker, though she'd deluded herself into thinking that she meant more. One thing for sure, she was no killer.

"How long you give her?" Erik asked Danny.

"Another few months or so," said Danny casually. "If she don't OD, she'll get caught up in some bad shit and get killed. Sad thing. She's a damned good speller."

They walked to their cars and saw the dealers come out of the restaurant talking into cell phones. They climbed into a black Cadillac Escalade and roared off.

"I give them until next week," said Danny. "So, tell me about the Castle group."

"Not much to tell," said Erik. "Back in the forties and fifties in Detroit, there was a group of black people called the Castle Society. They were elite blacks—doctors, lawyers, morticians. My grandmother used to tell stories about it all the time. It kinda of phased out because they used to exclude people on the basis of skin color . . . holy shit."

"You took the words right out of my mouth," said Danny. "So what happened to this group?" asked Danny.

"The Castle was frowned upon as blacks of all skin colors rose to power in the sixties. There's a story that it got so bad once that Dr. King himself had to issue an order to stop the infighting."

"These are the same kind of people who have been dying," Danny pointed out.

Erik and Danny said good-bye, promising to sort it all out tomorrow. Danny went home and called Fiona and was told rather angrily
not to bother her, that all would be revealed when she was ready.
Fiona didn't just work a case, she took possession of it and there was
no use in arguing with her.

Danny got a beer and turned on some loud, thumping music by
Eminem. He thought vaguely about his first day of school at Davison
Elementary. He recalled the sea of black faces and the strange looks
he got. Looks that asked, "what are you and what are you doing
here, here where you don't belong?" He wondered if Eminem caught
a lot of shit for being a white and performing rap music.

As the driving beat thundered into his head, he tried to relax and
not think about the killer, or Vinny, who had made another clean and
graceful exit from their home.

Danny caught sight of a family picture from 1981 on his mantel.
He was there with his mother and father. They all looked happy and
peaceful in the bright sunshine. Soon, he fell asleep, his mind covered
in peaceful darkness. Then he dreamed again of his mother's awful
death. He woke up in fright and never got back to sleep.

20

OASIS

The Bady brothers had broken into the office of the Oasis Halfway House with ease. For a place that dealt with criminals, it didn't take many precautions against theft.

It was probably some of that honor-system rehabilitation shit, thought Muhammad. The system was full of that kind of silly, human nature crap. He remembered the people who made those kinds of rules, pie-in-the-sky-type assholes who believed if they thought good thoughts they could turn shit into gold.

The brothers had waited for several hours on Eight Mile just west of Gratiot. Muhammad had sat on a bus bench and watched hundreds of people roar by in their cars. He was particularly watchful of families in their big SUVs and dumb-ass station wagons. But he was not angry or envious. He had his family, too. It was just a different kind of family. They were devoid of lies, hypocrisy, and secrets. Instead they lived on respect, truth, and yes, even love.

When it was dark out, Muhammad and his brothers walked down Eight Mile toward Livernois then onto a side street where the Oasis Halfway House was located. They forced open a window of the place and slipped inside without attracting any attention.

The facility was actually a converted apartment complex. It was a dull gray color and had remnants of what were once colorful borders. Now they were faded memories washed into bleakness by time.

The neighborhood residents had fought against the facility, but had lost. The city needed businesses, any kind of businesses, and so in the end it was commerce that placed the halfway house where it was.

Muhammad rifled through the thick files in an old metal cabinet against the far wall of the front office. He was looking through the B files for his father, to see if he had resided there. This Oasis had to be the place Cameron Cole had talked about.

They had been careful in casing Oasis. It was not too far from the home occupied by the Locke and his men. The word was out on the street that the Locke was looking for the brothers and had offered a generous bounty for any information leading to them. First things first, thought Muhammad. Find their father and kill him. Then they could attend to the man who had tried to kill them.

Rimba went through the office looking for anything portable that could be sold on the street. Akema looked out a window watching for intruders.

"Shit!" said Muhammad. "He ain't here." Muhammad tossed a file into the air angrily and slammed his fist into the concrete floor. He was not cut out for this, breaking into houses to look for information. He was a bull, not a private eye. Muhammad took what he needed, but in this there was nothing to take. He had to be smart, to think, and sadly that was not his strength.

Muhammad stood up. His brothers looked at him, waiting for him to speak. Muhammad felt the weight of his brothers' stares. He was the leader, the big brother, and he had to be strong. His outburst had probably rattled them. If he was not confident, then what chance did Rimba and Akema have?

Suddenly Muhammad's face brightened. He walked back to the file cabinet and pulled out the last drawer marked EMPLOYEES and opened it up.

"He couldn't use a made-up name," said Muhammad. "They

woulda got his fingerprints and found out who he really was. So the only way he coulda been here if he wasn't livin' here was if his ass was workin' here." Muhammad said this almost to himself as he searched the files. Muhammad scanned the contents of the folders until he found what he'd been searching for. Herman Bady had changed his name by the time he got to Michigan.

Muhammad pulled out the photo that had been taken so many years ago. He had indeed changed. His face was fuller and he had hair on his face. But he could not change his eyes. Muhammad grew hot as he looked into those cold eyes in the photo, remembering the death and pain he'd brought into their lives.

"There he is," said Muhammad. "We gonna take this and study everything in it so we can find out where he went—"

They heard a commotion at the door, the jingling of keys and a light flashing. Before they could react, the door was opened and in stepped a security guard. He was a man of about fifty or so. He held a gun in one hand and a flashlight in the other.

"Don't move!" yelled the guard. The light in his hand shook as he trained it on the trio before him.

Muhammad looked at Rimba, who stepped in front of the gun without hesitation. Faintly, Rimba's music could be heard from his stereo.

"You gonna have to kill him," said Muhammad.

"I will," said the guard. "Now, all of you put your hands in the air!"

Rimba took a step forward, and the guard cocked the gun. Rimba just looked the man in the eyes, steady, unflinching.

"Something else to kill a man," said Muhammad. "Especially one who ain't got no gun."

"Shut up!" yelled the guard.

"Go on and do it," said Muhammad. "As soon as you shoot him, I'll kill you."

"I said shut up," the guard hissed. "I want all of you to put your hands up."

Rimba moved closer. The guard's flashlight shook even more now. Then the guard took a step back.

At that moment, Rimba leapt at the guard, knocking him down to the floor. Rimba hit the guard in the throat; the man croaked loudly. Akema was then all over the fallen man, grabbing his gun and placing it to the guard's head.

"Stop," said Muhammad. He walked over to the threesome. He looked at the guard coldly, then took the gun from Akema. "It takes a lot to kill a man," he said to the guard.

"Please," begged the guard. "Take whatever you want, I won't say anything."

"We got what we wanted," said Muhammad.

Muhammad pointed the gun at the man, who had turned into a frightened child. Muhammad had seen that look many times, too many to remember them all. When the guard's eyes calmed, when he'd accepted that he would die, Muhammad turned to his brothers.

"We'll make too much noise if we shoot him," said Muhammad.

Rimba tugged off the guard's belt, wrapped it around his neck, and pulled it tight. The guard struggled, but Rimba held on fast until the man stopped kicking. Muhammad was not taking any chance that someone would find out what he was up to.

Muhammad pulled out a can of lighter fluid and set fire to all of the files. He couldn't let anyone know which file he'd taken. He was planning a family reunion and he wanted it to be a surprise.

As the flames rose, Muhammad and his brothers looked at the picture of their father. The firelight bounced eerie light off the glossy photo. Akema and Rimba stared at the visage with awe and anger. Muhammad's plan was to make their father suffer before killing him. Now that he'd seen his face, he knew in his heart that it would be a very difficult thing to do.

21

FIONA'S TOUCH

Danny, Erik, and Janis got to Fiona early the next morning. They grabbed newspapers at the *News* and *Free Press* boxes. Both papers had front-page headlines about the latest killing. Mercifully, the story did not lead in either paper, but it was front-page news, and there was a strong suggestion that there was a link between Olittah Reese and the Bakers.

Danny, Erik, and Janis entered Fiona's office and found her waiting for them. Jacob was in a corner office poring over a stack of files, muttering to himself. Fiona had given him some kind of shit assignment to keep him out of her hair.

Fiona told the three officers how Olittah Reese, thirty-three, had met her demise. The fact that she'd been in the river made everything a little speculative, but Reese had probably been beaten, bound, and gagged and then shot in the same manner as the Bakers. This time, no chloroform was used.

Danny inquired if there were abrasions on her face as if the killer had lifted the gags as he'd done before. Fiona answered yes to this. The murders were identical, only this time the killer had the river to help cover his tracks.

Olittah Reese had known the Bakers as political allies of the current mayor. If the mayor was somehow a target, it was a mystery to everyone but the killer. More interesting was the fact that Olittah had helped the Bakers with several investor parties for New Nubia.com. Danny felt certain that somewhere in that group was Janis's so-called serial murderer.

"So, do we have anything we can use?" asked Danny.

"Yes, there is one thing," said Fiona. "Our deceased had a little prize in her stomach, some male sperm."

Danny and Erik both reacted, but not with shock. They were happy. Tangible evidence was always appreciated.

"Excellent," said Janis. "We can definitely use that."

"Sperm makes us girls excited," said Fiona. Janis visibly blushed.

"Got a type on it, yet?" asked Erik.

"I sure as hell do," said Fiona. "Get me a match, and maybe we got your killer."

"Wait," said Danny. "Reese was married. It could belong to her husband."

"One way to find out," said Erik.

They said a quick good-bye to Fiona, who promised a full report soon.

Danny was thinking that the prize in the deceased, as Fiona called it, could not have been done forcibly. That kind of sex was not the thing that a rapist/killer would engage in. Too dangerous to put it in some woman's mouth. What it did indicate was that this killing was not as clean as the Bakers, and usually when a killer slipped up you could follow the mistake to a clue. They were on to something, and Danny tried not to be too excited as they drove uptown to Sherwood Forest, a fashionable, upscale black neighborhood in the city.

They entered the spacious home of Thomas Reese, the deceased's husband. Reese looked like shit. Since his wife had been missing, he hadn't slept much and was on leave from his job at DaimlerChrysler. However, even stressed out and grieving, Reese was a handsome black man of about forty or so. Olittah had been a beautiful woman, and they had probably made a striking couple, Danny thought.

"Mr. Reese," said Danny. "I know this is hard for you, but we need your help, sir."

"Sure, anything," said Reese. "You guys want a drink, oh shit, right, you can't. You mind?"

Danny, Erik, and Janis shook their heads as Reese went to the bar and made a drink. He downed it and quickly poured another.

"Olittah was a great woman," said Reese. "She and I had our shit all together, you know. She was connected downtown with the brothers, and I had the white folks. Oh, no offense, man," he said to Danny.

"None taken," said Danny. "Mr. Reese, we have something to ask you, and it's pretty sensitive. It's about what your wife did before she died."

"Well, I really don't know," said Reese. "I told the police all I could. I was working late, and when I came home, Olittah was gone."

"Was it normal for you to work late?" asked Janis.

"I do it sometimes but usually I'm home by nine or so. Why?"

Danny took a moment to let him feel the seriousness of what he was about to ask. "Mr. Reese, did you have sex with your wife the day she disappeared?"

"What?" asked Reese, wide-eyed. "Wha— Why is that—?" His eyes got larger, and a rage filled them. Reese sat down hard in a chair, and even before he said it, Danny knew. It was not his semen they'd found in his wife's stomach.

"Fuck," he said. "How could she?" He shook his head and looked at his feet.

"Do you have any idea who it might have been, sir?" Erik asked.

"If I knew, he'd be dead!" yelled Reese.

Suddenly Danny was thinking about Vinny and her new study partner, his body language, and the almost plastic smile on his face. A man may not know the truth, but he always has suspicions of what the truth is. He also thought about how Olittah Reese had flirted with him so openly. Thomas Reese had to know something.

"Mr. Reese, your wife was a nice-looking woman," said Danny. "I'm sure you noticed men who were more than just friendly with her. A man who you just felt had the wrong intention?"

Reese downed his second drink, then another, and looked up at the ceiling. He lowered his head. "Charles," he said.

"He got a last name?" asked Erik.

"Eastergoode," said Reese. "Judge Charles Eastergoode."

Danny and Erik shared a look of recognition. Danny pulled out his notebook and checked the notes from the Longs' interview. It was there, Charles Eastergoode, the man who had gossiped about Mr. Baker's lover. Danny fought the urge to smile at what was their first real lead in the case. Mr. Reese was in pain, and Danny didn't want him to think he was insensitive.

"Thank you, sir," said Danny.

"Mr. Reese, a doctor will be here shortly to ask for some blood to compare to the fluids we found in the body," said Janis.

"Why?" said Reese, fighting his tears. "It wasn't me, okay? My dead wife was fucking some guy and it wasn't me."

"We just have to be sure," said Janis. "Whoever it was will claim it was you in court."

"Okay," said Reese in a low voice that contained his surrender to all the grief in his life.

Danny felt for the man. Not only was his wife dead, she'd been having an affair, and to add insult to injury, he now had to prove it by being stuck with a needle.

Danny, Erik, and Janis left and drove back downtown to Recorder's Court, the special criminal division of the Circuit Court. They parked their car on St. Antoine along with the other double-parked police vehicles and went inside. They flashed their badges, passed the security station, then took the elevator up to the seventh floor.

Judge Charles Eastergoode was one of those men who had probably always been destined for greatness. He was the son of two black physicians, which in the 1950s was a big-ass deal. He was a track star at Cass Tech High School, a special public magnet school where Detroit's smartest kids went. Eastergoode attended the University of Michigan undergraduate program, then later the law school.

He worked briefly for Mayor Harris Yancy, becoming one of his rising stars, then he opened a law practice that specialized in civil litigation. He made a ton of money suing insurance companies and corporations. After spreading his wealth around, he got an appointment from then-governor James Blanchard to the Circuit Court bench.

Danny had testified before Eastergoode on a number of occasions. He was smart, arrogant, and didn't take any shit. He was highly connected, so Danny knew that they had to tread softly with him. Messing around with someone's wife was not a crime, but Eastergoode might have some other information that would prove useful.

Danny, Erik, and Janis sat in the spacious chambers of the judge while he concluded a case involving an assault. Soon, they heard the commotion of people leaving and a bailiff signaling the end of the session. The door sprang open and the judge walked in, removing a pair of reading glasses. He was medium build, in great shape for a man over fifty, and his hair was turning gray.

Eastergoode was not a handsome man, but had a quality about his face that was not unpleasant. He was rugged-looking and carried himself with confidence.

The judge was followed in by a female bailiff, who had a mean look on her face. She gave Erik, Danny, and Janis a nod, then stood by the door.

Eastergoode removed his robe, put on his suit jacket, and then pulled out a pipe. "What can I do for you boys—and lady?" he added, looking at Janis. He lit the pipe and took a long puff. The sweet smell of the tobacco wafted across the room.

"We have a sensitive matter to discuss, Judge," said Danny.

"Is it about a case on my docket?" he asked.

"No," said Erik.

"Then no need to pussyfoot," said Eastergoode. "Out with it."

Danny glanced over at the bailiff, who was still watching. Then he looked the judge directly in the eyes, making sure he got his meaning.

"It's about Olittah Reese," Danny said.

Eastergoode's eyes grew ever so slightly wider, then he put down his pipe, and asked the bailiff to leave. When she was gone, he turned back to them.

"Sad thing what happened," he said. "How can I help?"

"We've got a problem, Judge," Danny began. "I can sit here and ease my way into it, but I don't think a man like you would appreciate that."

"I prefer candor," said Eastergoode.

"Yes, sir," said Danny. "We found semen in the stomach of Olittah Reese."

Eastergoode was now settled and his expression did not change after hearing this statement.

"And what does this have to do with me?" His voice had a mixture of concern and anger in it.

"We're trying to find out who it belonged to," said Janis.

Danny was surprised at this statement from Janis. It was blunt, and it also cut into his line of questioning. The last thing he needed to do was get into a power struggle in front of a suspect.

"How is it I've never seen you?" Eastergoode asked Janis. "I know all of the detectives in the SCU." He seemed upset at the not-so-subtle implication of her statement.

"I'm from the FBI," said Janis.

Danny saw Eastergoode show genuine fear now. State judges didn't want anything to do with federal power. It usually meant trouble. The Circuit Court had had a corruption probe a few years back and three judges had gone to prison.

"Olittah and I were friends, but she never told me her business," said Eastergoode, calming down.

"You don't think the semen belonged to her husband?" asked Danny.

Eastergoode looked afraid, then shifting some mental plan, he took on an angry look. "Okay, Detectives, there's no need to play this game anymore. You obviously think I'm the man you're looking for. Well, I'm not, so you can go now."

"We have a type on the semen," said Danny. "If we get a suspect, and this goes to trial, we'll have to do everything to find out who the man was."

"Are you threatening me?" asked Eastergoode.

"No, sir," said Danny, "but you can see our position. If we don't ask you our bosses chew us out. If we do, well, then we get on your bad side."

Danny and the judge locked gazes for a moment as Eastergoode contemplated his choices. Danny could feel him thinking. If he threw them out, that would raise suspicion, to say nothing of the FBI agent and what she might do. If he cooperated, then they would find out whatever it was he was hiding.

"I'm afraid I'm going to have to ask you to leave, gentlemen," said Eastergoode.

"If we leave here without your cooperation," said Danny, "people will talk."

"Talk is bad in Detroit," said Erik. "Has a way of getting around. All around."

Janis didn't say anything. She just looked angrily at the judge and that seemed to bother him more than what he was hearing from the two men.

Danny could see that Eastergoode was visibly upset now. He was caught and he knew it. He looked at Danny with anger in his eyes, and Danny wondered if he focused on him because he was white. Black men like Eastergoode had power in Detroit, and they didn't like to be under the authority of any white man, even if he was just a cop. Eastergoode turned his back on the detectives, lifted his head up and sighed.

"How can I trust you?" he said.

"Because we'll give you our word," said Danny.

Eastergoode thought about this a long time, assessing the cops before him. "I was at home with my wife and some friends when she died, so I have an alibi, you know."

"We know that," said Erik.

"Then you don't consider me a suspect," said the judge.

"No, we don't," said Danny and Janis, overlapping each other.

The judge sat down in his big leather chair and looked right at the detectives.

"It was going on for about a year, off and on," the judge began. "Mostly we did it here or in her office. We're both too well known to get some hotel room. Once, we hooked up in Canada across the river at a hotel after some gambling." He smiled ever so slightly at the memory. "Olittah was an exciting, passionate woman. We were both married and had a lot to lose, and so there was never any talk of divorce or any of that shit. We'd break it off, then we'd run into each other, and it was on again."

"What happened the night she disappeared?" asked Danny.

"Nothing out of the ordinary, really. Olittah came here, we talked, and then . . . we serviced each other. I went home. I assumed she did, too."

"Were you involved with New Nubia.com?" asked Danny.

"No," said Eastergoode. "Olittah keep trying to get me into it, but I'm a very conservative investor. Turns out I was smart, huh? People lost their shirts on that thing."

Danny and Erik looked at each other, making sure that neither of them had any more questions about the encounter. Danny then turned to Janis, who was looking at Eastergoode. She shook her head ever so slightly. Danny took this to mean that she didn't consider him a serious suspect. Danny had one more question on his mind.

"Have you heard of the Castle Society?" asked Danny.

"Castle Society?" The judge laughed a little, almost like a cough. "Haven't heard that name in a long time. Sure, I've heard of it, but it's defunct now. Why?"

"We can't say, sir," said Danny. "Is the name still used at all?"

"Not unless you're eighty years old," said Eastergoode. "It's ancient history."

"Did Ms. Reese ever mention the group?" asked Erik.

"No, never," said Eastergoode. "She was much too young to even know about it. The only reason I know is that my grandparents were involved in it."

Danny was confused. Eastergoode was a dark-skinned man and that was counter to what he'd heard about this Castle Society. Then Danny noticed an old picture on the judge's shelf. It was a couple who were as fair-skinned as his own parents. Danny went over to it and picked it up.

"Are these your grandparents?" asked Danny.

"Yes," said Eastergoode.

Danny stared at the picture of the two people. They were as light as you could get without actually being white. Eastergoode's grandmother actually had freckles.

"Look, I don't want this situation to hurt my career," said Eastergoode.

"To say nothing of your wife," Janis added with venom in her voice.

"There's no need to ruin a man because of a little indiscretion, is there?"

"Olittah Reese was kidnapped, beaten, shot, and dumped in the river," said Danny, looking directly at the judge. "Her husband is at home half crazy and half drunk with grief. And her killer is still at large. So, you gotta forgive us if your career ain't the first thing on our minds right now."

"I haven't made any confession about the DNA sample and it can't be matched without a court order and a test," said Eastergoode. "So as far as I'm concerned, you don't have any evidence connecting me to the murder."

"Is that your official position?" asked Erik.

"Yes," said Eastergoode. "You can let yourselves out."

Danny and his partners didn't say anything. They just exited the office and made their way through the courthouse. When they got to the lobby, Janis took a deep breath as if she'd been unable to breathe in Eastergoode's presence.

"He's right, you know," said Janis. "We can't connect him unless we have a case. We can press, but I'm betting he's the kind of guy who has friends in high places."

"Fucking around on your wife ain't a crime," said Danny.

"Tell that to my wife," said Erik.

"He didn't kill Olittah Reese," said Danny, "and so I bet he didn't do the Bakers either. That's all I really care about."

"We don't know that," said Janis. "This is exactly the kind of man who might fit the profile of a serial murderer. He's intelligent, connected, and knows that forensics and science have to be thwarted in an investigation."

"She's got a point," said Erik. "A judge would know how to fuck up a crime scene and raise reasonable doubt."

"I won't argue with that," said Danny, "but when we got his name from the Longs, he had an alibi."

"Maybe we need to check it again," said Janis.

"Let's do it," said Danny. "But I think we'd be wasting our time."

Danny walked out of the building ahead of his partners, aware that they were watching him. He was filled with thoughts of the victims and their color, and how it kept coming up in the investigation. There was a malignancy in the history of black people in Detroit, and somehow it had turned fatal.

22

CONFESSION

Danny knew there would be trouble even before he went inside his house. There were three strange cars parked in front at the curb. One he recognized as Clarence's, Vinny's study partner. The others he did not know.

Danny walked inside his home and found Vinny and three other people in the living room. There was Clarence, of course, and a woman, a black girl about Vinny's age, who had long braids that stopped at her shoulders. The last person was a black man who looked younger than the rest. He wore glasses and sported an African hat made of Kinte cloth.

But what held Danny's attention was not these people or the table filled with empty bottles of beer. It wasn't even Vinny herself, who was sitting between the two men dressed in a skirt so short that he wondered how she kept anything hidden. Danny was struck by the mood of them all—the nature of the evening. There were no books on the table. It looked like a date, a date in his house.

"Wha'sup?" said Danny as he entered.

Clarence immediately turned his frame away from Vinny. He was so transparent that Danny found him harmless. The girl with the braids said hello as Vinny got up to greet him. The man in the hat said nothing. He just looked at Danny with a distinct anger in his eyes.

"We just stopped here after school for a minute and a party kinda started," said Vinny. "Oh, this is LaRisa and Roger." She pointed to the two people on the sofa. "You know Clarence."

"Hey, man," said Clarence.

Danny was getting a disturbing picture. Two pretty black women and two black men all from law school, just hanging out and who knew what could happen. But he knew Vinny wasn't dumb or evil enough to do anything right here in their house. No, she was still in denial about what was happening between them.

"Do you talk, brother?" Danny asked Roger, who still hadn't said anything.

"Yeah," said Roger, and there was a nastiness in his voice. "We gotta get going, Vinny."

The others agreed and hustled to the door over Vinny's protests. When they were gone, she turned back to Danny.

"What is it with you?" she asked.

"All I did was come home," said Danny. "You threw the party."

"What you did was come in here and glare at my friends until they became uncomfortable."

"That Roger brother, I suppose I made him sit there and give me the evil eye."

"Well, I know he was acting funny. He's got issues with white people," said Vinny.

"Then he should stay the fuck out of their houses."

Danny took off his coat and went into the bedroom. He wasn't surprised when Vinny came in the room behind him.

"I live here, too, you know," she began. "I should be able to have some friends over if I want."

"What if I brought over some white racist cop who sat on your sofa and looked at you like you stole something from him? Would you like that?"

"You don't have any white friends," said Vinny. "And you know, maybe that's the problem."

Danny was silent a moment. He didn't want to walk through the door that had just been opened, but he had to. He thought of Gordon and his incessant prodding over this very issue.

"What does that mean?" he asked.

"It don't—doesn't mean anything," she corrected herself. "I'm sorry."

And now he wanted to push her, make her tell him why she'd said that, why she'd said the same thing to him that Gordon had said. But that didn't bother him nearly as much as the way she corrected her English just now. The fact that she cared about speaking properly when it was just the two of them terrified him.

"You tryin' to say that I need to stick with my own kind or somethin'?" asked Danny.

"Can we just drop it?" said Vinny

"No. I want to know why you said that."

"Look," said Vinny. "I just wanted to hang out with my friends, with people who can help me with my career. If I'm going to make it, I have to associate with different people than I'm used to. Maybe you should, too."

"That's Renitta talking," said Danny. Vinny was beginning to think of herself as outgrowing him, of their way of speaking as somehow wrong.

"Are you trying to say I don't have a mind of my own?" Vinny jutted out one of her hips toward him, a gesture that was meant as aggressive, but which came off as sexy, making it worse than intended.

Danny was looking at this woman he loved and thinking about the killer, a man who was disposing of human beings because of their color. Was that any different from what was happening to him right now? His color and Vinny's had been part of the attraction, but also part of the problem. Vinny's suggestion that his color was something of a hindrance was awful, sickening and it hurt just as bad as anything he'd ever experienced growing up. But he was not going to allow that to stop him from making an attempt to make things right.

"Who's it gonna be, Vinny, me or them?" asked Danny.

"You talking about my family?"

"I'm talking about all of it. Family, school, career. Where do I fit in?"

"I don't see a choice to be made," said Vinny.

"I chose you over my family," Danny said. "Do you think anyone likes the idea of me and you together? I didn't have to even think about it. I chose you and to hell with all of them. I figured I don't sleep with them and share with them the way I do with you, so I couldn't give a shit how they feel. I owe my favor to you because I know you've given up just as much for me, or have you?"

"Don't make me do this now," she said.

"We don't get to choose where shit finds us, Vinny. I'm not going to leave here until I know how you feel."

She looked Danny straight in the eyes. Vinny was not one to falter under pressure. She'd taken all the shit the streets had to offer. She was not going to be afraid of a situation like this.

"I don't know," she said finally, and Danny felt the room shift under his feet for a moment. "Maybe we both should think about it. Take a break from each other."

"A break?" said Danny. "What the hell does that mean?"

"It means I stay with Ivory for a while. Since your mother passed you've been hard to live with. God knows I feel bad for you, but life eventually goes on, for all of us. I don't need the space. You do." She was still looking Danny in the eyes, unwavering, but it was only making him want her more.

There were a lot of things he wanted to say, ranging from anger to some smart-ass response. In the end, silence was the only thing that seemed appropriate. It stated his hurt, anger, and shock all at once, and it allowed Vinny to make a graceful exit from the room.

Danny stood for a second, not moving. Then he sat down and took off his shoes. And silently, he thought that maybe Gordon was right. Maybe he did hate what he was just a little bit.

Danny returned to the SCU the next day to find an urgent message from Fiona on his desk. It read simply: MUST SEE YOU—JUST YOU! He started to tell Erik, but thought better of it. Fiona was not the secretive type, so if she wanted just him to come, she probably had a good reason.

Danny slipped away and was soon back in Fiona's office. She was at her desk drinking from a small plastic cup.

"Hey," said Danny, bounding into the room. "We got something new on the killer, I hope."

"There's whiskey in this cup," said Fiona calmly.

"Okay," said Danny. "Why are you drinking at the job in the daytime?"

"You might wanna have one," she said.

"I'll pass," said Danny. "Are you okay, Fiona. You're making me nervous about being here."

"You remember that kid Jacob, the pain in the ass? I made him read over some old autopsy files. It was really just a way to get him out of my hair. Jacob is an asshole, but he's smart, real smart. So, earlier today, he came to me all excited. And he has a file in his hand—your mother's file . . ."

Danny was rocked by this simple statement. This was a woman who worked with dead people who were killed violently each day and she was unnerved. His mind immediately filled with images of his worst suspicions. And before she said her next words, he knew what they would be.

"—something wasn't right about the way she died. I shouldn't have been so damned nosy, so fucking professional," said Fiona.

"The fall didn't kill her, did it?" asked Danny grimly. He was looking off at the far wall, seeing the faces of his parents. His mother tumbling down the stairs and his father shoving her.

"No," said Fiona. "She was probably already dead before she took that fall."

"What was it, then?"

"She took an overdose of medicine. The report showed that there was organ damage conducive to a drug overdose, but the doctor who did the case conveniently buried it in the file."

"Who was the doctor?"

"Tim Lester. Old-timer. Retired and conveniently moved out of town."

"Dr. Lester was friend of my father from the old days," said Danny. "They did a lot of cases together." Danny's face took on an even more alarmed look as the evidence mounted.

"I'm sorry," said Fiona. "I know you got a lot of shit going on right now, but I found out yesterday and I beat myself up all night. Me, I wouldn't want to know, but I know you."

"You're right," said Danny. "I'm too stupid to leave it alone. Thanks."

Danny hugged Fiona more out of grief than gratitude. She held on to him, patted his back like a mother, and whispered that she was sorry again.

Danny moved to the door of the lab and his feet felt as if they weighed a ton, as if the earth was holding on to them, not wanting him to go.

Danny walked out of the lab and into the hallway. He'd been in the space a hundred times but now it seemed like a different dimension. His worst fears had been realized. He saw the image of his mother again, falling, and he was filled with frightening questions about how it had happened.

Danny started to run, the surge of motion mirroring the churning emotions in his heart. In his tortured mind, he was already seeing himself in a confrontation, trying to find out why his father covered up his mother's suicide.

23

WEIGHT

Danny sat for an hour in a stairwell before he paged Dr. Gordon and asked for an emergency session. Gordon told Danny he'd be at his office as soon as he could. Danny beat Gordon there by twenty minutes and Gordon arrived to find Danny sitting on the floor outside the locked suite.

They went inside and Danny quickly unloaded on his doctor. He told him about the breakup with Vinny, which seemed like good news compared to what he'd learned from Fiona. Gordon just listened with the same passionless expression he always had.

"Do you feel your father had something to do with her death?" asked Gordon.

"He lied," said Danny. "He covered up the death with a friend of his, a doctor. He consciously got another man to commit a felony."

"That's not an answer," said Gordon calmly.

"My answer is no," said Danny, "but that don't change the fact that something is wrong. I'm going to find out why she died. He's going to tell me, or I'll—"

"What?" asked Gordon.

Danny calmed himself and let his grief subside. He loved his father and he would never do him any harm. Besides, Danny thought, Robert Cavanaugh could probably still take him.

"I just need to know the truth," said Danny. "All of it. My father was in that house punishing himself each day and there has to be a reason for it. A man doesn't do that kind of thing unless he's got sin in his heart. I know, believe me, I know."

"You think interrogating your father will make you feel better?" Gordon asked. Danny got the feeling that this question was more for Gordon than it was for himself.

"My mother is gone. I'm never going to see her again." Danny took a long pause, fighting all the things he was feeling. "I have to know why."

Danny shifted in the chair and felt like a child in the principal's office. Gordon knew every embarrassing thing in his life, and now he knew his mother might have been killed and his father involved in some kind of cover-up. Danny knew there was a doctor-patient privilege, but he always wondered if it was kept.

"My life is falling apart," said Danny. "My father . . . Vinny . . . and I'm no closer to catching the killer of the Bakers and Olittah Reese than I was yesterday. I got nothing. Asking my father what really happened is all I have right now."

Gordon put down his pad and looked directly at Danny, something that suggested he was no longer his doctor at this moment.

"Do you think that your problem with Vinny is the same as your concerns about your father?"

"How?" asked Danny urgently and with a little anger in his voice. "How are those two things the same?"

"You have to find that out," said Gordon. "All I know is you seem to be drawing from the same pool of emotions for both problems. You've reacted to the loss of your mother and Vinny in the same manner."

Danny didn't argue with Gordon. He was a smart man and had helped him immensely since he'd started coming to him. Gordon was trying to be objective, to lead him to what he thought the problem was.

"I can see that, I think," said Danny. "They are so much alike, those two. I was the only one who could see it."

"If that's the case, then how does that make you feel about talking to your father?"

"Like it's maybe the place to begin to solve all of my problems," said Danny.

"Normally, I would never ask a patient to explore these matters without supervision, but I confess that this is new to me, and you—" Gordon stopped as if he were trying to choose his words carefully. "—you're a unique man."

Danny talked for a few more minutes then left Gordon's office. He stepped out of the office complex into the coolness of the night air. He had been with the doctor for a long time and night had fallen. Danny was thinking that he'd faced many dangerous situations in his life, but nothing seemed as frightening as the prospect of knowing what had driven his mother to her death.

24

EXODUS

Reverend Bolt was worried. The detectives who had come calling asked embarrassing and dangerous questions, poking their noses around in his financial business. In addition, the losses he'd sustained from New Nubia were threatening to crumble his empire and maybe get the authorities looking at those same finances. He could not let that happen. He'd worked too hard for too long to let it all slip away now. So many years of struggle had been put behind him, he thought. He could not afford to be stupid or weak now. His people needed him more than ever and he would not let them down.

He examined the gun carefully as he loaded a clip and placed it into a holster under his suit coat. He was never a man to take chances. He'd taken many precautions since his days in the South. He went to his bar and poured himself a scotch.

That was a long time ago, a lifetime. He thought sadly about the man he used to be, the evil, pathetic human being who had destroyed lives and taken from others. But God did indeed move in mysterious ways. He had led Bolt to prison, where he'd found The Word and the way. He was transformed and when he was released he set out to give back some of the joy that he'd stolen from the world.

Bolt had discarded his old name and identity. He'd left Herman

Bady in a Texas prison cell and tried never to think of him again. He'd transformed himself into a self-ordained minister and covered up his tracks, going through three states, assuming a new identity in each, slowly changing his look while changing his life. The last name he took was that of his religious mentor, Cleophus Boltman. Cleophus, then deceased, was a former basketball star, hardened lifer, and prison minister. Rashus, his new first name, was taken from a religious book he'd read while in prison.

Bolt ended up in Detroit, where he briefly worked at a halfway house while he preached on the streets on the weekends. Eventually he got a storefront church and started a full-time ministry.

Soon his church began to grow, and with the growth came controversy. Holyland was cited by many as too extreme in its practices. Men and women sat on opposite sides of the church, and women who wore dresses above the knees were told to go home. They also held fasting vigils and all-night prayer meetings and encouraged followers to donate part of their salary to the church, no matter how little they made.

More controversial was Reverend Bolt's outreach program to the state's prison. Prisoners were recruited while still incarcerated, and once they came out, the church took them in, making them family. The reverend saw this as essential to the making of his ministry, and he was known to keep these men close to him.

Despite controversy, the congregation was loyal. Reverend Bolt's fiery sermons and layman's approach to The Word mesmerized the hopeless and gave them hope. Bolt was now deemed a living work of God's power. He was where he had always wanted to be in God's light. So, he could not let the Bakers and their evil scheme end his ascension. He was going to build his religious empire and nothing would stop him.

He was going to see a man who admittedly worked on the other side of the law. He hated to do it, but these were desperate times. The players in the hood were really no worse than a banker, he told himself, and he'd exhausted all his legitimate resources. He walked the edge of law with his prison ministry, but now he was crossing back over. He had made a solemn promise long ago never to reenter the world of crime. He'd done terrible things in the past and the memories of that sinful life clung to him no matter what he did. Even giving his life to the church had not cleansed him. So what he had in mind today hung heavy in his heart.

Bolt finished his drink. He said a prayer, then exited his office. He walked through the sanctuary, taking his time to gaze at the pictures of Jesus and the apostles on the stained-glass windows. When he got to the back of the room, he was joined by two of his deacons. They flanked him as he walked out of the church into the night. A white Cadillac DeVille was parked at the curb. Bolt got in and the car sped off, headed toward Woodward Avenue.

Across the street, the Bady brothers watched their father come out of the church surrounded by men. Muhammad had carefully read the file he'd stolen. It wasn't hard to find him after they burned the office at Oasis.

Muhammad could barely contain himself. He wanted to press a button and blow the Cadillac off the face of the earth. But that would be too easy, he thought. Too good for the man who had spawned death and sadness in their lives. No, their father's death would have to be as glorious as the pain he'd inflicted.

"Don't lose him," Muhammad said to Rimba as Bolt's car pulled away.

The brothers started off after Bolt, following him down Woodward to the boulevard. Suddenly, the Cadillac pulled over and stopped by Clairmount Avenue. The Bady brothers stopped behind Bolt, parking a block away.

Bolt's car sat for ten minutes, unmoving. Muhammad became nervous. What was their father up to? Had he seen them?

"Get ready to take him," said Muhammad. He reached under his seat and took out his weapon. Rimba pulled out a knife, and Akema took out a 9 mm and checked the magazine. "Hold up," said Muhammad.

Two other vehicles had pulled up next to Bolt's car. One was another Cadillac, an Escalade. The other was a green Jeep. The Escalade pulled in front of Bolt's car, the Jeep settled in behind it.

Muhammad remembered a white Escalade was present the day the would-be killers came to their old home. He focused on the new vehicle, waiting for the occupants to emerge.

Desandias Locke pulled himself out of the passenger side of the SUV and into the backseat of Bolt's car. He moved quickly and had a distinct air of fear about him.

"Shit, somebody loves me," said Muhammad. He laughed a little, which surprised his brothers.

"Who's that?" asked Akema with interest.

"Just another dead man," said Muhammad. "Just another dead man."

25

COLORISM

Danny knocked on the door of Marshall's house in Palmer Woods and waited. He was always a little jealous when he came there. A friend always likes to think of his peers as equals. But Marshall had done so much better than he had in the money department. The house was massive and well kept. The kind of place Danny could only dream about. The door opened, revealing Chemin, Marshall's wife.

"Danny," she said brightly, flinging open the screen door. "Come on in." She pulled him inside. "How are you? Come and see the kids." She smiled a smile that he could only describe as happiness itself. Danny realized that Marshall had done better than he had in the life department, too.

Danny stepped inside thinking how different Chemin was these days. About a year ago, he would not have recognized this pleasant woman. Chemin and Marshall were having a terrible problem that resolved itself and ended in the birth of a baby boy. She was now the person Danny remembered when they'd first met, a feisty, distractingly beautiful woman, who was funny, sensitive, and strong.

"So, how's Vinny?" she asked. Then finally she noticed his expression. "Are you okay?"

"Not really," said Danny.

"Is it that case?" she asked. "The murders?"

"Yeah, and other stuff."

She looked at Danny and he felt that she knew everything. Chemin had always been a formidable woman and one of the smartest people he knew, maybe smarter than the man he had come to see.

"Marshall's in the back," she said. "I'm sure he'll want to see you. We have company, but they're about to leave."

"Who is it?" Danny asked. He didn't want to socialize unnecessarily.

"Just Marshall's mama and her friend."

They walked through the house to the den, where they found Marshall on the floor play fighting with a little boy of three. His mother, Beatrice, was sitting on the sofa next to a black man in his sixties.

Beatrice held Marshall's son while Marshall played with his nephew, Kadhi, who was his brother Moses' illegitimate son. Moses was bad news, a hard-core killer and career criminal who was Marshall's fraternal twin. He was the black sheep, or maybe that should be white sheep, of their family, Danny thought.

"Look who's here," said Chemin.

"Danny," said Marshall. He started to get up, but couldn't with the kid in his arms. Chemin came over, took the child, and Marshall got to his feet.

Danny quickly walked over and kissed Beatrice as he said hello. He knew that if he waited too long to show her respect, she'd get on him, and he'd never hear the end of it.

"Hello, Danny," said Beatrice. She was a big woman with a good nature who always had a kind word for everyone. When he was young, he saw her as much as he did his own mother. Her husband, Buford, had died many years ago and although there had been suitors in the past, this was the first one Danny had seen in a long time.

"Hi, Ma," said Danny. She insisted that he call her "Ma" like a second mother since his own had died.

"This is Deacon Walton from my church," said Beatrice.

Danny shook hands with the deacon. "Hiya doin', Rev," said Danny.

"They're dating," said Marshall.

"Stop it," said Chemin. She put Kadhi down and took her own son from Beatrice.

"We gotta go now, Bea," said the deacon. He got up, stuck out his hand, and helped Beatrice up from the sofa. It was a simple, elegant gesture that spoke volumes about what they meant to each other.

Beatrice and the deacon said good-bye and walked out of the house. Marshall escorted them to the door. Danny checked his friend's face. He was happy for his mom to be seeing a man, but just a little resentful in that way that a son has to be.

"I guess you two want to talk," said Chemin. "I'll get these kids out of your way."

"See you later, man," Danny said to Kadhi, and they slapped five in the sloppy way a kid does.

"Daniel, say 'bye to Uncle Danny," said Chemin. She held the little baby out to Danny and he took the boy with a smile.

"That's Godfather Danny," Danny corrected. "Like Marlon Brando."

"Come on, honey," Chemin said to the baby. "Let's let the big men do their thing."

Danny gave her the baby as Marshall came back. Chemin gave her husband a concerned look, then she bounced out of the room with the two boys.

"Still can't believe you named him after me," Danny said to Marshall.

"She wanted to name him Lynn after her grandfather, remember that shit? A girl's name. Anyway, it's nice having both the kids here. Kadhi's mama is in school now, and he's here most of the time. All of a sudden, I got a full house."

"Chemin's still working from home?" asked Danny.

"Yeah, and she loves it. Personally, I don't think she's ever going back."

"I hardly recognize her. What a difference a baby makes, huh?"

"So, what can I do for you, man?" asked Marshall. "That look on your face is pretty serious."

Danny stared at his friend, wanting terribly to unburden himself about his father. Marshall was the only person in the world whom he really trusted, and he wanted to share his secret with someone. Hell, he thought, he wanted sympathy if nothing else.

"My mother didn't die in a fall," said Danny calmly. "I found out that she might have taken an overdose of drugs. And my father . . . he tried to cover it up."

Marshall reacted as if hit in the face by a blow. He looked at the ceiling for a second as if something were written on it.

"Jesus," said Marshall. "Are you sure?"

Danny just nodded and Marshall made another exasperated sound. Then he thought for a moment more.

"Talk to him," said Marshall finally. "Your father is a good man. My father thought so and so do I. I know he'll have an explanation. And keep an open mind." He gave Danny a knowing look. "Remember what you thought about Chemin."

Danny nodded, recalling that he'd suspected Marshall's wife of a similar crime over a year ago and he'd been wrong.

"I will," said Danny. "I just—this is a fuckin' nightmare."

They sat in silence for a while and Danny thought about leaving. He felt like an intruder in this happy home. But he knew that if he tried to go now, Marshall would not have any of it. They were too close for him to go running off trying to be the strong silent cop. Their friendship was based on turning away from that terrible habit of men avoiding their feelings.

"Vinny moved out," said Danny flatly. "It's been coming for a while I guess."

"Man," said Marshall. "What the fuck is happening to you, man?"

"I've been asking myself that same question," said Danny. "It's like a snowball. Vinny and me, we fell out over nothing, some friends of hers came by."

"It's never about nothing," said Marshall. "That's just the thing that broke it. So, what are you gonna do?"

"Nothing," said Danny. "I'll just let it go for a while. Do some work."

"Maybe I can talk to her," said Marshall almost to himself.

"No," said Danny. "She'll think I put you up to it and it'll only make things worse. Vinny said that maybe I needed some white friends, like I was closed off from reality or something."

"Shit," said Marshall. "I thought you two were over that whole thing."

"I think school and hangin' out with the black elite is doing it. And her sisters, of course."

"I don't know what to say, man." Marshall rubbed his hands together in frustration. "I know what it's like to have this problem. It's a hell of a lot bigger than me."

"Well," said Danny, "don't kill yourself about it. Maybe you can help me with my other problem—my case, the murders of the Bakers and Olittah Reese. All of the victims were light-skinned blacks, and I have this nasty feeling that it means something."

Marshall was quiet as he looked back at him. Danny searched for that hurt look he'd seen with Erik and Janis, but it wasn't there. All he saw in his eyes was concern.

"Maybe it's a coincidence," said Marshall.

"Maybe, but I think it means something, and so does the FBI agent who's on it."

"FBI?"

"She's a profiler from Quantico. She thinks it's a serial killer, a black one. It seems only white people usually do this kind of thing."

"Yeah, sick-ass white boys," said Marshall, laughing. "So, if it's important, what does it mean?"

"What I don't know is why it's relevant," said Danny. "I don't know a lot about skin color differences between the brothers."

"Colorism," said Marshall.

"There's a word for it?" Danny was surprised by this.

"Yeah, a writer made it up. Danny, you've stepped into some deep shit, deep *black* shit."

"I know. I caught the reactions of my partner and the FBI agent, who's black, too, by the way. They seem to be bothered by the subject in general and hurt by memories."

"Everybody's got a story," said Marshall. "I'll tell you what I know about it, but you've been seeing it all your life. I guess it never hit you the same way because you were white."

"So I've been told," said Danny. "What's your story?"

"Remember Ms. Rattin from Davison Elementary?" said Marshall without hesitation.

"Yeah, I remember. Third grade. Pretty lady."

"I had a big ol' crush on her. She was my favorite teacher with that long hair and those beautiful hazel eyes. Then one day, I overheard her talking to another teacher about her class. She said that some kids in her class were 'as dumb as they were black.' And she said it in that mean, nasty way that let me know she had a dislike for dark skin, my kind of skin."

"Ms. Rattin was very light-skinned," Danny said absently.

"Then about a year later I heard some teachers talking about her; they plotted to keep her from getting some kind of award. They made reference to her thinking she was too good already." And now Marshall's face took on that pained look Danny had seen before. "There are two revelations for black people," he continued. "The first comes when you find out what it means to be black, and the second is when you find out what it means to be dark or light."

"Light?" Danny asked.

"Yes, it goes both ways," said Marshall. "A lot of light-skinned blacks get shit for not being dark enough. Remember Tommy, the kid whose father drove that beat-up old convertible?"

"Tommy Sanders," Danny said, remembering the name. "He had freckles."

"But he was black," said Marshall. "The kids called him snow-ball, spotty, yellow-nigger, sweet pink, and all kinds of nasty stuff. I'm sad to say that I called him a few names myself. And that hurt look you talked about, the one your partner had on his face. I've seen that look on your face so many times, I'd like to forget them all."

"Really?" said Danny, and in that instant he knew Marshall was probably right. He'd endured the worst kind of colorism. "Yeah, I guess so."

"This all started with slavery, you know," said Marshall. "When we were brought here, voluntarily or not, the races mixed, voluntarily or not. The slave masters treated their bastard kids better than their darker cousins, and the shit has just been carried on down through the years."

Danny thought again about the victims and their faces. "And just what is the problem?" he asked.

"The lighter the skin, the better the person," said Marshall. "That's the stereotype. Reality is more complicated. And you know, a lot of the first really good jobs, doctor, teacher, lawyer, went to fair-skinned blacks who were more accepted by white society. Darker blacks had to take the backseat twice if you will, once to the white man and again to the light black man. Blacks of all colors married, but there was always a section of the race that intermarried and re-mained very light-skinned. Some even passed for white. My father told me about the parties with the paper bag by the door, and if you were darker than the bag, your ass couldn't come in."

"So, if my killer is all fucked up about color, what could have made him that way?" asked Danny.

"Could be a lot of things," said Marshall. "These days, we're all pretty much in denial about the shit. We're so busy trying to make it, that we've just let it slip under the surface of everyday life, and that's not a good place for something so painful."

"My gut tells me that the color of the victims is not a coinci-dence," said Danny. He took another drink of his beer. It was ever so slightly warmer from being in his hand for so long. "I think maybe the people involved were together for this reason."

"Then you got yourself a real problem, my brother," said Marshall.

Danny waited a moment, thinking, then asked, "Have you heard of the Castle Society?"

"Sure," said Marshall. "My grandmother used to work at their parties as a servant. Why do you ask?"

"I'm not sure yet," said Danny. "But it's involved in my case somehow."

Chemin came back in at that moment. She forced a smile, knowing that they'd been talking about something serious.

"Got them both to sleep," she said. "That's like a mommy holiday. So, everything okay?"

"Yeah, more or less," said Marshall. "Danny's come for some information about color. Chemin, tell Danny about your sister, Avon," said Marshall.

Chemin's face took on the by now familiar look of upset and hurt. "Marsh, why does he need to know that?"

"He wants to know about the color differences between black people," said Marshall. "It's for his case."

"You can tell him," said Chemin.

"It's different for women," said Marshall. "Help the man."

"You don't have to talk about it if you don't want to," said Danny. But he was interested in what Chemin had to say. He also saw that she wanted to speak on the subject.

The reference to her sister had taken hold of him. He'd met her sister, Avon before. Chemin was dark. But Avon was completely the opposite. He remembered thinking that maybe they were not even related or had different fathers, which they didn't. Chemin's mother was very light and her father was dark. The girls had been split between them almost right down the middle.

Chemin folded her arms and gave Marshall a look that suggested she'd get him later. "No, I'll talk about it," she said. "Avon and I got along fine when we were young," she said, turning to Danny. "In fact, we were best friends in that way that only sisters can be. Then, when I turned twelve we both got interested in boys. In a nutshell, she got more attention than I did. In our culture, the lighter the woman, the more she's favored by black men."

Marshall cleared his throat.

"With some exceptions," said Chemin, smiling at her husband. "And for a woman, that ability to attract men is everything. We're told all our lives that our beauty is our value as women, and then we learn that some of us are more valuable than others. It doesn't matter if you don't believe it. The world is what it is and nothing is going to change that. All the light-skinned girls got the best boyfriends in school, were favored by certain sororities, got married first—and look."

Chemin grabbed a magazine from a table and flipped through. She stopped at each ad featuring a black model, and in almost every case that model was light-skinned.

"The media lets you know what time it is every day," she said. "See how most of them are either really fair or that weird-ass golden color?" She laughed.

"Or maybe you just think about shit too much," Marshall laughed.

"No, I don't," said Chemin. "I know what I'm talking about."

"This is too fuckin' much," said Danny. "Dark brothers get dogged, light brothers get dogged, for what? This thing is crazy."

"Most of us try to be bigger than color, Danny," said Chemin. Her face showed her sincerity. "We try, but a lot of times we fail. So the thing isn't crazy. It's human."

"Finish the sister story," said Marshall. "I never get tired of hearing this."

"That's because you're sick," said Chemin, giving him a love tap on the head. "Anyway, Avon and I started dating boys, and soon she began to think she was better than me. Or at least that's what I thought. We never talked about it, but it was there, under our relationship, festering like a sickness. And then one day, we had a fight over, of all things, a sweater. She wanted to wear my red sweater because 'it looked better on her,' she said, and it wasn't right for me. I knew what she meant. I'd heard that old saying about how dark girls shouldn't wear red. I told her she couldn't wear it, and she wore it on a date anyway, so I ripped one of hers to pieces. We had a terrible fight, hair-pulling, the whole bit. I called her a thief and she called me a black bitch. Not just a bitch, a *black* one, as if the word black made it worse. We didn't speak for almost a year after that. We made up, but our relationship has never been the same." She looked far away for a second, reclaiming the last of the memory. "What kind of case are you working that you need to know this?"

"A murder case," I said. "All of my victims are light-skinned blacks."

"Damn," said Chemin. "I'm sorry." She made this last statement after searching for something appropriate to say. "Does it mean anything?"

"I'm afraid it might mean everything," said Danny. "This killer is sick in the head, and maybe he's seeing shit that the rest of us can't."

"Killers usually do, don't they?" said Marshall.

Chemin let out a little puff of air that echoed the exasperation Danny was feeling. Marshall said nothing. He just looked at Danny with the self-assured face of a friend.

"Whatever this whole thing is about," said Marshall, "you can handle it."

Danny nodded slightly, not knowing whether Marshall was talking about the case or the situation with his mother. He supposed that his friend meant both matters. In that regard he was grateful for his confidence.

Danny thanked Marshall and Chemin, then left them to their evening. He had brought a load of grief and heavy thinking on them, and he didn't want them to suffer any more.

Danny stepped outside into the cool night and immediately his thoughts went back to his father and the terrible burden he was carrying. He vowed at that moment that he had to face up to it and soon.

He got into his car and pulled off. He was vaguely aware of the car bumping over the road. He was processing all that he'd had just heard from his friends.

"... *it was my own people, not being my own people, and I felt like nothing.*"

He heard Erik's statement again. Danny saw millions of black people fighting against themselves and keeping it secret, like a shameful addiction.

Danny wondered if the deaths of the Bakers and Olittah Reese were what they seemed to be, revenge for lost wealth, or were born out of the affliction Marshall called colorism. And if it was, would it make the killer more or less deadly?

26

JOY ROAD

John and Lenora Baker sat with Olittah Reese talking quietly about something. Danny stood behind them straining to hear and worried that they would see him.

The Bakers looked robust and healthy and Ms. Baker wore a bright yellow hat. Olittah looked even better, sexy and vibrant as she laughed at something. Suddenly, Olittah Reese turned and winked at him. But now she was the dead Olittah, pale and water-damaged. Next to her, Danny saw his mother. Sorrow lined her pained visage and she held up her hands in a pleading gesture.

"Why, son?" she asked in sorrowful voice. Then she tumbled down a dark abyss, pulling the others with her. . . .

Danny awoke in bed alone, breathing hard. He got up and went into the kitchen and poured a big glass of water. He wasn't particularly thirsty, but needed to do something physical to remind himself that he was indeed awake.

Vinny had not called or left any message since her departure. He took this to mean that he should not call or leave a message at her sister's. In his head, he saw them all sitting around, talking about him, making those excited sounds women make when they're talking about something juicy. Worse were the pictures of Vinny in the arms and bed of another man, purging herself of guilt and celebrating her new life without him.

He wondered how he could mend his relationship with Vinny before it was too late. It's a fucked-up thing to be a man, he thought, to realize that most of what you're about is trying to figure out women—and you never will.

He decided to take his own advice and concentrate on the case. His evening with Marshall and Chemin had shaken him in ways that he could not fully explain. He'd always thought of black people as one people. Now, Danny was seeing them as gradations on a living line of color. Erik was very dark in complexion like Hamilton Grace and his sons; Marshall and Chemin were about the same dark color. Janis was a light brown, like Kelly, Hamilton's wife. Jim Cole, his boss, was fair-skinned, and the victims were all even lighter than that.

And then, me, thought Danny. Next on the line was white itself.

He got a pad and wrote down what he knew about the case so far. It always helped to see the shape of what he was up against:

The first thing he noticed was that he had a lot more suspects than victims. The killer wasn't a rabid dog, tearing his way through a list. He was cold, calculating, and sure of himself.

SUSPECTS	VICTIMS
Hamilton Grace (Lost millions. Disliked Bakers. Olittah Reese might have cost him in the election.)	The Bakers (Scammed their friends. Stole millions. John had hooker friend.)
Jordan Grace (Adopted. Overly protective of father.)	Olittah Reese (Solicited people for bogus company. Affair with judge.)
Logan Grace (Rebellious. Hates father?)	
Reverend Boltman (Shady past. Violent assistants capable of killing.)	
Virginia Stallworth (Lost money and social face.)	
Oscar Stallworth (Connection to underworld.)	

Danny thought that he could find the next victim by seeing who else had been involved with the company, but as far as he knew, only the Bakers and Olittah Reese had done the solicitations.

Then he wrote:

Money

Danny thought about the missing money that went through New Nubia. Everyone assumed the Bakers had stolen it, but in fact all of the money was never found.

Maybe the killer was looking for it. And maybe he was willing to kill anyone who he thought might have it.

That would explain the meticulous nature of the killer and why he might be asking his victims questions. Then he wrote:

Color

The skin tones of the suspects ran the gamut, from the darkness of Grace to the almost Caucasian hue of the Stallworths. But the victims were still all light-skinned. He wrote:

Baker thought Castle still existed.

Then Danny wrote:

What if it did?

"Stallworth," said Danny to himself. Oscar and Virginia were such snobs and she had that picture of her family with the Castle Society prominently displayed in her home. So there was a history. And Virginia had made it a point to tell him that it didn't exist anymore. He might have suspected Hamilton Grace, but he was too dark.

"Too dark," said Danny out loud as if he needed to hear it. And then he went back to bed.

Danny did not get any sleep before the morning came. He drifted off now and then, but the fear of another nightmare about his mother would pump adrenaline into his blood and he'd wake right up. Finally, he hustled out of bed and went into work early.

Thirteen hundred always seemed spooky early in the day, and this was no exception. Behind the clean interior was a long history of crime, death and struggle. In the academy, Danny had heard stories of the place being haunted, and he believed every one of them. Danny didn't think the troubled souls on both sides of the badge would ever rest peacefully.

He entered the office and was surprised to find Janis already there alone, looking at some papers. He said hello, then sat down at his desk and started to read the case file again.

The two sat in silence for a while, not looking at each other. In the distance, Danny heard sounds of other people in the building.

"You don't like me, do you?" asked Janis.

Danny looked up at Janis and was surprised to see her smiling a little.

"I'm not sure," said Danny. "But you seem like a good cop."

"I didn't come to take over your case."

"Doesn't matter. You did. You and your boss, but I'm a big boy. I can still do my job. But when I get this bastard, all the newspapers will care about is that the case got closed after the FBI got into it."

Janis adjusted her glasses. "And that bothers you?"

"No," said Danny. "The people who matter in the Department will know the truth."

"And what if I catch him first?" asked Janis with another little smile.

"Then the newspapers will have it right for once," said Danny.

Danny went back to his list and Janis read from a stack of papers. He wasn't even sure if she respected him at all. Like all feds, she was hard to read. They must teach them that, he thought.

"I have a profile of the killer for you," she said to Danny in a matter-of-fact tone. "I spent all last night putting it together."

"A serial killer profile?" asked Danny. There was a note of challenge in his voice.

"Yes. I still believe I'm on the right track," said Janis rather defiantly. "Do you still have doubts?"

"You're the doctor," said Danny.

"That's not an answer," Janis said, a little annoyed.

"I'm working on my own theory," said Danny. "There are solid, normal reasons for these killings. I think I've already met the killer on my interviews. I just need to narrow it down."

"Well, let me read the profile to you," said Janis. "Perhaps I can change your mind." She cleared her throat. " 'I am a black man, twenty to forty years old. I'm intelligent, possibly possessing a secondary college degree. I have had a tortured childhood, possibly traumatized or abused at an early age. As a young adult, this continual abuse mutated my normal pattern of thinking, and I began to experiment with venting my rage, first on inanimate objects, then on small animals. I found that violence lessened the pain I felt inside, so I kept killing animals and destroying things, changing my life to revolve around this occupation. I learned to appear normal to others, and I am even considered charming among my friends. I may have turned my tortured self into another personality, an avenger who carries out my will against my enemies. I plan each kill meticulously, and I am searching for an answer to the end of my internal pain. I am not insane. I am special.' "

Janis looked at Danny, pleased with herself. She slid the papers over to him, and took a drink of coffee from a cup on her side of the desk.

"And what about the color thing?" asked Danny. "How does that figure into your profile?"

Janis took a moment, and for the first time Danny noticed that they were in the place alone. The lights were kind of low, and she looked good with her hair falling down around her face.

"That may be part of the trauma," said Janis. "If he has a color fixation, it came about in a bad way."

"A friend told me all about colorism last night," said Danny.

"I don't like that word," said Janis. "I'd prefer a more clinical term for it. Prejudice is prejudice to me. So, what did you learn?"

"That everybody has a story," he said, then before she could respond, he asked, "What's yours?"

Janis's face took on that look of remembered pain for a second. Her brows fell and her smile faded a little. Danny didn't know if he was asking to continue his education, or if he just wanted to know more about the lady herself.

"Well," she began. "Your friend is right. As a psychologist, I can tell you that there is no greater sublimation in the black community than the problems with color. It has gone from overt conflict to a kind of foundation of the subconscious. When I used to take patients, I found that many of the problems of black people, particularly women, were at least in part linked to the issue."

"I'm waiting on the story," said Danny. He smiled a little to let her know that she had not deterred him with her interesting and clever digression.

"It's personal," said Janis.

"How about I tell you mine?" said Danny.

"I can't stop you, but I doubt it will change my mind."

"When I was a kid my father put me in a school where there were only three other white kids. I was the only one in my class. To say I caught hell would be an understatement. I . . . what do you call it when you adopt ways that ain't really yours?"

"Assimilated," said Janis.

"Yeah, I did that," said Danny. "And in the process, I guess maybe I lost myself. I was angry, I had a bad temper, and I was always looking to prove myself, even if I didn't have to, because I'd been doing it all my life. I've shot and killed men in the line of duty, but I wonder if I would have chosen another way if I wasn't so messed up inside. In the end, my attitude almost cost me everything, and now I'm in therapy trying to figure all this shit out."

Janis just stared at him for a moment, analyzing. Danny felt that she was assessing the truth of his story as well as its worth in trade for hers.

"In college, I dated this guy, Nelson, a teaching assistant in the psych department," Janis started. "We got along fine until his parents came to visit from Nigeria. When they saw me, I knew something was wrong. They were short with me and refused to make eye contact. Well, a week later, Nelson and I broke up. It seems his father and mother thought I was too light, 'too mixed up,' is what he said. They didn't understand American blacks, didn't know what they were. I argued with him, but his parents held the purse strings on his education. Then a month later, I saw his new girlfriend."

"Darker," said Danny knowingly.

"No," said Janis. "She was white. It seems the problem was that I wasn't *pure*. Nelson's parents could accept a dark black girl, or a white one, but not one who was somewhere in between. So, I thought to hell with him, right? I mean, if he couldn't accept me for what I was, then screw him, only I was the one who felt screwed. Like—"

"Like you were nothing?" said Danny, recalling what Erik had told him.

"Something like that," said Janis.

Danny let some time pass before he spoke again. The silence was almost poetic as he felt himself move closer to Janis. Even though she was kind of prissy and elitist, she was strong, and more interesting than he'd first thought.

"So," she said, breaking the beautiful silence. "Did that help you?"

"Yes," said Danny. "The killer is linked to the Internet scam New Nubia as well as the color of the victims. If we have another victim, he or she will be fair-skinned and in the same groups of investors."

"So where will you start?"

"I'll have Jim get security on everyone on the list. Then I want to see a lady named Virginia Stallworth. I think there's an elite secret society within the black upper class in Detroit, and I think she knows about it."

"So, when can we talk to her?" asked Janis.

"Erik will be checking with the Fraud guys on the Internet company when he comes in. Today, it's just me. I was planning to catch her early."

"Great, let's go."

"I thought you were stuck on the serial killer angle," said Danny. "I guess I've convinced you to give it up, huh?"

"No. I just want to see you in action," she said. "I want to see this deductive mind your partner talked about."

Danny and Janis got a car and drove out as thirteen hundred was filling up. He was hoping to take on Virginia Stallworth alone, but he didn't mind Janis coming as long as she didn't mess up his flow. If Virginia Stallworth would cop to there being a new Castle Society, then maybe he could find the next victim before it was too late.

Danny got on the Lodge Freeway and headed uptown. They passed the tangle of cars going into downtown.

"The freeway, thank God," said Janis. "The city looks so much better from here."

"You're a guest," said Danny. "Be nice."

"I can see why your childhood was so traumatic. Detroit is a hard town."

"Traumatic. Didn't nobody say nothin' about that," said Danny. "The city changes you, but it don't make you sick."

"If you say so," said Janis.

"We probably have some time to kill," said Danny. "In the meantime, let me show you what I mean."

"How?" asked Janis.

"I didn't have breakfast. I need a piece of fruit."

Danny got off the freeway at Grand Boulevard. They drove to Woodward Avenue. Danny watched as Janis looked at the area with amazement and scorn. This was the world her parents warned her about, and here she was in the middle of it.

"The mayor has a lot of work to do on this town," said Janis.

"Black people have run this town for the last thirty years or so. What do you think of that?" asked Danny.

"That's a complicated question," said Janis. "We're just now getting to the root of the problems of large urban areas. And there was a lot of trouble we inherited that was started by other people."

Danny turned left on Clairmount and headed west. The neighborhood was rough. Old gray buildings, potholed streets, and unkempt sidewalks, hopeless-looking old black men and dangerous-looking young ones. He felt invigorated by the sight of all these things. Janis's eyes narrowed and her face took on a look as if she smelled something bad. She could see that there was no joy on Joy Road in Detroit.

Danny stopped at a shabby-looking market on Joy. The parking lot had a few cars in it by the building. Two cars filled with black men sat in a corner away from the store, engines running.

"Why are we stopping here?" asked Janis.

"They have good fruit here," said Danny. "Come on in."

They went inside the market and Danny immediately smelled the strong aroma of fresh onions and produce. There were a few customers already in line. A young black girl holding a handcart of goods talked on a mobile phone. A white woman about thirty scolded her two kids in a voice that sounded decidedly black. Danny looked at her for a moment and saw the contrast. That was how people must react to me, he thought. He had to admit it was weird.

"This place is in a bad neighborhood," said Danny. "In fact, the crime rate here averages twenty percent higher than the rest of the city. But this store gets one of the first runs from the market, so their produce is the best."

Danny and Janis went to the produce section and took in the lush beauty of the fruit and vegetables piled high. The rest of the market looked shabby, but this section was immaculate.

Danny and Janis picked out fruit while behind them at the service counter a heavyset black woman argued with a Chaldean man of about forty. Danny noticed the man passed the woman a few bills then she stomped off, her big necklace swinging and making a jangling noise. The man laughed and put something in a drawer.

"Andy," said Danny to the man, walking over to him.

Andy looked alarmed at seeing Danny then locked up something behind the counter.

"A friend?" asked Janis.

"Not this time," said Danny.

"Danny the cop," said Andy. His Middle Eastern accent was thin, but noticeable. "What do you want?"

"I want to know why you just bought two Social Security checks off that lady who stomped out of here."

"Ain't no law against cashing a check," said Andy.

"Give them to me," said Danny.

Andy mumbled, then handed Danny the colorful checks.

"I think I'll call the owners of these," said Danny, "and see if they're missing their monthly. They're probably getting replacements from the government, but by the time they do, these will be processed, right? What did you pay for them, ten cents on the dollar?"

Andy frowned at Danny and said something in another language, which Danny took to be cursing.

"You have a nice day, too," said Danny. He left Andy some money for the fruit then walked out with Janis.

"Now when we get back out, both of the cars with those brothers in them will be gone."

When they got outside, sure enough, the two cars had vanished.

"Neat trick," said Janis. "So what's the deal?"

"I saw the government check paper flash when the big woman passed it to Andy. But there was a lot more than just that going on in there."

"I'm listening," she said. "Dazzle me with this gift of yours."

"The white girl with the two kids," began Danny. "The kids were black, but they looked nothing alike. Different fathers or she was baby-sitting for a friend with a job. And she was buying enough groceries for ten people. She could have more at home, which is not likely, or she stole food stamps and is buying the food to sell it, also unlikely. It's easier to just sell the food stamps. Or she's buying groceries for people who can't get out of the house and charging them a fee. That's the most likely thing. She was harmless. The young girl on the phone was a drug dealer. She had three pagers on her belt and two cell phones. Her jewelry was expensive and flashy, bling, bling. In her basket she had hot dogs, beans, white bread, and a large Faygo red pop. Her kids are about six or seven, and she don't like to make complicated food for them. When I busted Andy, she hung up one phone and dialed another. That was her calling whoever those men were in one of the cars and telling him some detectives are around. That's why both cars ghosted."

Janis was impressed. She took all this in with a measured and analytical look. "If I didn't know better, I'd say you were making this all up to impress me."

"Let's just say that I wanted you to see that I'm not traumatized like you say. This is just life, the life I'm used to. The ghetto don't discriminate. It's an equal opportunity muthafucka—" Danny stopped as he saw something across the busy street.

"What?" asked Janis.

"I don't know," said Danny. "Come on."

Danny and Janis got into the car and pulled out of the parking lot. He drove down a residential street, trailing a young black man wearing a warm-up jacket and a baseball cap.

"Who is it?" asked Janis.

"Jordan Grace," said Danny. "His father is—"

"Hamilton Grace," said Janis. "I saw his name on the suspect list."

"This kid Jordan is Grace's illegitimate son. He adopted him, but I get the feeling that he's still treated like an outsider kid by Grace."

"What's he doing in this neighborhood?" Janis asked almost to herself.

"That's what we're going to find out." Danny kept following him, trying to keep a good distance back.

Jordan Grace whipped out a cell phone, then got into a new SUV, and roared off down the street. Danny followed him until he got to the freeway, then Danny stopped and turned around.

"We're not going to follow him?" asked Janis.

"No," said Danny. "Whatever he was here for, he finished. He's headed back home."

"So what does it mean, Sherlock?" asked Janis.

"I'm not sure," said Danny. "Not yet." He didn't mind Janis calling him Sherlock because she said it with something akin to admiration.

Danny remembered how Jordan Grace was kind of the stepchild in that family, but eager to please his father. What if he wanted to take out the Bakers and Olittah Reese because of the embarrassment they caused his father? Danny noticed for the first time that Jordan was lighter in skin tone than Hamilton Grace and his legitimate son, Logan.

"I think maybe Jordan Grace has another life his family doesn't know anything about," said Danny. "I just wonder where that life takes him every night."

Danny headed back uptown, wondering what terrible thing could have lured a proper, polished kid like Jordan Grace into the worst part of Detroit.

27

THE CASTLE

Virginia Stallworth's backyard was filled with well-heeled supporters eating eggs and drinking mimosas around a sparkling pool. Water rushed from a marble fountain in a corner of the yard. The water's sound mixed casually with Ella Fitzgerald scatting a jazzy tune from small Bose speakers on the perimeter of the yard.

Danny and Janis entered the crowded party and looked for the Stallworths. Danny was already figuring out what he would say. He'd have only one chance at getting the information he wanted. He hoped it would work. If it didn't, he'd be back to shooting in the dark.

"Man, these people throw a lot of parties," said Danny.

"The NOAA convention is in town," said Janis. "She's courting the out-of-state voters. I recognize Mel Vinson, the civil rights leader from D.C."

Danny didn't spot Virginia in the crowd. He tried not to notice the color of the mostly black partyers, but he was programmed for it now. They covered the spectrum of colors, so he didn't think anything particular of this gathering.

Danny and Janis moved toward the house. In the kitchen, he saw Cal talking with his sister Gwen. Danny noticed again the difference in the color of their skin. Gwen's dark skin stood in stark contrast to

Cal's. He realized that he couldn't stop himself from these observations anymore.

Gwen was talking urgently to her brother, who listened without a word. Gwen held a prescription pill bottle in her hand. She raised it then gestured with it wildly.

Suddenly, Gwen spotted Danny and Janis. She said something to Cal, who turned and looked at them. Gwen ran off. Cal stood a moment then followed.

"Looks like we're being announced," said Janis.

"Yeah," said Danny. "Let's wait here."

A moment later, Virginia Stallworth came out, dressed in a stunning white dress and sun hat. She was pissed off and didn't mind showing it. She scowled at Danny and Janis as she approached them.

"I can see that I'm going to have to call the Chief again about you," she said. "You don't seem to take hints very well."

"And you've been lying to me and impeding my murder investigation," said Danny harshly.

"I'm Special Agent Janis Cates of the FBI," Janis broke in. "I'm here because of Detective Cavanaugh's concerns."

"FBI?" Virginia said with visible fear. "Why would the FBI be involved with me?"

"We should talk inside," said Danny, wanting to get her alone to grill her about his suspicions.

"Yes, that would be best given the setting here," said Janis.

Virginia turned to Gwen, who was standing behind her looking upset and concerned. Danny didn't even remember Gwen coming back in the room. Virginia said something to her, and Gwen reluctantly walked off. Cal was gone, apparently not wanting any part of the confrontation.

"Is your husband around?" asked Danny. "We'd like to talk to him, too."

"He's in his study," said Virginia. "We can talk there."

They walked into Oscar Stallworth's well-appointed study to find him having a drink with another man. Oscar's face turned sour at the sight of Danny. He recovered, continuing to smile at the man he was talking to. Oscar made an excuse to his guest, who left after saying a friendly hello to everyone.

When the man was gone, Oscar's face converted back to the angry look. He instantly focused on Danny. "What the hell are you doing in my house again?" asked Oscar.

"This woman is from the FBI," said Virginia quickly.

That made Oscar stop short. He looked at Janis with unmistakable fear in his eyes and absently took a swallow of his drink.

"What's this about?" asked Oscar.

Danny saw his chance. Both of them were upset and off-balance. He had to shock them, upset them with a piece of information before they could get together and form a wall of resistance.

"We know about what you're doing with the Castle," said Danny. "It took us a while to put it together, but after Olittah Reese died, it all made sense. There's a new version of the group operating in Detroit. We believe the killer's victims are being selected from this group."

"Castle?" asked Oscar. "That's preposterous. The organization was divisive to black people and died out years ago. . . ."

Oscar continued his speech denying Danny's statement, but Danny barely heard it. He was focusing on Virginia, who had not said a word. She was looking down at her feet.

"Ms. Stallworth," Danny cut in. "You want to deny it, too?"

"And I'd think carefully about your campaign before you answer," said Janis.

Virginia looked at the officers with guilt in her eyes. She steadied herself on the edge of her husband's desk. Her eyes dropped again, and she glanced at the hardwood floor as she spoke.

"We didn't want to hurt anyone," she began.

"Virginia? . . ." said Oscar, shock and worry in his voice.

"Let her finish," said Danny.

"She doesn't have to talk to you!" snapped Oscar.

"Then we'll arrest her," said Danny. "Right here, right now. I'll take her out in handcuffs past her guests out there."

"He's not kidding," said Janis. "Whatever it is you know, ma'am, it's better to tell us now, voluntarily."

Virginia gave her husband a reassuring look then continued. "We started the group about three years ago. I was talking with the Bakers about their ancestors, who are white, black, and part Asian. We realized that black people are all lumped together without regard for their actual background. We found it dehumanizing. The Bakers and I were the first to join. Then Dr. Vance, Raymer Farrell, the Trentons, Olittah, and the Collinses."

"Jesus Christ," said Oscar. He sat on the edge of his desk.

"And they all had to be fair-skinned to be in the group, right?" asked Danny.

"No," said Virginia. "That was the old way. In the new group we were all multi-ethnic."

"But were there any dark-skinned members in the group?" asked Danny.

"No," said Virginia. "But that wasn't by design."

"That's not much different," said Janis. "It's still a color bias."

"You think so?" said Virginia. "The country is going to be completely multi-ethnic in the next fifty years. There will be no more racism or discrimination, and all the garbage people fight about will be moot. Then we can go about the business of living, Detectives." She made this last statment like a politician giving a speech.

"I need to know all the names of the people in the group," said Danny. "They'll need protection."

"They already know," said Virginia. "After Olittah died, we all panicked. Everyone hired guards."

"Where are yours?" asked Danny.

"I have my family to protect me," said Virginia.

"Why didn't you tell me about this?" asked Oscar. He was clearly angry and embarrassed by his wife.

"I knew you'd disapprove," said Virginia.

"You're damned right I do!" bellowed Oscar. "You just won't give it up, will you? Haven't our people suffered enough from this nonsense? Haven't *we*?"

Oscar seemed to be angry with her, but Danny couldn't tell if he was faking or not. Oscar glared at his wife with an emotion beyond embarrassment or even anger.

"It was just a social group," said Virginia. "We met, we talked, we shared, that's all."

"Then why is someone killing your people?" asked Danny. "Why are three of them dead for just talking and sharing?"

"I don't know," said Virginia. "It doesn't make sense."

"How did New Nubia fit in?" asked Janis. "Was it part of the group?"

"The Bakers started it," said Virginia. "They promised that they would use the profits from the company to help my campaign and expand the group."

"Expand?" asked Danny. "You mean start more chapters of the Castle?"

"No," said Virginia. "We wanted to get the NOAA to accept more kinds of people, all minorities, not just blacks. That's what my candidacy is all about. But yes, the company was important to us. We needed that money."

"Did the Castle get New Nubia investors to join the group?" asked Janis.

"Yes," said Virginia. "But why does that make a difference?"

"Maybe a disgruntled investor is taking revenge," said Danny. "And that means he'd have to know about the group. Who knew, Ms. Stallworth?"

"Just us," said Virginia. "We kept our secret well. As you can see, even my own husband didn't know."

"Mr. Baker had a friend who knew," said Danny. "He told this friend, so I can assume that Olittah Reese did, too, and maybe some of the other people. Someone knew and he or she is our killer."

There was silence at this. Virginia looked stunned and afraid.

Danny guessed that it never occurred to her that her select group was corrupt. She was a woman who needed standards for people, but based them on artificial criteria. Of course secrets get told. People have loose lips. But not her people. They were supposed to be better than that, he thought.

"What have you done?" Oscar asked his wife. He had a look of guilt on his face that was frightening to Danny. "What have you done?"

"Something you want to say?" asked Danny.

"No," said Oscar. "We're finished talking."

"I want that list of names," said Danny.

Virginia went to her husband's desk, wrote out the list, and then handed it to Danny:

JOHN AND LENORA BAKER

OLITTAH REESE

RAYMER FARRELL

DR. HENRY VANCE

JIM AND KELLY TRENTON

QUINTEN AND SANDRA COLLINS

"Any of these people here today?" asked Danny.

"No," said Virginia. "This party is for out-of-town delegates."

"You forgot to put down your name," said Danny.

"You already know that," said Virginia.

Danny jotted her name down anyway, and this seemed to annoy Virginia. He hadn't found his killer yet, but he felt as if he were closing in. He had to interview the other members on the list as soon as possible.

"Mr. Baker was afraid of something," said Danny. "He told a friend that your group was afraid. 'Fear stalks the Castle,' is what he said. Do you know anything about that?"

"Someone sent him a threatening letter because of New Nubia," said Virginia, "but it had nothing to do with our group. He was mistaken."

"Hard to make that conclusion now that he's dead," said Janis.

Danny had a sudden wave of revulsion for Virginia. He thought about Vinny's sister Renitta, and her self-righteous racism. He thought about all the stories of pain and hurt he'd heard from his friends relating to color, and he thought about how underneath all his trouble with Vinny, there was an unstated question of whether they were not right for each other because of their races. The connection between the perception of color and the reaction to it was a frightening mystery. The foreboding nature of darkness and the purity of lightness were things that became ingrained in people, stamped on their minds and hearts. But it seemed that someone's grasp of this phenomenon had turned his heart to murder.

Danny and Janis left the Stallworth house as Virginia and Oscar walked out to the party to polite applause. They smiled and looked adoringly at each other like the President and the First Lady when they made public appearances.

Danny was wondering how they could look so loving and secure with each other after what they had just revealed. But he was more concerned about the people on the list and which of them might be the next victim.

28

SAVING GRACES

Bellva looked at the graveyard with fear and excitement in her heart. The sun felt warm against the back of her neck, but a cool breeze blew in her face from the cemetery. For a second, she felt caught between two worlds, the heat of hell, and the coolness of heaven. Ironic that the heavenly feeling came from a place of death, she thought.

The wind from the graveyard smelled of flowers and cut grass, not the smell of death that she'd read about so much. In fact, she didn't really know what death smelled like. Was it putrid and thick like old blood or was it sharp, piercing, and suffocating like fear? She imagined it was the latter for that was what she faced each day, the fear and uncertainty of life in the street with nothing but her addiction to move her from one place to the next.

Bellva had managed to fool the two detectives who'd picked her up, even though she had been coming down from a high. The black one was not hard. He'd looked at her with the familiar sense of sorrow and disgust that she was used to. But the white one, the one who sounded like a black man, had been trying to get inside her head, to know what made her tick. He looked *inside* her and that was scary as hell. He suspected something and that was not good.

Ever since the cops had told her that John Baker was dead, she'd been running hard and fast. Running because she knew why he was dead and because she had a good idea who had killed him. John had told her about the scam he was running, the money he was stealing, and from whom. She had been his confessor. She didn't understand what the Internet company was, or how he'd taken the investors, but she did know they were pissed about it.

John Baker had been much more than the occasional boyfriend she'd told the cops he was. They were lovers, friends, and more like father and daughter than she wanted to believe.

She stood outside the gates of the burial ground on the far east side. She wondered if she would be here one day soon, tucked into the cold ground, looking up into the darkness of eternity. Not if she took care of her business, she thought. John Baker had left something and she planned to get it. But she was a frail, weak, drug-dependent woman who was out of money and almost out of time. She turned away from the gate as the attendant rode by on a golf cart, his tools rattling noisily. She walked away from the graveyard and decided she needed to eat.

Bellva walked up to Eight Mile and strutted until she flagged down a fat white man in a Toyota. They pulled onto a side street and ten minutes later she had her lunch money. She stuffed the cash in her bra away from the money she'd saved for drugs. As desperate as she was, she still obeyed the first rule: never use your drug money to eat.

Bellva went into a Taco Bell and ordered a combination meal. She ate thinking about how she could get to what John Baker had left behind. She was convinced that he'd told her about it so she could have it when he was gone.

She barely tasted the food as she forced her mind to focus on a solution to her dilemma. The food was warm, thick, and salty. It tasted neither good nor bad. It was what she did to keep going between highs. Food was like a battery in her car. Heroin was the fuel.

A greasy-looking man in a shirt with the telephone company logo on it walked by her table and winked at her. She still had it, she thought. She was still pretty enough to get a man's attention. But for how long? she thought. How long before she was like her friend Lilly, tired and dead-looking? And what would happen to her when the men stopped looking?

If she could just get to what was in the cemetery, she would never have to worry about getting high again. She would have all the drugs she wanted.

She saw herself floating, dressed in fine clothes, high on the best shit on the planet. It would be a good life, filled with an addict's dream to be endlessly fucked up.

Then in her tortured brain a plan emerged. It stepped from behind her dreams and the ever-present need for drugs, and she saw it. She could make it happen, she could get to John Baker's treasure.

If she had a partner.

Bellva finished her meal and got on a bus, riding east. Eventually she jumped off and walked a few more blocks. She turned down the street she was looking for. Her heart was pumping and she was feeling the need for a hit again. But she held it off. It didn't happen often, but there were some things that were more important than getting high.

Bellva stopped short as she got halfway up the block from the house she was looking for. There were men all around it, and she'd been on the street long enough to see that they were armed.

A man in a puffy jacket walked to her quickly. She froze, knowing that any sudden movement might be interpreted as offensive. Her life in the street had taught her a great many things, chief of which was to never challenge someone unless you were ready to back it up. Bellva waited as the man moved toward her. She smiled feebly as if this would calm him. But he kept coming at her with the same mean expression on his face.

The man in the puffy coat got to her and looked her up and down. His face was young but hard-looking, and above his right eye there was a wound that was still healing. Without saying a word, he reached inside his coat and pulled a gun. After he was sure she saw it, he cocked it and pointed it at her face.

Danny had been sitting outside his father's house for over an hour. He'd started to go in more than once but lost his nerve. He had officers out to warn all of the people on the Stallworth list, and for the first time, he felt that he could do what he had come here to do.

Danny was thinking that maybe he didn't need the knowledge that was in his father's head, maybe there were some things better left unknown in this world. His mother was gone and nothing would ever change that. Nothing he could say or do would bring back that half of him that had fallen down those stairs with her, or give him the chance to tell her all of the things he'd never said.

His hand shook as he realized that he was holding the steering wheel so tightly his knuckles had turned white from the force of his grip. He let it go and watched the blood flow back into them, turning them pink.

A police cruiser rolled slowly down the street. It stopped by a house, then kept going, passing Danny. Inside, there were two uniformed officers who eyed him suspiciously.

Danny watched the cruiser for a moment. He remembered the first time he saw his father in his policeman's uniform and how proud he felt when he knew what it stood for. He saw him marching under the morning sun into the elementary school with the young boy he used to be. Robert Cavanaugh was the symbol of what it meant to be in law enforcement, bold, unerring, and strong. The thought of what those things meant to him filled his heart and he started to move. Danny had always known that his father was a better cop than he was, but perhaps he was a better son.

Danny got out of the car and went to the door of the house. He knocked only once before his father answered. Robert saw his son and didn't say a word. He looked at him for a moment then he just walked away from the open door.

Danny came inside and saw that the house was messier than the last time he'd been there. He followed his father into the kitchen, where it seemed he lived these days.

"Got some food if you want it," said Robert.

"No thanks," said Danny.

The two men sat and just looked at each other as Robert finished off a sandwich he was eating. In that moment Danny realized that he never talked much to his father, that all the things they needed to say had been said. Theirs had always been a quiet connection, one that had made both men comfortable.

"I came about Ma," said Danny.

Robert looked up from his plate with a start then he looked back down. "What about her?"

"I know."

Robert didn't say anything. He finished the sandwich, then started on a beer he had on the table.

"And what is it that you think you know?" asked Robert. He sounded official, as if the part of him that was a cop had suddenly awakened.

"I'm not in the mood to play games," said Danny. "I saw the report you and Dr. Lester fudged. I know she didn't die from the fall she took in this house."

Robert put down his beer and stared at his son. His green eyes were fierce from within the wrinkles on his face. This was the Robert Cavanaugh of old, Danny thought, the man who could walk through fire and stop the rain with a glance.

"You sure you want to come in here, in my house, and do this?" asked Robert in a voice that was as mean as it was strong. "You sure you want to challenge me, accuse me about this?"

"I'm here," said Danny. He could not back down when his father got like this. If he did, his father would bury him under a mountain of strength and paternal guilt. Most men have to challenge their father one day of their lives. He never thought his time would be about the death of his mother, but he had to do it. Fate had left him with this and he was not about to walk away from it. "I'm not leaving until I get the truth."

"Truth?" Robert laughed bitterly, a sad sick thing that was more like a rasp. "Is that what you want? Everybody thinks they want to know the truth until they hear it. You think it's some kinda medicine that'll cure all the shit that makes you sick, until you realize what the truth really is."

Danny just stared at him, unwilling to give an inch. Inside, he was dying. Everything he knew as a cop told him that his father was hiding some terribleness. And no matter how bad it was, he had to know it.

"What is it?" asked Danny. "What is the truth to you?"

"It's pain," said Robert without hesitation. "It's the hard, fucked-up reality of what we all really are, what we really feel and do to each other . . ."

Robert pushed away the beer and started to get up from the table. Danny saw water in his eyes, and now he knew the world was ending for sure. Robert Cavanaugh had never cried in his life, even when his family was falling apart from his alcoholism.

The old man turned his back on his son and moved to the doorway. Danny wanted to grab him, to plead with him to give him the terrible truth that he so desperately needed. Just then Robert turned around to his son, his eyes now clearly filled with tears.

"I did it," he said. "I killed your mother."

Bellva could not take her eyes off the gun the man in front of her held in his hand. He pulled the gun down away from her face, then kept it in front of him, still partially inside his coat as if he'd been taught to do so.

"You don't need to be on this street today," said the man in the puffy coat.

"I need to see the man," said Bellva. She choked on the words.

"Man ain't seein' no hos. Bounce."

"This ain't about no fuckin'. It's about bid'ness."

"What kinda bid'ness you got, bitch?" Puffy Coat laughed. And now sure of her harmlessness, he put the gun away.

Bellva was getting angry, but it didn't pay to mess with these thugs. They had no respect for themselves let alone some drug-addict prostitute.

"I'll tell him in person," said Bellva. "You tell him that it's Bellva. You tell him that and see how fast he comes outta that house."

Puffy Coat looked at Bellva and he could see she did have something to say, but more important, she was desperate. He checked out her ass and legs, then brought his eyes back to hers.

"You wax my shit and I'll tell him."

"What?" said Bellva before she could stop herself.

"Suck my dick," said Puffy Coat. "I'm sho' you familiar with how it's done, bitch."

Bellva looked at the young man with contempt. She knew from experience that if she did it, he would just laugh at her then send her away, and she'd never get to the man she needed to see. She was not tough like many of her friends in the profession. She didn't carry a knife or a gun and if a man gave her trouble, she usually cried and ran off. But this was too important to be timid. She had to make this thug respect her. And there was only one way to do that.

"Fuck you," she said.

"Then get yo' stank ass off dis block," said Puffy Coat. He opened his coat to show her the gun again.

Bellva didn't move. His obvious dependence on the gun told her that he was inexperienced. A real killer took it out only when he intended to kill, and then it was the last thing you saw. Puffy Coat had shown it to her twice and she was still alive. He could be intimidated if she did it right.

Bellva took a step toward him and to her surprise, the man moved back.

"You throw me off this street and you can be the one to tell your boss how you fucked him out of a score. Maybe he'll kill you, or maybe he'll make *you* suck some dick."

Puffy Coat looked at the woman before him and saw the determination in her eyes. Bellva saw the hardness in the man's eyes fade. He didn't really have the stomach to shoot her. Whatever his job was, it didn't involve thinking or making his boss lose money.

"Come on, bitch," he said. Then he turned and walked toward a house.

Bellva followed, smiling a little. Even though he had called her a bitch, the way he said it dripped with respect.

She followed Puffy Coat to the house and was patted down for a weapon. Something was up, she thought. There was more than the usual security here and the faces were new. Bellva walked inside the house and waited by the door. Soon, the Locke came out, munching on a candy bar, looking at her with curiosity.

"What the hell you doin' here, woman?" he asked. He looked pissed, as if she had interrupted something important.

Bellva knew the man well enough to know that it didn't pay to beat around the bush with the Locke.

"I know where John Baker's money is," she said.

Danny followed his father into the living room. Robert sat on the sofa. Danny took a chair next to him. His knees were weak and he almost collapsed into the seat.

Danny sat there for a while looking at this man he'd known all his life as if seeing him for the first time. He felt sorry for him, and at the same time he wanted to pound him for what he'd done. Part of him wanted to leave, to go and forget what he'd heard. But it was too late. The truth was here and now he had to have all of it.

"Why?" asked Danny. "Were you two having trouble?"

"You got your answer. Just go," said Robert.

"You confess to a murder, my own mother, and I'm supposed to just walk out and have a cup of coffee? No. I demand to know why you did it." Danny took a moment, then added, "And when you're done, I'm going to arrest you."

Robert's face didn't change at this statement. He shifted on the sofa as if he were about to get up, but he didn't.

"Your mother took a bunch of pills," said Robert. "She sat in the bathroom for a half hour and just waited, all the while slipping deeper and deeper into darkness, I suspect. Then I heard her fall down on the floor." Robert's face took on a scared look as he relived it. "I ran up as quickly as I could and there she was on the floor, out like a light. She wasn't moving, but I thought I felt a pulse, just a faint one. She wasn't going to make it, you see. No ambulance would get here in time to save her. I tried resuscitation, but it didn't work."

And now Robert was crying, trying not to lapse into sobs. He pushed his face into his hands and for a moment he was gone. In his place was a broken old man who had done the unthinkable and could not live with himself. Finally, he raised his head and wiped his face.

"I ain't never been a good Catholic," Robert continued, "but your mother was, and I knew what she'd done was a sin, and she'd never get into heaven if she died like that. I didn't have a lot of time to think about it. I dragged her to the staircase and I pushed her down. Then I called Tim Lester and made sure he was on the case to help me. I didn't want Father Cullen to know she'd tried to take her own life. So, you see, I didn't have a choice. God will forgive me for killing your mother, but he'd never forgive her for killing herself."

Danny moved over next to his father, who looked like he'd lost his mind, like a man who had just one hand on reality. He put a hand on his shoulder and he could feel him still trembling.

"Dad, she was probably already gone, you didn't—"

"Yes, I did!" yelled Robert. "If I didn't, your mother ain't in heaven, and I failed her again. I don't accept that. I killed her."

Danny didn't say anything for a long time, and the silence between them was good, like all the silences they'd shared over the years.

"I'm sorry," said Danny. "Look, you should come and stay with me for a while. You can't be alone at a time like this."

Robert laughed his bitter, half-crazy laugh again. "You don't get it, do you? There's more. Don't you want to know what kind of pills she was taking? Pills for depression, Danny. For five years she took them."

Danny was speechless. His mother had never been a happy woman. She was consumed by worry and totally dependent on religion to hold her together, but he never suspected she was so badly off that she needed medication.

Robert got up and walked over to a table and pulled out a drawer. He took out a thick book and tossed it to Danny. It was his mother's diary. A pink-and-white book with frilly trim on it. On the cover was written "LC." Toward the back, there was a yellow Post-it, marking a passage.

"She started writing in this thing about a year ago," said Robert. "The pain I talked about was not the truth of knowing what I did. It's the truth in here." Robert pointed at it as if it were Original Sin. Then he walked out of the room, leaving Danny with his mother's last words.

Danny didn't know how long he stared at the diary. When he finally opened it, he went to the marked passage and heard his mother's voice, clear, and terribly sweet:

> By the time anyone sees this I will be gone. I know it's a sin, but I am past caring about that. Each day I wake up, and my first thought is of dying and how much better it would be if I was not here. I can't bear the awful pain I feel each day, the pain of knowing that my life has meant and continues to mean nothing.
>
> Thirty years of it I've spent trying to make sense of my choices, and all I have to show for it is memories of a drunk husband, two lost sons, and all the paths I never walked down. Robert's drinking killed part of all of us, and I've never been able to get my part back. I lost my first son to crime and drugs and hatred. He is dead to me now.
>
> It drove me to despair and kept us living in the heart of a city that was hostile to us, that didn't want us. I know

we're supposed to love all men no matter what their color, but there are things that people do that are awful and beyond the reach of the Lord's hand.

Each day my son would come home, bruised and crying, beaten by black kids because we could not get away from the legacy of hate in this city. Soon he embraced black people and their ways for fear that he'd never survive, and that decision turned him away from what our family was and into something that I didn't understand. I have no grandchildren and I wouldn't want any from either son. And that may be the most terrible thing of all.

Danny almost dropped the book. He and his mother had rarely talked about any of this. She was a woman who obviously learned to suffer in silence. Danny thought about his talks with Gordon and his question concerning how Danny felt about himself. The doctor had somehow sensed the truth. He wanted to know if Danny felt about himself the way his mother had, if he resented being so imbued with a culture that was not his own.

Danny heard a faint rustling and saw that he was wrenching the pages in his hands that he was reading. He wanted to burn the diary, watch it turn to pretty black ashes and fly away on a current of air, but instead he forced himself to continue.

Danny is a policeman like his father, has the same hardness of his father, the same coldness, and worse he's not really like us at all, not the happy son I always imagined I'd have. He's like all those black people he grew up around. He sounds like them, feels like them, and I can't stand it. We used to argue about it, but I gave up. In the end, he loved them more than me.

Danny lives in sin with a black woman who I cannot bring myself to like. You always think your son will marry a younger version of you. Not in my case. She is a good person, but she is not me. She is black and my heart breaks to say it, Father, but I can never love her.

All of my friends show pictures of their grandchildren, pretty little girls who look like them, or little boys who are wild and lovely. I have nothing. The poison in this family has killed my hope and my heart, and some days I just want to rip it out of my chest and squeeze it until it stops beating.

I have nothing to hold on to, nothing to keep me here on God's good earth. Please pray for me, pray that my soul will be released from wherever it goes when you take God's most precious life from yourself.

Danny stared at the pages, trying to will the letters to disappear, but there it was, his mother's will and testament to her life of pain, denial, and regret.

His mother had taken her life in part because of what he was, what he'd always felt was special. Danny thought of all the times his mother had fought with him over the way he spoke and his choice of friends and women. He never thought he was doing anything more than standing up for himself. He wished he could take back a million things he'd said and done.

He thought about the killer, his terrible campaign against a color of skin, and his mother's despair over his internal color. He wanted to wrap himself into a ball and close in, draw into himself until there was nothing left, until he was gone and none of this had happened. And finally, most terribly, he thought that surely he had killed his mother as much as his father thought he did.

Danny got out of the chair and lay down on the floor. He felt a cool draft settle over him. His father was right, he thought. The truth was a terrible thing, and the pain resonated through him like the shock of being born.

He saw himself standing on the edge of great void. But it wasn't a hole, it was the shadow of life, the terrible painful truth of the world, and in it were his mother's life, his innocence, and all of his hope, swirling like lost children.

Bellva sat down and munched on a handful of candy. The Locke eyed the desperate-looking girl and smiled. There was something wonderful about a woman who would do anything to get what she wanted, he thought.

"What money?" asked the Locke. "I thought John Baker was just a trick to you."

"Johnny had money," said Bellva. "Money he stole from some people on the Internet. He was skimming and hiding it from his wife and everybody."

"How much money?" asked the Locke. He took a seat next to Bellva.

"Johnny said it was over a million dollars. When he knew that his company was fucked, he got scared. He was planning to leave his wife."

"And marry you?" asked the Locke with derision.

"That so hard to believe?" asked Bellva. "Johnny and me had an understanding."

The Locke looked at Bella with unmistakable disgust in his eyes as if he was repulsed by the idea that she thought of herself as desirable. "Where did he keep the cash?" he asked flatly.

Bellva stiffened in her seat. This was the moment she dreaded. She was shaking and that moment she wished she had gotten high before she came inside.

"I can only show you," she said.

"Don't trust me?" asked the Locke. He put his hand on her thigh and squeezed. "Me and you been close, girl. You don't trust a man you used to fuck?"

"I did that with a lot of men," said Bellva. "Don't mean nothing. I can only show you where it is. We split it fifty-fifty. It'll be easy."

"No," he said.

"No?" Bellva's face showed her shock. "But it's a lot of money, and you don't gotta do nothing for it."

"See that's my problem," said the Locke. "Ain't nothing for free in this world, least of all a million dollars. It's too good to be true."

"The money's real," said Bellva adamantly.

"Oh, I believe you," said the Locke. "It's the easy part I got trouble with. If it was easy, your ass would have that cash and be on a bus out of town."

"Well, there is kind of a hitch," said Bellva.

"Uh-huh," he said. "And for that I want a bigger cut. Seventy-five percent."

"What?!" Bellva stood up and just as quickly he pulled her back down.

"Don't you even think about trying to pull some hard shit on me, bitch," said the Locke. "I'm the king of hard shit and you ain't got it in you. Now here's what's gonna happen. Tomorrow me and you is gonna go to where that money is and get it. And we'll split it just like I said and you're gonna be glad that I don't leave your ass in a garbage can somewhere. And tonight, you're gonna stay here and take care of me."

"Wait," said a man's voice from behind Bellva.

She turned to see a big man emerge from the back of the house.

"That money is mine," said Reverend Bolt. Bolt's men walked in beside him, menacing.

"Get out of here," said the Locke.

"No," said Bolt. "That money was stolen from me. It's the reason I came here to borrow from you."

"And you will," said the Locke. "Right after you get your ass out of here."

"Who is this?" asked Bellva.

"Nobody," said the Locke. "Just be cool." He turned an angry face back to Bolt.

"Young lady," Bolt said to Bellva, "come with us." And with that, Bolt's men grabbed her.

"Ain't this a bitch," said the Locke. "Do you think I'm gonna let you get out of here with her—?"

Bellva recoiled from the touch of Bolt's deacons as the first gunshot sounded. It was a big boom like a cannon. The Locke ran across the room so fast Bellva was amazed behind her fear.

Bolt and his men all drew their guns. The Locke ran to a closet as Bellva heard more shots and screaming from the front of the house. Bolt and his men pulled her toward the back of the place.

The Locke grabbed a rifle as the first man came through the door. Bellva hit the floor as the bullets flew. She covered her eyes and screamed until her lungs were empty. She heard more shots and a body hit the floor hard. She heard the pleading of the Locke's voice, then another loud boom. More bodies fell then she heard Bolt yell, then someone else fell hard beside her.

Silence.

Bellva saw only darkness. Her hands shook violently as she pulled her legs into her chest. She was afraid to look, afraid she'd open her eyes and see only the barrel of a gun in her face, a flash, then the sweet hereafter.

She heard voices, but they were a mumble to her as someone trashed the room around her.

Suddenly her hands were pulled from her eyes. She was crying and so her sight was blurry. She wiped the wetness from her vision. First she saw bodies all around her covered in blood then she focused on the angry face of Muhammad Bady. He was joined by two other young men.

Next to her, she saw Bolt with a wound in his leg but very much alive. Muhammad walked over to Bolt and smiled.

"Your sons have come to take you home, Daddy," he said.

Jim Cole didn't know who'd be ringing his doorbell at the ungodly hour of two in the morning. The young lady who slept next to him rustled under the covers and smacked her lips as he got out of the bed. He threw on his robe and grabbed his service revolver from the nightstand. The bell rang again.

"It'd better be God or his son," he mumbled as he checked the gun and put a bullet into the chamber.

He moved through the house barefoot, the coldness of the floor sending waves of reality through his body. He walked into the living room and carefully approached the front door as the person on the other side rang the doorbell again. He stood so that his visitor could not see his figure through the little glass windows at the top of the door. He eased his frame by the wall, then slowly moved to the peephole. He was still half asleep and had to focus a minute before he saw who it was.

"Jesus," he said as he opened the door.

Danny stood in the doorway, slouched over. He was unsteady on his feet, and Jim could tell he'd been drinking.

"Cavanaugh," said Jim. "What the hell are you doing here?"

"Had to see you, boss," said Danny. "Needed to talk to you."

"You're drunk, man. Come on in."

"No," said Danny. "If I come in you'll reason with me and shit and keep me from doing what I came to do. Nope, I need to stay out here with *my* reason, where I know I'm doing the right thing."

Danny reached into his jacket and pulled out his badge and gun. He stuck it out like a kid who been playing with his father's pocketknife. "I'm done," he said. "I quit."

Jim was shocked. But he was a man who'd seen just about everything in the job, so he kept his face resolute. "What's this all about?" he asked.

"Everything," said Danny. "I can't be sure that I'll function right anymore. See, I let this job become everything to me, and now I ain't got nothing left."

"Look, man, we all go through this at one time or another. You fought too hard for it to walk away."

Danny teetered a bit, then put the gun and badge on the floor of the threshold.

"I know, but I was fighting for the wrong thing."

Danny turned and staggered off into the dark as Jim walked out into the cold night trying to reason with him. Danny barely heard Jim's voice. Danny was looking up into the night and saw the vastness of the dark sky, littered with distant stars and suddenly, awfully, he was aware of how small he was.

PART THREE

Color of Justice

Murder's from the heart.

—DANNY CAVANAUGH

29

MESSENGER

Dr. Henry Vance pulled into a parking space in the underground garage downtown and turned off his car's engine. He sighed as he unstrapped himself from his seat belt. He had an urgent meeting with a wealthy patient that he did not wish to take. These days, he didn't even want to venture out of his home. Three people were dead from his inner circle, and he was, to say the least, a little stressed about it.

The passenger door of the car opened, and a big man got out. He walked over to Henry, who was still seated in the car. Next to them, an overhead light flickered off, struggling against its malfunction.

"Ready, Dr. Vance?" asked the big man.

"Yeah, Rudy," replied Henry. He searched for the button on the fancy remote that locked the high-tech car and set the alarm as he got out. "Cheap-ass office building, can't afford to fix a broken light."

Henry stood next to his bodyguard, aware of being in his shadow. Henry was just under six feet tall, and weighed a thin one-sixty. Rudy was taller and larger, weighing in at about two-forty. Rudy stood in a defensive posture, checking out the area around them. The garage was quiet and smelled of gasoline and exhaust. The jingling of Henry's keys was like discordant music.

Henry heard the car's locks click. "Jesus," he said. "Damned Japanese cars."

They heard footsteps. Rudy turned and saw a figure come out of the elevator area and start toward them. Rudy moved out a few steps in front of Henry and took on a crouching stance.

The figure walked only a few steps then got into a car in a handicapped space near the elevator door and drove off.

Rudy eased in his stance, straightening up. "Let's go, sir," he said.

Rudy and Henry quickly made their way across the garage. The sound of their footfalls bounced off the hard walls, making a hollow, popping sound.

"Shit," said Henry, stopping. "I left my medical bag in the backseat. Go on up without me, Rudy. I gotta go back to my damned car."

"I can't do it, sir," said Rudy.

"Then you go lock the car and I'll go up."

"Can't do that either," said Rudy. "I don't get paid to leave you alone. Let's go together, sir," said Rudy.

"I guess I'm safe whether I like it or not, huh?" said Henry, laughing.

"That's the plan, sir," said Rudy. Rudy didn't care why the doctor needed protection. In Detroit, it could have been a million reasons. All he knew was that he had been a third-rate football player with a bad knee and this kind of work paid well.

They walked back to the car. Henry got to the car and took out his keys. The flickering of the broken light made Henry's job all the more difficult as he fumbled with the remote. Henry found the button and pressed it. Nothing.

"Dammit," said Henry.

"Let me, sir," said Rudy.

Rudy reached for the key chain as a man rose from behind the car next to them. The blinking of the light made the killer seem as though he were moving in slow motion. He came forward, his hand swinging outward toward Rudy's face. Rudy saw a dark object cover his vision, then sharp pain as something crashed into the bridge of his nose. Rudy yelled and dropped the key chain. A second later, the killer was slamming Rudy's head into the concrete pillar next to it. There was a dull cracking sound then Rudy slumped and fell to the ground.

Henry had already turned to run, but the killer was on him. Henry could see him more clearly now. It was a man, dressed in dark clothes. He was wearing something over his face with eyeholes in it. The killer raised a hand and brought it down toward Henry's face.

Henry stumbled backward to avoid the blow. He turned and moved away from his attacker, knowing that if he was caught, something terrible would happen. This was what he'd been afraid of, what Rudy was for. He was foolish to have left his home, he thought.

The killer pivoted on one foot under the flickering light. He looked strangely graceful as he turned and inched closer to Henry, who was now terrified beyond reason. He opened his mouth to yell, but only a dry choking sound came out.

The killer slowed, taking measured steps, not wanting his prey to escape another blow. Henry backed toward the elevator, looking at the exit door. He was wondering whether he could make a mad dash for the door, but he knew he was not fast, and some lunatic was in front of him and surely quicker than he was. Still, his body was pumping adrenaline, and he felt that he could do it.

Henry was about to run, when a car pulled into the garage. The headlights flashed dully off the stone pillars, and the sound of its engine echoed off the stone walls.

"Hel—!" was all Henry got out before the killer clamped a hand over his mouth. A quick blow to the stomach followed, emptying Henry's lungs of air. Henry crumpled like paper. The killer dragged Henry between two vehicles as a Mercedes pulled up on the driveway. The Mercedes rolled right past Rudy's body, which was wedged between Henry's car and the one next to it.

The killer struggled to keep Henry quiet as the driver of the Mercedes found a space. It was across the aisle and to the left, close enough that the occupants might hear them.

A well-dressed couple got out of the Mercedes and walked toward the elevator door. Henry made a muffled scream, which was cut off by another blow to the stomach. The man and woman stopped and looked around. The man took a step toward the killer and his captive, then stopped. The woman pulled on the man's elbow and the couple walked to the elevator and got in.

As soon as they were gone, the killer pulled Henry up and knocked him out cold.

The killer was breathing hard. This man was the hardest yet to get. They were on to him now, but he had expected this after Olittah Reese was taken. His mission was almost done, and he would not be deterred. He grabbed Henry's keys, popped the trunk on the car then stuffed him inside.

30

BEDFELLOWS

Danny sat with his father in the kitchen reading the *Detroit News* with dread. On the front page was a picture of the crime scene at Dr. Henry Vance's house on Edison Street in Detroit. The place was swarming with police and press when the snapshot was taken. The police department had kept a lid on the case, but this time, the media were all over it.

Henry Vance had been killed by the same killer who was stalking the members of the Castle.

Danny cursed silently as he realized that calling for protection to be put on the listed names had been too late. He'd left the case at the worst possible time.

Danny was staying with his father these days, the two men sharing a room and their guilt over Lucy's death. It was difficult living in a house with his mother's face on every wall and some memory of her in each corner. In a strange way it was a good thing, he thought. He was being forced to live with what had happened.

Danny had quit the case, but officially he was on leave. Jim Cole was not giving up. He wanted Danny to come to the most recent crime scene as his last official act. Danny knew what he was doing. He was hoping to give him the scent again, get his blood hot to get the killer. But it didn't work. Danny had to step away from the job to find out what the hell in his life made any sense.

Danny's attention went back to the news story. Dr. Vance's body had been found by a neighbor. He had disappeared while on his way to see a patient early yesterday morning. Dr. Vance's companion, Rudolph Garrison, was seriously injured and was in critical condition at Receiving Hospital. The article went on to say that Henry Vance's death was at the hands of a serial murderer. Danny could see Janis somewhere smiling about this.

The news story also contained a report from sources in the police department that the killings of Olittah Reese and the Bakers had "shockingly similar details." Then it went on to cite an unconfirmed report that Dr. Vance's crime scene had been despoiled after the killer had covered the crime scene with flour. Dr. Vance was a widower and there were no witnesses.

Jim Cole and Chip Unger had formed a joint task force of SCU cops and FBI. They would mobilize and start the manhunt today.

Danny fought the burning in his gut to run out and take back his job. But his father needed him. Robert was all he had now, and that seemed to be much more important.

"He's a smart one," Danny heard his father say. Robert was reading the *Detroit Free Press*. Henry Vance was front-page news there as well.

"Yeah," said Danny. "I felt like I was closing in on his ass, too."

"Sounds like he kidnapped that man and took him to his own house to kill him. He had a reason for that, don't you think?"

"I don't know," said Danny, not wanting to get into it. "Let me fix you something to eat."

"Why ain't you out there?" asked Robert.

"Because I'm here with you," said Danny. "How about some eggs with cheese in them?"

Robert looked at his son and blinked once. Danny knew that look. He was processing something, analyzing his son's evasive response.

"You quit, didn't you?" asked Robert, " 'Cause of what I told you about Lucy."

"Yeah," said Danny. "Last night." He watched his father. Even though Robert had turned away, Danny could feel him thinking about him.

"Marshall know?" asked Robert.

"Not yet. I'll tell him today. I'm sure Erik has been trying to get hold of me all day."

"You know, every time I got it bad in life, I blamed the job, too. Shit, I musta quit or thought about it more than fifty times."

"I know what I'm doing," said Danny defensively. "So, don't try to talk me out of it."

"Didn't plan to," sad Robert. "The job is more than an occupation. You get into it for whatever crazy-ass reason then you realize that you never had a choice, that you didn't choose the job, it chose you. You think you can make your life better by quitting it, but you find out that the job is life."

Danny didn't say anything. He made his father breakfast and felt like a good son. He cleaned up the house and drove his father to church.

Danny walked his father into the cathedral and felt a sense of relief. Robert was going to confession. Apparently, he'd been going every day since Lucy's death.

Danny watched Robert disappear into a confessional. He turned to walk away when he caught sight of an angel in the stained glass. Suddenly he was ten again and his mother was standing next to him in the packed church. She was telling him that the angel with the red hair was him when he was in heaven. Danny recalled the story with great joy. He actually believed that for a while.

But soon his happiness was pushed aside by grief. Her memory was going to haunt him forever, he thought.

Danny took a deep breath, turned on his heel, and walked into a confessional.

"Bless me, Father, for I have sinned," said Danny after the priest entered the other side.

There was a moment of silence as Danny tried to remember the rest of what he was supposed to say.

"How long has it been since your last confession?" asked the priest. He sounded young to Danny. His voice was light and reedy like a girl's.

"It's been most of my life," said Danny. "Since I was a kid."

"And your sins?" asked the priest, urging Danny on.

"Yeah, right. I, uh, I killed a few guys, but you know it was in the line of duty. I'm a cop. I beat down some other people pretty bad, and that wasn't exactly cool, you know. I drink too much, but I'm trying to cut down. I live in sin with a woman, but you know, I love her."

There was more silence as Danny could hear how badly he was screwing this up.

"Why don't you tell me why you came here?" asked the priest.

Danny was taken a little aback by this. He didn't remember everything about confession, but he did know that the priest wasn't supposed to push you.

"I kinda killed my mother," said Danny.

There was a long silence then, "How?" asked the priest. The shock was apparent in his voice.

"I guess you could say I disappointed her to death."

"So you only think you killed her?" said the priest, calming down.

"Yeah. I—she invested a lot in me and I just let her down. And while it ain't my fault, I still feel bad about it."

The priest took a long moment and Danny guessed he was at a loss as to what to say to this.

"Death is only the doorway to salvation, my son." said the priest. "I am more concerned with your soul than your life. Life is fleeting but it is the pathway to the greater glory of God. Therefore, when death comes, we must get back to life."

Danny was quiet as he contemplated the priest's wisdom. The priest told Danny to say a few prayers and sent him along his way.

Danny walked out of the church into the bright sun of the day. And all he could think about was getting a drink. He knew how bad it was to leave God's house and drink the demon rum, but even the philosophy of the church could not do what a stiff scotch could. He headed to the one place you could get a drink early in the day and no one would think you were a lush.

Danny tossed back his drink at the bar in the Motor City Casino. The place was surprisingly full for a weekday morning. The musical sound of slot machines filled the air, and the chatter of the patrons was like sweet whispers rather than the tired, drunken mutterings of gamblers.

The casino sat in place of the old Wonder Bread factory. Danny could remember driving into downtown on any given morning and smelling the heavenly odor of freshly baked bread. Across the street, old houses from the neighborhood stood in the contrast to the new building. The tiny, aged homes seemed to look at their new neighbor with envy. The image was clear. The city was determined to rise from its urban ashes.

Danny thought about what his father had said, about the job being life. He was probably right, but for now he was a civilian and that was just fine.

More interesting was what the priest had said to him. "*When death comes, we must get back to life.*" But which life? Danny thought. Police life or some other life taking care of his father, a life without Vinny?

Danny finished his drink and wanted another, but thought he'd better cut himself off. He was relying on the stuff more than he should anyway.

Danny got up to leave then stopped short after he opened the door. He literally jumped back as he saw two men talking on the street. Danny stayed inside, but watched the two men with interest as they strolled toward the casino parking lot. Danny didn't know what to make of it, but it was an intriguing picture. Thomas Reese was talking with Judge Charles Eastergoode, the man who'd had an affair with Thomas's dead wife, Olittah Reese.

Now in his automobile, Danny followed the unlikely couple as they got into separate cars and made their way uptown. Reese led the way and Eastergoode kept behind him.

Danny was on fire with what it meant for these two men to be together. He was off the case, but it seemed his father was right. The job was bigger than his tiny intentions about quitting and his pitiful guilt about his mother.

It could be Reese had forgiven Eastergoode for what the latter had done. Danny didn't know much about Reese, but he was not betting on that one. The average man will at least think about killing the man who slept with his wife.

Suddenly Danny grew nervous. What if Reese planned to kill Eastergoode? Maybe this ride was the last one Eastergoode would take. One thing was for certain, whatever the real story was, it was rotten. There was no good reason these two men should be together.

Thomas Reese turned on Seven Mile and Woodward, rolling into Palmer Park. Eastergoode followed. Resse and Eastergoode parked their cars then got out.

Danny drove past them, and parked on a residential street. He caught back up with them as they walked through the park. Their backs were to Danny, but it looked as if Reese was doing all of the talking. He was gesturing and looking at Eastergoode, who kept his hands at his side, and stared straight ahead.

Danny ducked behind two trees as they found a park bench and continued to talk. He wished he had some high-tech listening device, so that he could hear what they were saying. But in the real word, all a cop usually had was his brain, and his knowledge of people involved in crime.

It was possible, Danny thought, that Reese and Eastergoode had killed Olittah and made it look like the Baker murders. That was nice and neat, but it didn't explain why the Bakers and Dr. Vance were killed.

Danny noticed an old black man stroll out and take a seat near Reese and Eastergoode. Reese immediately shut up, eyeing the old man with suspicion. The old man sat a moment, then got up and left.

This gave Danny an idea. He took out a pad and pen and made a note of the old man, what he was wearing and the like. Then he looked around to see what else he could use. There was a kid on a bike wearing a red striped shirt. He zipped by the suspects. A garbage truck stopped nearby and emptied a basket. Danny got it all down.

The two men talked for another twenty minutes then they got into their cars and drove away in different directions.

Which one? Danny thought. Who would his target be? Eastergoode had already exhibited guilt for being in an affair with the deceased. On the other hand, Reese was clean in the eyes of the investigation so far. This made him a more likely person to have something bigger to hide. He was the man to go after.

Danny followed Reese back to his office at DaimlerChrysler. Danny waited until Reese was inside, then he left, hanging around the city, giving himself the rest of the day to make his story plausible.

Danny came back to Reese's office building at six and waited. Soon Reese emerged from the building, got into his car, and went home. Danny followed closely, practicing what he was going to say, talking to himself like a crazy man.

Reese drove into Sherwood Forest and Danny was not far behind. He was always mindful of the rich folks in the city. The homes were huge and fancy and the cars in the driveways made you wish you earned more money. Danny noticed for the first time that Reese was not driving a fancy car, but a common one, a compact Chrysler.

Reese went inside his house. Danny waited another half hour to let him get comfortable, then he walked up to the door. He rang the doorbell and waited for him to answer it.

"Officer?" said Reese innocently as he looked out a little window in the big wooden door.

"We need to speak with you, Mr. Reese," said Danny in his most official tone. "It's about your wife's murder. We have a suspect."

"Really, who—?" He stopped himself and opened the door to let Danny in.

Danny moved in quickly, drawing him away from the front door so he wouldn't see that there was no "we" as he'd just stated. Danny went into Reese's living room and stood by the sofa.

"Who is it?" he asked urgently. "Who killed my Olittah?"

Danny stood there for a moment, not speaking. He wanted Reese to become anxious.

"You know I'm not here about a suspect, Mr. Reese," said Danny finally.

"What?" said Reese. "Then I don't know what you're talking about. You say you have a suspect—then you say you don't. What the hell is this all about?"

"It's about you and Judge Eastergoode and what you talked about today."

This hit Reese like a dead weight. He even took a step back away from Danny, as if the cop were going to grab him and slam him into jail. This was the reaction Danny was hoping for, but he still didn't know a thing about where he was going. He had to be cool, or Reese would see through him.

"Right now," said Danny, "my partner is questioning Judge Eastergoode. Normally, we'd pick one of you up, then squeeze you, but there's no need for that after what we got today at Palmer Park."

"You were there?" he asked, his eyes filled with terror.

"We sure were. It was hard to get all of it, so we had to use several operatives. The old man who sat by you was used to distract you, while the kid on the bike put our microphones in position."

Danny saw Reese's eyebrows go up, remembering the people in the park. Realization washed across his face, then stark fear.

"The garbage men had video cameras on their truck," said Danny. "And they left another listening device when they put the trash can down. It was hard, but worth it for what we got. What I don't know is why you did it." Danny was going out on a limb, but he felt it was worth a shot.

Reese was floored. His knees wobbled, and he grabbed the mantel for support. He walked over to a black leather chair and sat down heavily. He buried his face in his hands, and started to cry, sobbing like this was his last hour on earth.

"I wasn't going to do it," he said. "I was mad, but I wasn't going to kill Olittah."

"You wanted to kill your wife," Danny said forcefully as if he had known this all the time. "And then she turns up dead. Do you see why we're so interested in you and your buddy? We're going to close this case, and I don't care which one of you goes down for it."

"I didn't do it!" he yelled suddenly. "She was fucking Charles, and I didn't like it. I was angry. So I called this guy."

"Look, man, if you tell me everything, maybe I can help you," said Danny. "Otherwise, we can just go downtown right now."

"No, no, no," said Reese, still crying a little. "I want to tell you. I can't hold on to this anymore." He took a breath, then looked at Danny with his red eyes. "I knew Olittah was having an affair. She told me it was Charles Eastergoode. She and I had been fighting a long time about my gambling at the new casinos. I'm in way over my head. Every night I'd be at MGM, Windsor, or the Motor City, losing money hand over fist. It reached the end when Olittah's car and mine got repossessed and we fell behind on the mortgage. She was going to leave me. I got desperate for money, you know, and I lost my head."

"What did you do?!" Danny demanded. He was no longer acting, he could tell where it was going and he was angry about it. "You wanted to kill her for the insurance?"

"No," said Reese. "Olittah didn't have any. She dropped her policy when my gambling got out of control. I wanted the money she and John Baker stole."

"John Baker and Olittah stole money from the New Nubia investors."

"Yes, a lot of money. Two million or so. I heard her talking with him about it. She did it with him, but then she didn't want any part of it. John Baker offered her a half million to keep her mouth shut.

But she said no. So, I hired a guy, this guy I met at a casino, to do it for me. His name was Clint, although I think it was a phony name. Anyway, Clint was going to kidnap Olittah and get the information out of her, only he took the thousand I gave him and disappeared. Then Olittah turned up dead."

"This Clint killed her?"

"No. Olittah came home the night he was supposed to grab her. Clint got picked up on an old arrest warrant and went to jail, so I know it wasn't him."

"Who then?" asked Danny. "Who did it?"

"I don't know," said Reese.

"Don't give me that bullshit," said Danny. "You wanted your wife dead. I know you're tied into this thing."

"No," said Reese. "I swear. I didn't want to kill her. I just needed the money."

"So, since you didn't get the money," said Danny, "you were black-mailing Eastergoode, threatening to tell his wife about the affair."

"Charles gave me a measly five thousand. Today, he cut me off, said it was over, that he was going to tell his wife everything." Reese shook his head and looked down. He was pitiful in his addiction to gambling and too crazy from it to see that he'd moved beyond rational thought. "I knew I picked the wrong person," Reese said calmly. "Olittah was really a decent person when you got right down to it. I should have gone after the prostitute."

"What prostitute?" Danny asked. And before Reese answered, Danny knew he had made a mistake long ago in this case.

"Some whore John was seeing. I remember Olittah yelling at him because John told this ho about what he was doing. And he was planning to skip town with her. I assumed John Baker told the prostitute where the money was."

Danny eyes grew wider. Bellva. She was the one all along, he thought. She'd played him and Erik good when they had her. She was the stupid drugged-out whore who knew nothing, a poor unfortunate girl in over her head. But she knew all along. She was waiting to get to that money. And now he had to get to her.

"The prostitute, do you remember her name?" Danny was making sure he was on the right track.

"It was Xena or something like that," said Reese. "What a damned fool John Baker was."

"Don't talk to anyone about this," sad Danny. "Someone from the police will contact you."

"You mean I'm not under arrest?" asked Reese.

"Just keep your mouth shut," said Danny. He ran out of Reese's house hoping that Bellva, who was certainly a lot smarter than she had let on, was not smart enough to have already gotten the money and skipped town.

Danny sat next to Desandias Locke in his hospital bed. He'd gone looking for information on Bellva. He'd checked the drug houses and her old haunts, but no one had seen her. Then Danny went to ask the man who knew everything and found the Locke's home had been turned into a crime scene.

The Locke had been shot up pretty good and left for dead, but he was still alive. He had sustained damage to his liver and spleen and had lost one of kidneys. Part of his spine had been shattered, and he had only partial movement on the right side of his body. If he lived, he'd most certainly need specialized medical attention forever.

Danny looked at the man with tubes running out of his body. One of the many monitors attached to him beeped softly. Danny managed some sympathy for the beaten man. He was a criminal but no one deserved this. It would have been better if he'd died.

"I need to talk to you," said Danny. "Can you manage?"

The Locke drew in a breath then let it go. It was a strained, frightening thing to see. He nodded his head.

"I'm looking for Bellva," said Danny. "I need to know where she is."

The Locke looked over at Danny and shook his head.

"She's dead?" asked Danny.

The Locke hunched his shoulders to say he didn't know. Then raised one hand and gestured to himself.

"The same people who did this got her?" asked Danny.

The Locke nodded.

"So, they got her, then they shot you up?"

The Locke shook his head then pointed to a pad and pen by his bed. Danny held the pad and gave the pen to the Locke, who scribbled as best he could:

bady brothers   killers   crazy mfs

"Bady brothers, killers, crazy muthafuckas," Danny said out loud. He took this to mean that the Locke was racked up by the Bady brothers.

"Where can I find them?" asked Danny.

He gave Danny a pissed-off look, as if to say, if he knew that, he would not be where he was.

Danny said his good-byes to the Locke and was about to go when he made a loud grunt. For a second, Danny thought he was having a seizure or something. But when he turned to him, he was pointing to the pad and Danny held it out for him. The Locke wrote something on it:

kill them

Danny drove back to his home, thinking that he should call his old boss and tell him what he knew. It would be the smart and sensible thing to do. But he also knew that by the time the cops got out a task-force to look for the Bady brothers, they'd get wind of it on the street, kill the girl, and skip town. He couldn't risk that, and he didn't have much time to get to them. Men like the Badys, men who would challenge a man like Locke, were not to be trifled with.

Danny stopped at his house and took out his other gun, the S&W .45 ACP. He stared at the gleam of the steel body against the darkness of the black handgrip. Contrast, he thought. All of a sudden it was everywhere in life.

He put on the second gun, trying not to think of what Gordon had said about them. He also remembered what the department said about carrying both weapons, the danger involved. But everything about what he was going to do was dangerous.

An unofficial investigation could lead to casualties and because of that, he didn't have a lot of time. If Bellva was still alive she wouldn't be for long. So he had to get on the street and get answers to a lot of questions about her abductors. The only thing he did know was that he didn't want to do this alone.

31

JOHN R

The big house on John R Street stretched up into the sky. It was one of those pre–World War II places, three stories high. Even in its current state of dilapidation, it towered above the other homes around it, like an ancient titan weary from battle.

Danny didn't know much about architecture, but he'd seen this kind of house, with its stone columns and pointy corners, before. They'd called them spooky houses when he was a kid. As Danny got out of the car, he could see that this house had kept the reputation.

Danny left his car a block from the place. He'd gone to several sources and found that the Bady brothers were all the Locke had said and more. They'd come from the South and had left a path of murder and destruction in their wake. Danny was concerned about this fact. The only thing more dangerous than a man willing to kill was one who was not afraid to die.

"That's a big house," said Marshall as he got out and stepped next to Danny.

Danny had called on his best friend to assist him in this endeavor. He had almost called it off when he saw Marshall's kids playing in the living room, then witnessed him take the child lock off the gun in his office. Marshall was a capable man and certainly he didn't trust anyone on earth more, but he was now a father and the thought of him dying was more terrible that what was in the big house down the street.

Danny hadn't told Marshall what he'd learned about his mother's death. Lucy Cavanaugh's letter blamed Danny for her depression and death and he didn't want those who cared about him to look at him differently. Even between friends, there had to be secrets.

"My people say one of them always watches for intruders. They sleep in shifts and they are all deadly."

"Then there's no room for mistakes," said Marshall.

Danny wanted to ask him if he was sure about this but Marshall would take that as an insult. Marshall was tough, and together with Danny had taken down a man who was a professional killer. Danny was feeling as if he'd lost so much lately. If he lost his friend he'd never forgive himself.

"You go in behind me and remember they'll be ready for us." Danny went into his trunk and pulled out a wooden box. He handled it carefully.

"Thank God you defend lowlives," said Danny. "I don't know where else I coulda got something like this."

"Believe me, he wanted to do it," said Marshall. "I walked him on arson for hire and that ain't easy."

Danny reached inside the box and flipped a switch, then he and Marshall took off running toward the Bady brothers' house.

Muhammad hit his father again. Bolt's head snapped back from the impact. He was on his knees kneeling before the brothers. Bolt's hands were tied in front of him and his feet were similarly bound. Muhammad had been beating him for a half hour. Letting each blow sink in before inflicting the next.

Rimba watched, listening to a rap tune and holding a machete he'd been sharpening. Akema stood next to a window with Bellva tied up on her side. Rimba had ripped her blouse and fondled her breasts until Muhammad stopped him. There would plenty of time for that he'd told Rimba. Their priority was dealing with Bolt, making sure their goal was achieved.

Akema Bady was angry. She'd wanted to kill the woman they'd found at the home of their enemy. They'd gotten their father, so they didn't need that woman. She knew her brothers occasionally liked to have sex with women. She refrained from the act herself, so she couldn't understand why they couldn't, too.

Whenever her brothers had some woman around, they never paid attention to her. She was supposed to be first in their lives, not second to some sick, loathsome act. They were going to kill their father then have sex with the filthy woman. She only looked forward to the first thing on that list.

"Why . . . why are you doing this?" asked Bolt through his swollen lips.

"Don't you recognize us?" demanded Muhammad. "Look at us!" he yelled. "Can't you see the faces you spit on so long ago?"

Muhammad had already seen the recognition in his father's eyes. Bolt was trying to save his life by denying who he was. And it was a game that was going to be played out to the end.

"I'm a reverend," said Bolt. "Don't you kids have any respect for the Lord?"

"Fuck the Lord!" yelled Muhammad as he kicked Bolt in the ribs.

Bolt coughed up blood as he lurched over. Rimba put the machete under Bolt's chin and forced his head back up.

"We can be here all night," said Muhammad. "You say you believe in God. This is what I believe in." Muhammad pulled out a gun. "This is our god. This is what you left us when you killed our mother and left us to rot in foster homes and jail. Black men run out on their kids all the time and never think about what happens after they leave. We are what you planted, Daddy. This is the tree of your sin. So if you believe in God then you gotta know he brought you here to pay for what you did. But don't you lie to us anymore."

Bolt hung his head and cried. Blood dripped from his mouth and nose. His big frame shook as he heaved in his pain and grief. On the other side of the room Bellva cried also and was hit by Akema and told to shut up.

"I am your father," said Bolt. "But I'm not that man who left you. I'm a better man. I've dedicated myself to—"

Bolt was cut off by a kick to his face. Muhammad smashed his foot into his jaw and Bolt fell over on his side.

"I don't want to hear your confession," said Muhammad. "I just wanted to know that the man we killed was the right one. Yes, you gonna, Daddy. We are going to make your death as painful as you made our lives. All we've had is time to think about how to do it, and now it's time to put that knowledge to use." Turning to Rimba, he said, "Tie off his arm."

Rimba took a rag and tied it tightly around Bolt's left arm. He pulled it until he saw Bolt's palm go white.

Then Muhammad got on his knees next to his father. He put his mouth next to his ear and whispered to him the horror of what had happened to his children in the foster care and penal systems.

Boltman started to cry again as he heard stories of Akema's sexual abuse for over a year, Rimba's beating and torture at the hands of a sadistic couple, and Muhammad's own beating by white supremacists in prison. With each terrible tale, Bolt grew weaker and weaker, and Muhammad could feel him accepting his fate.

"Each day," said Muhammad, "we're going to take part of you off, until there's nothing left. We will take you apart until you die, then we will keep cutting you until there is nothing left but your evil-ass heart."

Bolt started to say the Lord's Prayer, closing his eyes to shut out his tormentors. For a second, Muhammad believed that his father was a changed man. The sincerity of the prayer was sweet and genuine, the words of a man with God in his heart. But whatever mercy Muhammad might have once had inside him was gone. He felt only the need to rid the world of this poisonous man and the pain he felt in his own heart.

Muhammad nodded to Rimba, who took Bolt's arm with the tourniquet on it. Akema stopped her watch to see the spectacle. Rimba raised the big knife, his arm shaking with anger. Then he brought the blade down, cutting off his father's hand.

Bolt's scream was unearthly as the limb was lopped off. The brothers watched as Bolt writhed on the floor. Muhammad hugged Rimba, telling him that his blow was good.

"Men coming!" said Akema, looking out of the window. She saw Danny and Marshall running toward their home.

Without a word, the brothers armed themselves. Muhammad looked at his father on the floor. The blood had stopped flowing from his arm and he'd passed out from the pain.

Akema tied Bellva to a doorknob on a closet. She slapped her viciously across the face and was about to hit Bellva again when Muhammad grabbed his sister and pulled her out of the room.

Danny slid the small wooden box onto the front porch of the house. Then he and Marshall continued moving to the back of the home. The place was falling apart and someone had torn off the city sign condemning it. All that was left were the letters DEMNED. Danny thought of the word *damned* as he passed by.

Danny and Marshall arrived at the back door and found a panel of plywood that had been pulled back. They got on either side of the door and Danny ripped off the flimsy piece of wood. Then he pulled out his other gun and waited.

Suddenly, there was an explosion at the front of the place. Danny waited a few seconds then moved into the doorway, raising both weapons.

Danny entered a small pantry. When he got inside, he saw Akema Bady running out of the room to see what had blown up the front door.

Danny sensed someone to his right and swung the .45 out and fired. Danny felt Marshall move to his left behind him.

Danny's first shot with the .45 missed Muhammad Bady, but forced him to move away into the kitchen. Danny fired the Glock and hit Muhammad in the arm.

Rimba tossed the machete at Marshall at the same time Marshall squeezed off a shot at him. Marshall leaned to one side as the blade flew by his head. His shot hit Rimba in the gut and Rimba fell to one knee.

Muhammad's gun fired, and Danny heard the bullet go by his ear. Danny fired the .45 again and hit Muhammad in the chest, sending the man flying into the air. Muhammad's gun flew out of his hand, but Danny couldn't see where it went.

Danny jerked his head over to check on Marshall. He saw him moving in on Rimba, who was still on his knees.

"Don't get close to him," said Danny.

Marshall took a step back as Rimba pulled out another knife. He looked up at Marshall, then plunged his own knife into his heart, killing himself.

Danny ran by Rimba's dead body into the other room. He entered and was backed out by a volley of gunfire. He had seen brief muzzle flashes from a corner.

Danny took a only second, knowing that if he waited a standoff would ensue. He ran back into the room and pumped several shots from both weapons toward the place where he had seen the muzzle flashes. The sound was deafening and he moved forward trying to see if the last Bady brother had been hit.

He found Akema in the corner, hit twice and not moving. He felt for a pulse. There was none. She was gone.

Danny heard a muffled cry. He turned and saw Bellva tied to a door across the room. She was half naked and crying.

Danny moved toward her when he heard a noise from behind him. He turned to see Muhammad crawling next to another man on the floor. Muhammad's face had an expression of pain and determination. He crawled to the man on the floor, raised his bloodstained hands, and started to choke him. Wounded, Muhammad was very weak but he used every ounce of his strength to choke the fallen man.

Danny yelled for Muhammad to stop, but he could see that he was not going to. Danny ran over and pulled Muhammad off the other

man. Muhammad grunted loudly then rolled over on his face and collapsed. He took in a couple of sharp breaths—then nothing.

Danny checked on Muhammad. He was dead. Danny looked at
the fallen man and saw that it was Reverend Bolt. He was lying in a
pool of blood. On Bolt's arm was a dirty rag, which was tied off just
above the elbow. Then Danny saw why. Bolt's left hand had been cut
off. Danny checked Bolt for signs of life. He felt a weak pulse.

"This one's still with us, Marshall," said Danny.

Marshall walked over and saw the man Danny referred to.

"Well, I'll be damned," said Marshall.

"We need to call an ambulance, right now."

"I'm on it," said Marshall.

Danny moved back over to Bellva as Marshall whipped out a cell
phone. Bellva was tired, beaten, and scared, but she was in good
shape compared to everyone else in the house. Danny quickly untied
her.

"Good to see you again," said Danny to Bellva. She smiled a little
sick smile and wiped her eyes.

Danny helped her to her feet. Bellva stood on shaky kegs and tried
to cover herself up.

"Can you make it?" asked Danny.

"Yes," said Bellva. "Yes, I can."

32

FRANKIE

Danny and Marshall watched as the attendant at the pet cemetery dug up John Baker's dog, Frankie. The Rest-in-Pets Animal Cemetery was a dismal patch of land jammed in the back of what used to be a strip mall in Ferndale just outside of Detroit. Darkness was settling on the city, and the tiny headstones sprouted up around them like a miniature vision of some hellish dream.

Like most people, Danny thought of pets as kind of human, so this place, this ragged piece of land filled with the carcasses of once-loved family members, was very quietly giving him the creeps.

Danny had called in the cops and an ambulance for Reverend Bolt. How and why Bolt was there and had been mutilated was something that he did not know. They were all curious but Bolt was in no shape to talk yet.

The morgue's meat wagon had come for the Bady brothers. They would not be talking at all.

Bellva had confessed to everything she knew. John Baker had stolen a lot of money along with Olittah Reese, who'd had a last-minute change of heart. When the heat was on, he buried it with his dead dog before he was killed.

The cemetery attendant, a young man named Wilson, dug up the grave of John Baker's dead dog. Wilson told Danny that Mr. Baker had insisted on buying the casket himself and would not let him see what was inside it. By law he had to know, so after a little haggling, Baker had bribed him with a hundred bucks to keep his mouth shut.

Wilson hit something solid and stopped shoveling. "That's gotta be it," he said. Wilson put down his spade and scooped away dirt with his hand, revealing a black metal casket. Lifting it up, he pushed it out of the hole.

Danny took over at this point. He forced open the lid and waited for the stench of the dog's rotting corpse. Instead, he smelled nothing. Inside the coffin were two black vinyl bags. Danny opened the first one and saw it contained neatly bundled packets of bills.

"A buried treasure," said Marshall. "This shit could only happen in Detroit."

"You got that right," said Danny. Danny opened the other bag and found Frankie's carcass. He quickly zipped it closed.

Wilson sighed and whistled as he realized that he took a measly hundred to pass up a fortune. "There a finder's fee or somethin' for this?" he asked.

"No such luck," said Danny. He lifted the bag with the money in it, then noticed that there was something else in the coffin. He removed several mini cassette tapes and a recorder with a tape inside. It also had a small microphone still plugged in. He stared at it, understanding that John Baker had hidden more than stolen money; he'd buried a secret with his beloved dog. Whatever was on these tapes had driven John Baker to extremes and perhaps caused his death.

"If you don't play it, I sure as hell will," said Marshall.

Danny searched the small machine for the play button.

"I should get one of these bundles of money." said Wilson.

"There's no reward," said Marshall.

"There should be," said Wilson. "That's a lot of money for there not to be no reward. Maybe you fellas can fix it so's I get hooked up with one."

"We'll do what we can, sir," said Danny. He pressed the tape recorder's play button and nothing happened. "Batteries are dead," Danny said to Marshall.

Marshall couldn't help but laugh a little as Danny fumbled with the tape machine. Danny saw Wilson run to his attendant's cart, then come back with several small batteries in his hand. Wilson seemed as eager to know what was going on with the desecrated grave as Danny was.

Danny took the batteries and put several of them in the tape machine. He rewound the tape, then played it. Danny was mesmerized as he listened to the voice emanating from the tiny speaker. He popped in tape after tape until he got it all. When he was finished, he took a deep breath and looked up into the darkening sky. Now he knew everything.

33

HEART OF A PEOPLE

Virginia Stallworth breathed nervously as she finished practicing her speech for the third time. This was going to be a historic night in her life. It had been a long, hard, and dangerous road, but she'd stayed the course, and it was finally going to pay off. Even though someone had found out her secret and struck down her companions, she was safe and ready to take her place in history.

"... and when history is recounted, we will look back to see that this day was not the end of something," she said to the mirror, "but the beginning of truth and prosperity for us all." She smiled for an imaginary crowd. It was good, she thought, perfect.

Virginia was in her bedroom, waiting for the NOAA Premiere Night festivities to begin downtown. Though her speech wasn't for some time, she was taking no chances. She'd come too far for that.

Her family waited downstairs, celebrating. But even they didn't know what she was going to announce tonight. To meet her goal, no one could know what she was planning, not even her loved ones. The police detectives had discovered just one small part of what she was planning. The Castle. It was silly to resurrect the name, but it had served her purpose. Oscar had been angry as hell, but he didn't know it went any farther than the Castle.

It had all started years ago, when the Japanese received reparations from President Reagan for their internment during World War II. That led black activists to ask for the same. The cry of "Where's our money?" rose from the beleaguered face of black America. But the trillions it would have cost to repay blacks would have bankrupted and demoralized the country. Internal focus groups in the NOAA, liberal think tanks and other organizations went through the practicality of doing it. Each time they came to the same conclusion. There were too many people to ever find a control group small enough to make it feasible. Many people in America were mixed with African blood, and answers about who was black and related to slaves were cloudy due to racial mixing. Millions could claim protected status, swelling the numbers out of proportion and killing the effort.

The NOAA had had a bitter internal struggle about this for several years. Finally they'd decided to abandon the agenda for reparations. Virginia had been upset, but not because she believed in reparations. In fact, she'd opposed them, thinking it to be just another political handout leveraged by white guilt and black weakness. What upset her was that a small number of blacks within the group had determined the issue. They'd arbitrarily decided who was black and what that term meant. They called the shots for everyone and lumped the entire race into a single mind-set that they had predetermined.

Virginia realized that this was the case not only within the organization but within the race in general. The many were dictated to by the few and select. It perturbed her even more that this control group was comprised mostly of dark-skinned blacks who considered themselves to be the "real" voice of the people.

The black race had been saved by its elite class, she thought. From W. E. B. DuBois to the legions downtown waiting for her speech. And that savior class had always been racially mixed for the most part. They were the first doctors, teachers, professors, lawyers, and intelligentsia, the backbone of the race.

And for this they had gotten only grief. The notion that the color of a black person didn't matter was repugnant to her. Color was everything in this country, and she was tired of being dragged down by those who didn't see that, those who didn't want to work, suffer, and strive for success.

So slowly, over time, she had sought out like-minded individuals within the NOAA, and found that her beliefs were echoed by a small, yet very powerful group of racially mixed blacks like herself.

Virginia had gotten them all together in a series of clandestine meetings and formulated a plan to give life to the reality of their ancestry and the necessity of their cause.

She was fighting with Hamilton Grace over leadership of the NOAA, but that was just a clever diversion, a ploy to put her in a leadership light. Her newly formed Castle group was going to be the real power.

Their agenda was to create a separate race within the black race in America, a new race of people who were multi-ethnic. She would split off all those of mixed blood and create an elite minority, one that would be fueled with money, power, and a single vision, her vision.

Her family was black, Irish, and Swedish. And yet, no one wanted to hear about those nonblack parts of her heritage. The idea that any black person with more than one race's blood in his veins was something different was met with derision and anger. When she talked about it, the overwhelming attitude was, "Shut up, you're black like the rest of us." The bullshit theory of the black "dominant gene" had made everyone, black and white, just assume you were one thing, and that thing was wretched. But she did not buy that limitation. It was dehumanizing to be forced to forget vital parts of your heritage, and it was time for it to end.

The Bakers had thought her mad at first, but over time they began to see the possibilities. John's Internet company would provide the money they needed and together they drafted the resolution she was going to read tonight at the meeting, one that would free her people from another generation of Jesus-and-corn-bread philosophy, liberal finger wagging, and the political begging of her organization.

The seeds for this change had always been there within the race, the silent, secret resentment based on color. She would lift it up, expose it in the light of day, and turn it into something good for all people. And her race, the new race, would be strong and proud. It would accept no handouts, and thrive on hard work and the depth of heritage. In time they would be joined by mixed-raced Latinos, Asians, and others would fill the ranks of her group until they were no longer a minority but the one, true voice of America.

And it would all begin tonight. She smiled to herself. After she took the podium and told everyone of her plan, she and her followers would stage a walkout that would throw the organization into disarray and focus instant media attention on her. She saw herself on the *Today* show, *Nightline,* and *Larry King Live,* leading the crusade and opening the mind of America in the new millennium.

From there, she would get funding for her new organization, which she planned to call the MEPOA, or the Multi-Ethnic Persons of America. They would start chapters in each city where there was an NOAA base then seek out certification from all of the powers that be in this country.

It was time for this, she thought. Hundreds of years in the making, a new day had come. She'd barely been able to contain herself these last few weeks. She didn't have time for her family, who had noticed the change in her, the nervousness and sleeplessness. They wrote it off to anxiety connected to the murders.

Virginia didn't know who had killed the members of her secret committee in Detroit. This had frightened her beyond belief. First she thought that it was a disgruntled investor in New Nubia, but that didn't make sense. Then she thought it was Hamilton Grace, but it was not his style. The one thing she did know was that John Baker had gotten cold feet about the Castle and her cause. He began to question what they were doing, threatening to stop the flow of money. But she'd countered with her own threats to expose his shady business dealings and he'd quieted down.

Still, that didn't explain what was happening. With each death, she'd grown more afraid to continue her quest. But no great revolution came without a price. Dr. King, Gandhi, and JFK had all paid for their vision. She knew there might be dangers, but she was willing to face them.

Even the death of Dr. Vance would not deter her. She would win the day, she thought. If all mixed-race blacks left with her, the so-called African American agenda would be weakened to the point of nonexistence. No more government set-asides, no more political clout, no more affirmative action. There would be a multibillion-dollar fallout, and groups like the NOAA, NAACP, and the Urban League would crumble into dust. Nothing in this country would ever be the same.

There was a knock on her door, which took her out of her wonderful reverie. She tucked her speech away in her purse and opened the door, revealing her son Cal, standing there in his elegant tux with a wild look on his face. His eyes bulged in their sockets and his face was twisted into a smile so wide and tight that it looked as if it would split his face.

"Son, are you okay?" she asked.

"We are fine," he said coldly. Then he raised his arm, and brought his weapon into her face with all his might.

34

NIGHT STATION

Danny had tracked down the Stallworths to their home, but security reported that they'd found all the members of the family unconscious, except Virginia and Cal, who were missing. Someone had put some kind of drug in a bottle of champagne, knocking out the family members. There were guards posted outside the house but they reported seeing no one leave the home.

The police were working on the theory that someone had abducted the two, but Danny didn't think so. One of them had taken the other, and he was betting that it was Cal who was the abductor. Why was what he didn't know.

John Baker's tapes were recordings of meetings of Virginia's new elite group. All of the people on her list were accounted for. Danny listened in shock as he heard Virginia's plan for race domination. She was crazy but, apparently, her son Cal was equally as bent.

Danny had turned in the money and told his boss what he'd been up to. Jim had covered for him as usual, saying that he was on a special mission. This was chiefly due to the Bady brothers' situation, which was a bloody mess.

They'd run a check on the brothers and connected them to a series of crimes stretching across the country. In the face of closing a lot of cases, no one was asking questions.

Reverend Bolt was in the hospital, unconscious and in critical condition. For now the police assumed Bolt had been kidnapped or carjacked by the brothers.

Danny had called for backup from the SCU team and the FBI. Marshall had gone back to his family, safe and sound.

Danny arrived at the home of Virginia Stallworth to find an angry Janis and an angrier Erik waiting for him. Erik's arms were folded across his chest and Janis's hands were on her hips. Their faces held the same expression, pissed off.

"This is completely unacceptable," said Janis.

"Damned right it is, partner," said Erik,

"I can't explain right now," said Danny. "I had some problems, but that's behind me."

"And we're just supposed to forget about you leaving us out to dry?" asked Erik.

"Yes," said Jim from behind Erik. "You can kick his ass tomorrow, but right now, we have a killer at large." Jim reached into his pocket and handed Danny his badge and gun. Danny took it quickly and no more was said.

Danny explained to Janis and Erik what he had learned. They both seemed unwilling to accept that the whole case hinged on matters of color. As they went inside the home, Danny could feel the anger radiated by Janis and Erik. He had to get back into the case and if he knew them that would be all they needed to forgive him.

The Stallworth home was neat and undisturbed, except for one thing. Someone had defaced many of the family pictures. Virginia's face was scratched out of picture after picture. But not Cal's. His face was left intact. They also found two bottles of prescription pills for Cal. Janis noted that the medication was given to stave off severe mental depression. The bottles were full.

"It's the son," said Danny. He called everyone over and they examined the pictures.

"All the pictures upstairs are the same," said another cop. "Mom's X-ed out."

"Got any theories on this?" Danny asked Janis.

"He hates his mother," said Janis. "But why? They're the same color."

Chip, the FBI boss, was engaged in a serious conversation with Jim across the room. He motioned to Danny, Erik, and Janis. Danny lingered behind, his attention drawn to another picture on the wall.

"Our canvas has to be tight. The Stallworth woman is probably gone by now," said Chip. "So, we have to find Cal before he can flee the city or kill himself."

"We'll have to coordinate with other law enforcement," said Jim. "And the county and state boys will want to be brought in,"

"Fine," said Chip. "As long they obey the chain of command. Our other offices will lend us more men. He's got to be somewhere in the city, and we're going to find him tonight."

"I got something here," said Danny.

Jim and the others moved over to a picture of Virginia and her husband when they were much younger. Oscar was smiling, and Virginia looked happy. Behind them was the sprawling train station on the city's south-west side. Back then, it was still open, though in the process of closing down. None of this was what had caught Danny's attention. In Virginia's arms were two little babies dressed in white jumpers. Danny grabbed the picture and took it out of its frame.

"Danny, what are you doing?" asked Janis. "That's evidence."

"This picture," said Danny. "It's the only one in the house where Virginia's face is not crossed out, and look at the kids' faces."

They all looked at the picture. Virginia held the two kids. One of them was pink, the other dark brown.

Danny examined the back of the photo, and read what was written there:

My angels: Colson and twin brother Callent.

"They told me Cal's brother died," said Danny. "But they never said how. And they sure as hell didn't say he looked like this. Throughout this case the color of the victims has been an issue. Virginia's group was composed of mixed-race people. She was obsessed with it and somehow it poisoned her family. I'd bet everything that Cal thinks she killed his brother because he was darker."

"Jesus," said Erik. "Would she do that?"

"Doesn't matter," said Janis. "If her son thinks she did."

"That explains the medication we found upstairs," said Janis. "The bottles are full, so he hasn't been taking his medicine. He been growing more and more depressed."

"Me and Janis saw Cal and his sister Gwen arguing about something at their house," said Danny. "And Gwen was waving a bottle of pills at him."

"He was not taking his medication and she knew it," said Janis.

"Yes," said Danny. "And this picture proves it. He couldn't deface it because—"

"He loved her back then," Janis finished for him.

"The train station," said Danny. "That's where he is."

"We can't gamble the entire investigation on a hunch, Detective," said Chip.

"I don't think it's just a hunch, sir," said Janis. "This picture held special meaning for him. The building here is where he would go."

"Maybe we should break off a detachment and check this out," said Jim.

Jim and Chip moved aside and began to talk in private. They stepped back just as quickly and each looked directly at Danny.

"Let's do it," said Chip. "My people will lead the unit."

Danny looked over to Jim, who subtly nodded his head. Danny

agreed and Jim and Chip went off to coordinate. It was law enforcement politics at its best.

Danny moved over to Erik and Janis. He didn't want to end this case with them angry at him. But he couldn't tell them why he'd vanished and went on to get Bellva without them. The matter of his mother's death had to end with him and his father.

"I don't have any excuses," said Danny. "Just know that this has been the worst time of my life. These last few days I couldn't come to you. If you're gonna have a problem with me for this, Erik, I understand."

"Trust was broken," said Erik.

"And you sure as hell didn't make me my boss's favorite," said Janis.

"I know," said Danny. "But this was not about the job. It was personal."

Erik quickly moved to his partner and placed a hand on his shoulder. "Fuck it," he said. Danny clapped a hand on Erik's shoulder and smiled. "It ain't like I needed the extra work, you know."

"The next crazed killer is all yours," said Danny. He looked over at Janis, whose eyes told him that she was not as ready to forgive as Erik.

"If you two are done being in love," said Janis, "maybe we can go arrest our killer."

Detroit's old train station sits on Sixteenth Street and Vernor, on the city's lower west side. It is a massive building, both grand and pitiful, a beautiful old structure neglected by time and abandoned by the great city that built it. It was scheduled for demolition and it stood by like a condemned man waiting for execution.

Danny and the tactical team moved in several blocks away, then proceeded on foot. Danny, Erik, and Janis took the lead, supported by a team of FBI and SCU cops. Chip, Jim, and the other big bosses fell back.

On the way to the station, the SCU had learned that Colson Stall-worth, Cal's twin brother, was killed at the age of ten in a boating ac-cident on the river off St. Clair Shores. Virginia and young Colson had been together in the boat when it tipped over. It was ruled a death by accident, but apparently Cal didn't think so. Several times he'd tried to get the police to investigate the killing, but no one would listen to the rantings of a ten-year-old.

A year after his brother's death, Cal Stallworth was put into a ju-venile rest home, a fancy name for a mental facility. He had been in and out of treatment houses for most of his life. The shock of losing his brother had kept him on the edge of sanity.

The feds wore flack jackets with FBI emblazoned on the back. The Special Crimes Unit wore similar jackets with their letters. To Danny, they looked like two well-armed softball teams running through the night.

Chip and Jim had arranged to have the streetlights turned off so that Cal could not see their approach. They hoped that he would be-lieve that it was a power outage. They also pulled up blueprints of the station so that Danny's team would know the basic outlay of the place.

The train station was dark and stretched out over what could have been three city blocks. Its facade was aged and gray, littered with cracks and holes. The pitch windows looked like hundreds of black eyes. It was a colossal haunted house. Across from it Roosevelt Park where three men sat around passing a bottle. The darkness didn't deter them from their little party.

Danny went over to them and pulled out his badge. "Yo. Y'all seen anybody go in there?" Danny pointed at the train station.

"Naw, Mr. Po-leece man," said an old black man with no teeth in the front. "Ain't nobody crazy enough to go in that muthafucka. It's got ghosts."

"I thought I saw somebody," said another man. "I thought I saw him drag somethin' up in there."

"You outta yo' mind, man," said the first man. "This whiskey ain't that damned good!"

They all laughed and the toothless man choked a little, then killed it with a drink.

"We got a car in the rear off the side street," said an officer on the radio.

"Copy that," said Erik. "He's inside just like you said."

"Okay, we go in and get him," said Danny. "The place is big, so we'll have to stick to the blueprint. If we stay quiet, maybe he'll make some noise and lead us to him."

"Nobody get cocky," said Chip on the radio. "Proceed with caution."

Danny pulled out both of his guns. After the incident with the Bady brothers he was not about to go in with one hand empty. Danny turned off his radio and instructed the backup team to do the same. Then he nodded to Erik and Janis, and moved toward the train station.

Danny and his team edged over to the front of the building and saw that someone had forced open the door. Danny, Janis, and Erik went inside, careful not to make any noise.

The lobby of the old train station had lost none of its grandness. It was a cavernous, crumbling mess. The place was dim, and the only light was from the door that Danny had just come in. They were assaulted by many smells, none of them good.

Danny waited until their eyes adjusted to the darkness. Then he could see that the floor was covered in debris, plywood, broken glass, beer cans, and the carcasses of dead rats.

They stood in the lobby for several minutes, waiting to hear something. A rodent scurried from a wall and stopped to pick at the dead body of its brother, then moved on. Danny heard gagging behind him, but it was not Janis, it was Erik, who detested rats.

"Sorry, man," he said. "I hate them damned things."

They huddled together in a tight circle and were motionless as the thickness of the stench assaulted their lungs. It looked like a good place to die, Danny thought grimly.

They heard a sound from above. It was soft, but audible. A voice. Someone was yelling. They could not make out the words, but that was beside the point. Their killer was here.

Danny pointed to the decrepit upper floors of the building and slowly broke the circle by moving toward the stairs. Erik and Janis followed. Janis took out a small light and the shrunken copy of the train station's blueprints. Erik called for the backup team to move in closer as they proceeded.

There was not much time, Danny thought. If Virginia were not the killer's mother, she would probably be dead already, or maybe she was dead, and Cal was ranting to himself over her corpse.

They went to a stairwell. The farther they moved into the place, the darker it got and the louder the voice became. Danny didn't know which was making him more nervous. He stopped when he got to a long stairwell. Looking up, he saw only murky darkness.

Danny peered at the stairwell and saw his own mother at the top of the flight, tumbling through air, twisting and falling, her descent racing against the poison that she'd put into herself. He saw his grief-stricken father, crying, broken by his own murderous mercy.

Danny's mother was a wrecked vessel at the end of her life, ruined by fate, choices, and limited love. Lucy had severed the emotional bond and taken her own life. Somewhere up those stairs, another son and his mother were engaging fate, only this time it was the son who had crumbled and was going to take his mother's life.

Danny pulled himself back into reality. Virginia was not his mother, he told himself. She was the killer's mother and whether he saved her or not, it would never bring back Lucy Cavanaugh or change the things she'd written about him.

Danny carefully stepped up the stairs, trying to keep quiet. He placed one foot down slowly and waited for a sound. When he heard none, he moved on to the next. This process took a long time, but it was the only way to go. Danny moved closer to the top and he noticed that there were now two voices.

Danny reached the second floor and leaned in and peeked around the corner to the hallway. No one was there. Then he heard the voices again. They were higher up.

Danny, Erik, and Janis entered the hallway and Danny immediately went to the next flight of stairs. It was covered in debris, the kind that would make noise if he stepped wrongly.

Then they heard the "pop" of a small-caliber gun and Virginia cried out loudly. Danny tensed and started up the second flight. Erik followed. Danny went as fast as he could, not wanting to hear another shot.

"Slow down," Erik whispered.

Virginia cried out in pain, but now it was muffled. Cal ranted, and Danny could hear him clearly.

"Why did you do it?" Cal yelled. "Why did you kill us?"

Virginia did not answer, she just cried. Then she grunted, a sick hurt sound. "Cal, please," she said. "I'm bleeding. . . ."

"There is no Cal! You killed him when you murdered his brother! We don't respond to those names."

"It was an accident," said Virginia. "An accident," she repeated in a lower voice.

"Accident!" screamed Cal. "You tortured us, nothing we did was good enough for you. And you hated Colson's skin, you despised his color. We heard you, talking about it, your filthy sick words about how he was not one of the family."

"I was wrong," said Virginia. "I was too young back then, I'm sorry but I didn't kill him, son—"

"Don't call me that!" yelled Cal. "Can't you see what I am now? Can't you see the glow on me? I am an angel, just like you used to call me when I was little."

"Yes, I can see," Virginia cried. "I can see, please don't hurt me anymore."

"You killed my brother and tore our family apart."

"No!" said Virginia. "Oscar came back to me, and we went on with our family. When Gwen was born there were no problems."

"I knew about your plan to create a race of people just like you. A new race, Mother?" He laughed. "Only you in your sick dementia would even think to do that."

Danny didn't hear an answer from Virginia. She just cried. Then he hear another loud pop, and Virginia screamed in pain.

Danny reached the landing and swung his head into the hallway. He saw them. Cal had his mother tied up in the middle of a hallway next to a railing. It must have overlooked the lobby below, which was why they had heard them from downstairs.

Virginia was sitting down and Cal knelt next to her. Near them was a small light.

Danny swung back and looked at Erik. He searched for Janis, but she was gone. Erik checked behind him. He saw nothing but darkness.

Danny didn't want to chance calling out to Janis. He nodded his head, then stepped into the hallway.

Cal jerked around and held up the gun. He eyes were wild and his face contorted. He was putting a tape patch on Virginia's latest wound.

"Get away from her, Cal," said Danny. He could see just Erik at his side.

Cal saw Danny and put the barrel of his weapon into his mother's eye socket. Then he lifted her to her feet.

"Get away!" Cal demanded.

Danny and Erik advanced slowly. Danny had both guns out. One pointed at Cal's head, the other at his leg, but he still didn't have a clear shot. If he hit the leg, Cal and Virginia would fall to their deaths. If he hit him in the head, Cal would die, but he would probably pull the trigger and kill his mother.

Cal pushed his mother closer to the railing of the balcony. The rusted steel creaked. Virginia teetered close to the edge with Cal right at her side.

Danny and Erik stopped. If Cal let her go, she'd fall, and he might jump over with her. As much as it pained Danny, he had to take Cal alive if he could, and he certainly couldn't let him kill his mother.

"Get out of here," demanded Cal. "We have a right to take her life. She killed my brother. Murdered him because . . ."

"I'll make sure she gets punished," said Danny. "I promise."

"Your promise means nothing," said Cal, and he pushed Virginia closer to her death.

Suddenly, Danny and Erik saw something move beyond Cal and his mother. A shadowy figure loomed down the hallway. Danny and Erik tensed as the shape came closer. It was Janis. She moved closer to Cal. Danny knew what he had to do. He needed to make noise so Cal wouldn't hear Janis.

"She killed your brother Colson because he was dark," said Danny.

Cal stopped. He looked at Danny with a mixture of shock and elation in his eyes. Cal's grip loosened on Virginia and he pulled the gun away from her face. Virginia let out a deep breath and sobbed softly.

"How did you know?" he asked.

"I put it all together. I've talked with her—anyone can see it." Danny took another careful step closer, lowering his guns.

"No," said Cal. "You're with her. I know it. Look at you, you look white, but you sound black." Cal started to raise the gun.

Janis stepped on a piece of glass. The crunch was like thunder to Danny's ears. Cal jerked his head around to look at her. He took his eyes off Danny, who raised the Glock and fired it into Cal's left arm, which held the gun. Cal flew back and his gun hand lowered, but somehow he was able to hold on fast to the butt of the weapon.

Cal and Virginia smashed into the railing. The weak metal buckled. Virginia managed to grab the railing using her two bound-up hands for support.

Danny seized Cal as the latter swung his gun toward Danny and fired. Danny was leaning into him and the shot missed.

Danny heard Janis yell then her body hit the ground. A second later, Danny saw Erik kick the gun out of Cal's hand.

Erik was reaching for Virginia when Cal pushed Danny, off and holding on to his mother, sent them into the railing and over the side.

Danny caught Virginia, but Cal kept falling. Virginia grabbed her son by the arm with her two hands and held on.

Danny was almost pulled over by their weight, but he hung on, pushing himself back. His armed strained and he felt as if it would dislodge from its socket.

"Let go!" Cal screamed. "Let me die!"

Erik caught Danny and held him fast. Together they pulled Virginia up, but the extra weight of her son made it difficult.

From behind them Janis yelled something.

Then Cal brought his mother's hand—the hand that held him—to his face and bit into it. Virginia screamed, but did not let go.

Erik and Danny dragged them both up just a little more. Danny could almost reach Cal.

Cal bit deeper into Virginia's hand and drew blood. Her index finger began to separate. Virginia screamed again, but held fast to her son, her body bleeding and tears streaming down her tortured face.

Erik grabbed Cal by his shirt and Virginia let go of him. Cal stopped biting Virginia's hand and looked up at Erik, who hit him as hard as he could in the face. Danny pulled Virginia to safety.

With Cal in a daze, Erik lifted him up and over the railing and handcuffed him. Cal struggled, cursing and muttering, but Erik had him subdued.

Janis walked over, holding her neck. Cal had hit her there. She was bleeding pretty badly. Blood poured through her fingers and she fell to one knee on the filthy floor.

While Erik cuffed Cal's feet together so that he could not move, Danny went to Janis and applied pressure to the wound on her neck. Erik radioed for the rest of the team to come in.

Danny didn't have time to attend to Virginia. Janis was bleeding too badly and Virginia wasn't as bad.

Then Virginia started to move on the floor. She dragged her body toward the collapsed railing. Danny was alarmed for a second, then she changed her path. Bloody and crying, Virginia crawled over to Cal, lifted a arm over her son, and hugged him.

The streetlights had been turned back on outside the station as Cal, Virginia, and Janis were put into ambulances. Medics, FBI, and cops swarmed all over the place. Not far away, reporters were held back by uniformed cops. Overhead, news helicopters circled.

Danny's boss was happy as he and Chip exchanged congratulations. Exhausted, Danny and Erik sat on the hood of a car. Around them were SCU team members, celebrating their good work.

Chip walked over to a TV news crew. The FBI would probably take all the credit, Danny thought, but it didn't matter. Danny felt a tremendous sense of closure. Cal would live and Virginia would not be taken from her other children. No matter what he thought of her, she was still someone's mother.

Jim Cole walked over to them and started talking to Danny and Erik about the press conference he and Chip would attend and how he wanted the information on the case to be given out. Erik said that he would rather not talk to any press. Danny echoed this sentiment.

Suddenly Danny saw something in the crowd of cops, paramedics, and FBI. He smiled then got up and walked away from the group that had assembled.

Walking through the crowd, escorted by a policeman, was Vinny. She'd been crying. They looked at each other for just a second and it didn't take more than that to know that they'd both made a mistake. Danny remembered that Vinny used to be a cop and had obviously called in some favors to be let into the crime scene.

He wondered what could have made her come here at this critical time. Maybe it was fate, he thought, some Great Hand that moved her to think of him at this crucial moment. Then Danny looked

behind Vinny and saw his father, Robert, in the background, talking
with several officers. Robert caught his son's eyes and smiled a little.
He'd lost his wife because his connection to her wasn't strong enough
for Lucy to tell him what was in her troubled heart. Robert didn't
want his son to suffer from the awful legacy that seemed to run in the
veins of the Cavanaugh men. Robert nodded a little, then disappeared into the crowd.

Danny went to Vinny and they embraced. Behind him, he heard
the clapping and jeers of his coworkers and chants of "kiss her,"
which he did quite gladly.

Epilogue

THE SCORE

Danny sat in silence in the hospital lobby, waiting to see Janis. She'd survived Cal's gunshot but had needed surgery. He hated hospitals and their clean smells, which covered sickness, pain, and death. Still, he had to be here.

Danny and Vinny had spent a busy night at home talking and making love. Robert had told her everything about Danny's mother and the diary. That had brought Vinny back to him. Maybe it was a little pathetic, he thought, but he was not about to ruin it.

Vinny for her part was sweetly silent about everything. All she really said was that she missed him. Danny had a thousand questions on his mind about their separation but he would get to them. It seemed that they had time now.

Danny decided to keep seeing Gordon. He'd called and set up a session for next week. There would be much to talk about.

Bellva had gone into rehab after the incident with the Bady brothers. The close brush with death had scared her back to normal thinking. Danny had escorted her to the facility himself. He watched her go in and it hurt him to know that her chances of making it through were not good. Most addicts failed their first attempt to clean themselves up. Danny hoped Bellva would be the exception.

Cal Stallworth was in custody. Danny didn't think he'd ever stand trial. He was obviously insane. Cal kept talking to the doctors about being himself as well as his dead brother and being some kind of avenging angel.

Cal confessed to questioning all of the victims about his mother's plan, trying to find out what she was up to and how she would make it happen. All he want to do was hurt Virginia. Cal didn't know about John Baker's money and he didn't care.

While he'd been at a mental health facility in Grand Rapids, Cal had had a roommate who'd killed an orderly by stabbing him with a kitchen knife and taping up the wounds. Cal had gotten his method of killing from a proven practitioner. He told the police that he'd learned to spoil the crime scenes from watching a forensics reality show on cable TV.

Virginia Stallworth was in intensive care. The image of her holding on to her son while he tried to literally chew off her fingers would be with Danny for the rest of his life. Her devotion to saving her son in that moment was only matched by her failure as a mother in the early part of her life.

The SCU reopened the case of Colson Stallworth's accidental drowning, but it remained inconclusive. Oscar Stallworth was leaving his wife for the second time in twenty-seven years. No one thought he'd change his mind this time.

The police found Virginia's speech for the convention. Danny was allowed to read it and was stunned and saddened by it all. Virginia was not so different from his own mother, he thought. People's feelings about color ran deep like subterranean rivers. Now he knew it was a force that, if not checked, could destroy.

The mayor was told about Virginia's speech and the tapes Danny had found in the dog's grave. The mayor turned them over to Hamilton Grace. No one in the NOAA would acknowledge being part of Virginia's scheme. So the speech was burned, and all of Virginia Stallworth's plans for a new race disappeared. Hamilton Grace was re-elected NOAA president unanimously.

Danny asked Hamilton Grace what his son Jordan had been doing over on Joy Road the day Janis and Danny had spotted him. Grace confessed that he'd dispatched Jordan to find Logan, his errant half-brother, who had shacked up with what he called an "undesirable" girl. Hamilton was unsuccessful in getting Logan to come back to the family, which seemed to suit Jordan just fine.

When Reverend Bolt regained consciousness, he made a full confession to all of his crimes and confirmed that the Bady brothers were his sons, who had come to Detroit to kill him. Bolt was being extradited to Texas to stand trial for murdering his wife. His church was taken over by one of his deacons, who said his ascension to the mantle of pastor was a sign from God.

The skin color of the victims was significant on the one hand, and on the other it was not. All of the members of Virginia Stallworth's secret committee were multi-ethnic and fair in complexion. She thought this would make them more agreeable to her grand scheme. Conversely, Cal didn't care what color his victims were. He would have killed anyone to hurt his mother and spoil her plan.

At that moment, a doctor came out of Janis's room and motioned Danny to go inside. Janis was sitting upright and had a bandage on her neck.

"You look like shit," said Danny, sitting down.

"At least I have an excuse," said Janis, smiling.

"You know that was a lucky shot he got off," said Danny. "One in a million he would have hit you."

"Just my luck," said Janis. "It severed an artery, but I'll be okay. And when I'm good to go, I'm leaving. I've been called to a case in Baltimore."

"That's great," said Danny. He took a moment to consider his third partner and what they'd been through. He felt a little sorry to know she was going. "Look, I know we didn't get along too good, but I'll miss you."

"Same here," said Janis. "Hey, I'm going to write a paper about the killer for the FBI. Cal Stallworth just might be our first verified black serial killer."

"You'll excuse me if I don't celebrate your discovery," said Danny. "And how can you be so happy about it? He tried to kill you, remember?"

"Nothing rare comes without a price. Say, I'm going to call him The Angel because of what was on the picture of the boys and their mother. I'm hoping I can turn it into a book."

"That's cool," said Danny. "Just make sure you describe me as tall and handsome."

"I'll do my best," said Janis. "Good-bye, Sherlock," she said sweetly.

Danny placed a hand on her shoulder, then she leaned over and kissed him on the cheek. It was a mild surprise to Danny, but certainly welcome.

Danny left, got into his car, and drove back to his old elementary school. He took just a second to look at the hard playground. Ghosts of friends and tormentors floated in his mind, and he was struck by how much of what we are is memory, and how much is forever unchangeable. He was who his life had made him and it was too late worry about it.

Danny saw himself walking along with Marshall, a white face in the ocean of black ones. Then the kid with the red hair stopped and turned. Danny looked into the memory of himself and saw that he was truly happy back then, happy as only a kid can be.

Danny watched as his memory faded into the red brick of the school itself and was gone.

He got back into his car, drove back downtown, and walked to the stairs of thirteen hundred. As he got to the top of the steps he stopped and looked out on to the city beyond him. He was acutely aware of people moving around him, rushing in the service of his chosen occupation. A couple of cops passed by, glancing at him strangely.

He remembered his father's words: ". . . the job is life." Robert was right, as usual. This place was part of him and he could never let it go.

Danny considered the color of all the people he saw and wondered if Virginia Stallworth wasn't right in her assessment of our society. Maybe if there was no color, people would have to invent it or find other ways to be biased against one another. Perhaps society needed these petty differences to be human. Virginia had been torn apart by a slavish devotion to these differences, and in the process, she'd created a monster.

He thought of Fiona and how nature had taken all of her color away. He never thought of Fiona as black or white, just as the person she was. Suddenly, he didn't think of her as afflicted.

Vinny and Danny were separated not by race but by class and divergence of aspiration. But what brought them back together was that thing which is colorless and bigger than the petty differences of individuals.

Danny was a man divided internally by external notions of color and perception. He thought about all that had happened, then what the psychologist had said about him and the two guns of different color. Quietly he accepted it.

He had Vinny back, but he had lost his mother and a part of his heart had gone into the grave with her. The memories of Lucy would make the days and nights a little harder.

Sure, he was keeping score, but didn't we all?

Danny turned back to police headquarters and left these heavy thoughts behind him. He walked in and went back to the job, the only thing he could never lose.